GRUMPILY *Yours*

OTHER TITLES BY TEAGAN HUNTER

STICK TAPS SERIES

Contemporary Romantic Comedies

Grumpily Ever After

SEATTLE SERPENTS SERIES

Contemporary Sports Romantic Comedies

Body Check

Face Off

Delayed Penalty

Empty Net

Top Shelf

Match Penalty

CAROLINA COMETS SERIES

Contemporary Sports Romantic Comedies

Puck Shy

Blind Pass

One-Timer

Sin Bin

Scoring Chance

Glove Save

"Game Changer"

Neutral Zone

TEXTING SERIES

Contemporary New Adult Romantic Comedies

Let's Get Textual

I Wanna Text You Up

Can't Text This

Text Me Baby One More Time

Textin' Up My Heart (novella)

SLICE SERIES

Contemporary Romantic Comedies

A Pizza My Heart

I Knead You Tonight

Doughn't Let Me Go

A Slice of Love (novella)

Cheesy on the Eyes

ROOMMATE ROMPS SERIES

Contemporary Romantic Comedies

Loathe Thy Neighbor

Love Thy Neighbor

Crave Thy Neighbor

Tempt Thy Neighbor

STARS SERIES

Contemporary Upper YA Emotional Romances

We Are the Stars

If You Say So

STAND-ALONES

Contemporary Romantic Comedies

The DM Diaries

Best Friends for Never

GRUMPILY *Yours*

TEAGAN HUNTER

Montlake

Published by Montlake, Seattle
www.apub.com

Amazon, the Amazon logo, and Montlake are trademarks of Amazon.com, Inc., or its affiliates.

EU product safety contact:
Amazon Media EU S. à r.l.
38, avenue John F. Kennedy, L-1855 Luxembourg
amazonpublishing-gpsr@amazon.com

ISBN-13: 9781662534065 (paperback)
ISBN-13: 9781662534072 (digital)

Cover design by Caroline Teagle Johnson
Cover image: © Wander Aguiar Photography;
© Mike Reid Photography / Getty Images

Printed in the United States of America

CHAPTER ONE

Ezra

"No."

"Please?"

"Absolutely not."

"But—"

"*No,*" I cut her off with a glare.

Odette crosses her arms over her chest, piercing me with a heated stare. "You're a real jerk sometimes, you know that, right?"

"I'm aware."

"And this doesn't bother you?"

"Not in the least."

She huffs. "All I'm saying is that adding an arcade would make this place absolutely *perfect.* Can you imagine how fun it would be to play pinball when you're tipsy?"

"Can you imagine how obnoxious that sound is going to be all day? No, because you're not here all day. Actually, wait, yes, you are."

I narrow my eyes at her, and she glowers right back.

The truth is, I like Odette Chambers. She's funny and bright. Plus, she puts up with Noah, her fiancé, who also happens to be my business partner. She's also done a lot to help make Stick Taps into not just one hell of a successful cidery, but a sought-after wedding destination too.

This new harebrained idea of hers, though? While it does have its appeal, I'm not completely sold on it. I already have a headache from staring at my computer for far too long. Adding the incessant noise from pinball and video game machines would only exacerbate the issue.

"What the hell are you complaining about?" Noah Stevens, my best friend and the man responsible for cooking up the idea of two former NHL players opening a hockey-themed cidery together, appears from the hall leading to the bathrooms and stands at the bar beside Odette. "You spend most of your time holed up in your office anyway." He turns to his fiancée. "And I thought we agreed that *I* would approach the sourpuss on my own first, then tag you in?"

Ah, so they planned this. Great.

Am I glad Noah found bliss and is now madly in love? Sure, I guess I'm as joyful as someone who doesn't believe in happily ever afters can be. But am I stoked that I'm now being ganged up on by his wedding planner fiancée *and* him? Abso-fucking-lutely not.

It's not the first time they've done this either. The last time ended with us getting miniature cows. While I admit they're cute, they're just another thing we have to add to our feed budget, thanks to all the other animals we have roaming around the picturesque Washington property.

But Noah doesn't always think about that side of it. Of the two of us, he's the doer, and I'm the numbers. While it works great most of the time, there are moments like these—like when Odette gets a "brilliant" idea—that I just want to hold his head over my ledger so he can take a look at our numbers and realize why we don't need to keep adding shit to the business.

We're doing good. *Really* fucking good. Why add the stress of more just for the sake of more?

Some days I feel like I'm already being stretched too thin as it is. Can I truly manage another thing?

"Did you tell him about the benefits?" Noah asks Odette.

"No, that was part of your pitch to him," she responds, as if I'm not standing right here.

"Why don't you just both get on with it so I can tell you no, and I can go back to my office. I was busy, you know. Working my way through applications. Something *important* since we need help around here."

With business picking up in ways none of us could have imagined, we officially need to expand our employee list. Not just to keep the cidery running, but also the farm. Between the chickens, goats, mini cows, and the cats that continue to show up, we're running thin on people to help keep it all in check.

Odette rolls her eyes, which only makes her fiancé grin, then he clears his throat and leans against the bar.

His face is hard, his eyes serious as he says one word: "Fun."

I quirk a brow. "Congratulations. It looks like hockey didn't beat everything out of that head of yours, and you know a three-letter word. Anything else?"

"I'm not surprised he doesn't get it," Odette chimes in. "He wouldn't know fun if it ran him into the boards."

"I know fun," I argue like a moody teenager, ignoring the way her words ring a little too true, all things considered.

My hand goes to my hip, and I press on the dull ache that always seems to be there, rubbing at the spot where I *did* collide with the boards, effectively ending my professional career.

Odette snorts disbelievingly. "Name one fun thing you've ever done."

"I played in the NHL."

She tosses her arms in the air. "That's a cop-out answer, and you know it!"

"I don't know, Odie. It's pretty damn fun," Noah says, and I'm not sure if she can hear it, but I certainly don't miss the longing in his voice.

In addition to running the Stick Taps cidery, Noah and I launched the Stick Taps Community Iceplex six months ago because we craved the game so much. Once it's part of you, it never truly goes away, and considering I started playing twenty-five years ago, it's damn sure a part of me.

While my answer might seem like a cop-out to Odette, she has no idea what it feels like to step out on two hundred feet of ice in front of a roaring crowd and get to play the greatest game on earth. There's nothing else like it, and I miss it more than I'd ever admit.

As if my body aches for it as much as my heart does, my hip throbs even more. I suppress the pain like I have so many times before and continue staring down Noah's fiancée.

"Fine," she relents. "But you still don't know fun. You never come out with us when we invite you."

Yes, because I want to spend my time hanging with my friend, his girl, and his family, acting like the . . . well, I'm not even sure what number wheel I'd be at that point, but I'm not doing it. I have better things to do with my time.

"Is 'fun' your only selling point?" I ask.

"Well, yes. Sort of. But also, it would be great for business. Help bring even *more* customers here. Imagine little Timmy running around the arcade, feeding quarter after quarter into the machine because his parents keep handing them to him so they can have a few blissful child-free moments."

"If you think bringing *more* kids into here is a selling point, you're barking up the wrong tree."

"You love children, and you know it. You wouldn't have started the iceplex if you didn't."

"I started the iceplex for a free place to skate, and that's it," I argue, though that's a lie.

I did start the iceplex for the kids. Hockey saved me when I was small, and I wanted to give that back in any way I could.

"Come on, Ezra," Odette whines, saving me before the memories of my childhood start rushing in and put me in a crappy mood. It's not that it was a bad childhood, but it isn't exactly something I want to reminisce about either. "Just say *yes* and stop torturing me. You know you're going to eventually."

"Oh, am I, now?"

She gives me a look that repeats her *Come on.*

And fuck me, she's probably right.

I'm fully capable of saying no—I do it all the time to my employees when they ask for extra days off—but saying no to Odette? It's a bit harder. Just about everyone is wrapped around her finger, including Noah, who is looking at her like she's the most beautiful woman in the world, and that's *after* she's been rolling in the dirt with the goats for the last thirty minutes.

Sometimes I wonder what it would be like to love someone like that. Then I remember that it's not something I'm capable of. I'm more equipped for flings or one-night stands. I could never give myself to someone fully when I hate what I see in the mirror every day. That wouldn't be fair to them, and the last thing I want is to waste someone's time.

"No," I tell her again.

She growls—actually fucking growls—then points to Noah. "You deal with him. I'm going to find Tootsie, who has somehow managed to escape her pen."

"Again? That's the third time just this week. I swear, that fucking chicken is going to end up as a nugget."

When we bought the property for the cidery, it came with a bunch of animals already, including Tootsie, our resident escape artist chicken, who we can't seem to keep locked away, no matter what we try. The number of times wedding photographers have had to photoshop her out of pictures is almost comical at this point.

Odette ignores me. "And tell him he has to have a plus-one to the wedding too!"

He presses his lips together, smothering a laugh as she walks away, muttering to herself about what an ass I am.

Noah watches her go, and once she pushes through the front doors of the cidery, he looks over at me. "So, we're doing the arcade, right?"

"It's probably a horrible idea because it means more work, more money, and more shit to take care of before your wedding, but can you imagine the stress relief after a long day of poring over ledgers? We should have thought of this sooner."

Noah chuckles. "We're starting a separate book for wagers on high scores, right?"

"You bet your ass we are." I point at him. "But you can forget the date for the wedding. That's not happening."

"Dude, come on."

"No, no way. I'm already caving on this arcade thing—"

"Because you want it too."

"—but I'm not budging on that. No date."

He rolls his eyes but lets me have it. He knows how I feel about love and relationships and shit. He was just like me before Odette came along, and just because he went and fell in love with his younger sister's best friend nearly two years ago doesn't mean it's "my turn now" or whatever. I mean it when I say no relationships. I'm doing just fine on my own.

My phone buzzes in my pocket, and I know without checking that it's an alarm to get on the road before I'm late for yet another physical therapy appointment.

This one will be different, they said. *It'll work. We swear it.*

I want to roll my eyes just thinking about it, but there's a small part of me that hopes they're right. I gave up the PT for a few years, but lately my hip has been bothering me more, so I decided to start it back up again just to see what happens.

"Listen," I say to Noah, "I've got to run, but don't tell Odette it's a yes to the arcade right away. Let her stew."

"Oh, I planned on it. She's hot when she's mad." He grins in a way that makes me want to roll my eyes again.

I grab the nearest thing I can find—a wet rag—and toss it at him. "You're disgusting."

He just laughs as he peels the cloth from his face.

I let tonight's shift leader know I'm heading out, grab my laptop from the back office so I don't have to stop by here after my therapy, then climb into my blue Porsche 911 GT3 RS.

I'm fully aware that folding my six-foot-three frame into a tiny sports car isn't the best idea, nor is the manual transmission, especially given my mobility issues thanks to my bad hip, but I refuse to give up my fun just because of my injury. I've already lost so much due to it.

Which is precisely why I gun it the moment I'm out of the Stick Taps parking lot.

Driving fast is about the only vice I have, so I take full advantage of it every chance I get.

I pause briefly at the stop sign at the end of the long dirt road that leads to the cidery, then steer the little sports car onto the blacktop, loving the squeal of my tires against the pavement.

My lips twitch as I watch the speedometer climb much higher than the posted limit, and instead of my heart racing, it calms. This is the first time all day that I've felt truly relaxed. I used to get the same high from playing hockey, but since that's not happening anymore, I find my peace doing this—going as fast as I possibly can, living life on the edge, even just for a few minutes.

I realize how messed up that is, but I can't be bothered to care, not when I push the gas pedal harder and the engine cranks up louder, the car eating up the miles as I zoom toward town.

In the back of my mind, I know I should slow down, especially since I've already gotten two tickets in the last three months, but I can't seem to make myself do it. All the thoughts that were racing around before this are gone. I'm not worrying about everything I'll need to do to make the arcade happen, how much feed I need to order for the animals this month, or the stack of applications I have sitting on my desk that I still need to look over so we can get a little more help.

Nope, I'm not thinking about any of that. I'm letting it go, and I'm focusing solely on the long stretch of road before me.

I fly past the **Welcome to Port Harbor** sign. Unlike Noah, I'm not from Washington. I followed him here when we decided to open Stick Taps. It didn't matter to me where we lived or built our business. I just wanted to do it and stop thinking about the game I was forced to give up.

I was surprised to discover that I liked small-town life far more than I thought I would. There are only roughly twelve thousand residents here, but man, they show up in droves when it counts. And it usually always counts. They have activities nearly every weekend, ranging from fundraising events to harbor races. While I think most of it is cheesy as hell and you won't catch me attending unless I'm absolutely forced, it still feels nice to know that if I truly needed anyone, people would be there.

It's a big change from what I had growing up, that's for sure.

I get about a quarter mile before I see them.

Red and blue lights fill my rearview mirror, and I groan, braking and downshifting as I navigate my car to the side of the road.

I flip my visor down and pull my registration and insurance card free before reaching into my back pocket for my wallet to retrieve my driver's license.

I hold all three out of the window before the officer even reaches the car. I've been through this routine far too many times to count.

That's when I see in my side-view mirror that I'm not dealing with just anyone.

"Put that away, Mr. Rawlings," Sheriff Turner says as he approaches the car. "You think I don't have your information memorized at this point?"

Relief sinks into me that it's him and not one of his deputies. They're always hyped up on a power trip, but not him. He oversees the two towns that make up our little county, and I swear he knows every single person who lives in each one. He's just that kind of guy.

"It's because you're so sharp at your job and surely not because you stop me too often." I offer him a grin as I put my papers back under the visor.

"Let's go with the first one." He rests his hand on the roof, leaning down so he can get a better look at me. "Do I even need to tell you why I pulled you over?"

"Because you wanted a closer look at my car?"

He sighs, but I still catch the twitch of his lips. Honestly, I think the only reason I've received tickets from his deputies and not him is that Sheriff Turner used to be a fan of mine back in my playing days. I heard it through the grapevine and have been using it to my advantage since.

"You were doing 110 in a 50. That's a serious infraction, you know?"

Really? Only 110 mph?

But I don't say that. Instead, I put on my best *Aw, shucks* face and say, "I'm sorry. I wasn't aware I was going so fast. Am I getting a ticket?"

"Sure you weren't," he mutters, then sighs again. "Look, I—"

"I'm sorry for speeding, Sheriff Turner, but I'm running late for physical therapy. Got that bad hip and can't play hockey anymore, remember?" I'm wrong to exploit people's emotions, but in this case, I'm using losing my NHL career to my advantage to try to drum up some sympathy. "Think I could be on my way?"

His eyes narrow ever so slightly, and something about it makes my skin crawl. I like Sheriff Turner, but I don't at all like the look he's giving me right now.

"Sure thing," he says coolly, and the words instantly raise my hackles.

"Sure thing?" I repeat.

"Of course."

He's acting too chill about this.

"So, no ticket?" I ask.

He laughs quietly. "No, you're getting a ticket, but that ain't all you'll be getting."

My brows slam together. "What else?"

"Oh, Mr. Rawlings, I have the perfect punishment for you."

CHAPTER TWO

Summer

Sheriff Daniel Turner is Port Harbor's favorite resident and their elected protector. He's basically a king in this town, and if my calculations are correct, that makes me a princess. The last time I checked, princesses aren't usually chained to tables.

"Is this cuff from Jenkins really necessary?"

My dad snorts from across the table in the interrogation room. "With you? You're damn straight it is."

"You know I can get out of this easily, right?"

"I have no doubt, Summer Anne, but you're not going to because you love your father and you care about his job, so you won't be causing yet another scene today. *Right?*"

"Right," I agree through gritted teeth.

We've gone through the same song and dance before. When I was growing up, my father was always worried about election season and collecting votes, which meant I needed to be on my best behavior. Which I guess also means I maybe shouldn't have stolen the mayor's microphone an hour ago and used it as an opportunity to start a rant about the patriarchy and how archaic it is that we're auctioning women off like cattle.

To be fair, I was right, and if their cheers were any indication, many people in the crowd gathered in Pine Square for the Mid-Summer Fling agreed with me.

Sure, we were raising money for repairs on the community center that was destroyed by a tree falling on it during a bad storm, but my point remained the same.

My father sighs loudly. "So, the Mid-Summer Fling, huh?"

"It's a crock of shit!" I explode. "Can you believe we're still participating in that thing? It's ridiculous! And so embarrassing. This town is so much better than parading women around for the sole purpose of selling them for dates. As if we *need* men. It's—"

He lifts his hand, putting an end to my tirade. "I agree with you, Summer. You know that."

I smile. I *do* know that. My father raised me as a single parent from the time I was eight, and for as long as I can remember, he instilled in me that women are strong and that we can do anything men can do, damn whatever anyone else says.

I'm sure he didn't expect those words of wisdom to be the reason I'm sitting handcuffed to a table today.

"While I'm very proud of you for standing up for what you believe in, I do think there were better times you could have chosen to relay your feelings to the entire town."

A flicker of guilt shoots through me. He's right. I shouldn't be riling everyone up, least of all him, given what happened last month and brought me back home in the first place.

I didn't think anything could be worse than losing one parent, but the idea of losing both might just be it. Getting the phone call that he was having a "heart incident" at 2:00 a.m. wasn't on my bingo card, and I booked a ticket back to Washington as fast as I could.

He swears he's fine, and I believe him to an extent, but it's not enough to send me back to Chicago anytime soon. Not like I have anything to go back to anyway. I burned too many bridges, and I have nobody to blame but myself.

Staying in Port Harbor just makes sense right now.

"It wasn't the entire town," I say, trying to cross my arms and failing because I'm *still* handcuffed. I lift my wrist, the metal clanking against the table. "Can we please take these off?"

He nods, rising from his chair and pulling the keys from his pocket. He undoes the lock, tossing the cuffs onto the table as I rub at my wrists.

"Fucking Jenkins," Dad mutters, talking about his deputy who likes wearing his badge just a little *too* much some days.

I have no doubt he'll be getting an earful from the sheriff later.

"Thank you." I fold my hands together on the table. "So, what's my punishment other than embarrassment from being cuffed in front of the entire town?"

"It wasn't the entire town," he echoes, grinning when I roll my eyes. "I'm sorry Deputy Jenkins did that to you."

"Not as sorry as he's going to be if I catch him around town again. I'll make him a cheesecake. He still gets the shits from dairy, right?"

"Summer . . ." my father warns, but I see the amusement in his eyes.

"Fine. I'll just politely jaywalk away from him."

"Do not jaywalk!"

"Why do you ruin *all* my fun, Father?"

He shakes his head, sinking lower in his chair like he's exhausted by me. "I swear, you remind me more and more of your mother every day."

I grin. "I take that as a compliment."

My mother passed away from breast cancer when I was young enough to remember only a few things about her, and one of those things was her tenacity. Rebecca Turner never let anyone off the hook, not even my father, and I always admired her headstrong nature.

Apparently I picked up the same trait.

"Good. It's intended as one." He clears his throat, and it's because he still misses her, even though it's been eighteen years since she's been gone. He's dated a bit over the years, but nothing long term, and while I wish he had someone so he wasn't so lonely, I understand it. He loved my mother more than anything, and love like that only happens once.

He's not looking to try to replace her, and I respect that. "Now, about your punishment."

I groan, tossing my head back and blowing air against my brown bangs that could use a trim. "Which old lady do I need to help across the street this time?"

"First of all, helping others is *not* a punishment."

"Of course not, Boy Scout," I mutter.

He cuts me a glare that has me sitting up a little straighter. "Secondly, it won't be anything like that. You're getting a job."

"But I'm on sabbatical. I'm here for—"

He raises one brow, and it's enough to shut me up. "I know why you're here, and I appreciate you coming to stay with me, but your problems began when you quit your job out of nowhere. Given what happened today, it's clear you're bored and need something to keep you out of trouble."

He's wrong. I'm not bored. And I didn't quit my job out of nowhere. I quit it because I could feel the joy slipping away day by day and I didn't want to end up hating the thing that once brought so much light into my life.

But I'm not exactly in a position to argue, so I don't. "I understand. I'll start looking around town, maybe stop by the library to see if they need help. I—"

"There's no need."

I tip my head to the side, confused. "No need? But I thought you said I had to get a job."

"You do. I already found you one."

My jaw slackens. "Wait, what? I don't even get to pick my job?"

"No."

He stands, opening the door to the small room with the two-way mirror. He motions for . . . well, I'm not sure what, but whatever it is, I'm assuming it's coming into the room, because he steps aside.

Suddenly someone is there, taking up every inch of the doorway, towering over my father, who isn't a small man at six foot one.

A simple gray button-up stretches over the newcomer's chest, and a pair of slacks that seem to have been tailored specifically for him hug his thick thighs. He's scowling yet somehow looks like he's ready to teach me math or something.

But that's not what draws my attention.

No, it's the slight limp in his step as he makes his way into the room.

I avert my eyes, trying not to notice, and the man doesn't miss it. I swear I see annoyance flash in his gaze.

"Mr. Rawlings," my father says, closing the door behind him as he steps into the room, which suddenly feels smaller. "I appreciate you coming in today. I'm sure you have better things to be doing on your Saturday."

"No problem, Sheriff Turner," Mr. Rawlings says, his voice deeper than I thought it would be. "Not like I had a choice, did I?"

Dad laughs. "With the very real possibility of a court taking your license away, no, I suppose not."

Interesting. This guy is a delinquent too.

Dad gestures toward me. "This is my daughter, Summer."

The man doesn't say anything. He just stares at me with hard, green eyes that remind me of a Granny Smith apple.

"She's your newest employee."

A single dark eyebrow is raised. "She is?"

"Yep. I've decided that, as your punishment for speeding down Harborview Boulevard yet again, you'll select my daughter's name from that stack of résumés I'm sure is sitting on your desk since putting that help wanted sign in the window."

Mr. Rawlings's jaw tics as he continues to stare at me, and I refuse to look away, even though I want to crawl under the table in response to the blatant nepotism my father is blackmailing this guy into.

"With all due respect, sir, she hasn't filled out an application."

"Oh, I assure you, that can be fixed quite easily, especially if you'd like to not take public transportation to and from your next *session*, Mr. Rawlings."

I can tell the man wants to sigh, but he represses it.

"I'm sure once Summer here fills out an application, I can make sure it's sitting at the top and that she's the one we call with the job offer."

"You can't be serious," I interject, annoyed they're talking about me like I'm not even here.

My father looks at me with amused eyes. "Oh, honey, I am *very* serious."

"You can't call me *honey* and be serious in the same sentence. That's not how it works, *Sheriff*."

He glares at me from the other side of the table, and I try my best not to smirk at his reaction. He hates it when I call him *Sheriff*.

Then suddenly he doesn't look so entertained after all. He looks furious as he leans over the table, and I have to tip my head back to look up at him. "Listen to me, Summer Anne, if you think you're going to run away from your problems and live in my house while terrorizing my town without any consequences for your actions, you're dead wrong. You're twenty-six years old. It's time to grow up."

His words are low, but not so quiet that I don't hear them loudly.

He's glad I'm here. I know he is. But he also knows I'm not just here for him. I'm here because I'm hiding from everything that happened in Chicago.

So I swallow down that rebelliousness that lives inside me, the part of me who wants to argue just because I can, and I nod. "Where exactly is it that I'm working now?"

Dad grins, leaning away from me as he motions toward Mr. Rawlings to let him explain.

"Stick Taps," the guy with the gruff voice says, running his hand over the stubble on his chin.

"What's that?"

I know what it is. I just like the way *Mr. Rawlings* narrows his eyes at me.

"The cidery-slash-farm on the outskirts of town."

"Never heard of it."

"Summer . . ." my father warns.

He knows I'm fully aware of what Stick Taps is. Even though I haven't come home often since the cidery opened, it's kind of hard to avoid with how much the people in this town won't shut up about it, since one of the owners is none other than the town's star, Noah Stevens. He played in the NHL for a long, long time, and the town rallied behind him all those years. Whenever he was in the playoffs, there wasn't a place you could go that wasn't blasting the game on the TV, including the library.

Now everyone can't stop talking about how he's engaged and has turned his cidery into a wedding venue on the side. It was supposed to be a onetime thing for his younger sister, Izzy, but even though her marriage never happened, it still became a sought-after location for other nuptials.

I'm happy for Noah and all his success. He was always a nice guy, and I ran in the same circles as his sister and fiancée, even though they were a grade older than me. But it doesn't mean I want to work for him.

I want to . . . well, I'm not entirely sure what I want to do anymore. I thought I knew. I spent years in culinary school and training in kitchens around Chicago before landing my role as executive chef. I made a name for myself. I had a good reputation, and I ruined it all with one bad day.

Lore was supposed to be the city's hottest new restaurant, and it was for a time. Then things got messy with their first chef, and they quit. I thought I could come in and rescue it, but all it did was break me.

What I believed would be my dream job turned out to be my worst nightmare. It made me question everything, including the passion that had driven me to cook or want my own restaurant in the first place.

Even still, working at a cidery in a small Washington State town feels like a step down after running a kitchen of that magnitude. My father must be serious about this punishment.

"What exactly will I be doing at this *cidery*?" I say the word with enough disdain that Mr. Rawlings's nostrils flare.

I'm being petulant. I know that, but I can't stop myself.

My father sends me another warning look before he announces he's going to grab the paperwork to release me, leaving me alone with the stranger.

The door closes behind him with such finality that it startles me.

The chair across from me scrapes against the floor as my new employer sits. He winces as he settles onto the metal seat.

He ignores it, and so do I.

"So," I say when he doesn't speak, "what'd he clock you at?"

There's *almost* a twitch to his lips. "One ten."

I let out a low whistle.

"In a fifty," he adds.

My eyes widen. "And he didn't write you a ticket that would land you in court?"

"Surprisingly, no." He leans back and crosses his arms over his chest. His muscles stretch against the material of his shirt like they're threatening to bust loose, but he doesn't seem to notice.

I do, maybe a little too much.

"I got lucky," he continues, "considering this would have been my third ticket in less than three months."

I arch a brow. "Lead foot?"

"I like to go fast." He shrugs, not looking the least bit apologetic, and I like that. "What was your crime? Had to be bad if Sheriff Turner hauled his own daughter into the station."

"Actually, that was Deputy Jenkins."

"Fucking Jenkins." He repeats my dad's words, and it makes me grin.

"I might have *stirred up the crowd* at the Mid-Summer Fling."

Another near twitch of his lips. "And how, exactly, did you do that?"

"Went on a bit of a rant about the patriarchy."

He nods. "Makes sense."

"Excuse me?"

"The patriarchy sucks." He sits forward and folds his hands together on the table. A piece of his black hair falls over his eye, and I have the strangest urge to reach across the table and brush it back. I resist. "Why, what'd you think I meant?"

"I was waiting for you to call me an insufferable feminist."

No twitch this time. No reaction at all.

Okay then . . .

I clear my throat. "Anyway, I guess I hit a button with Jenkins, and the next thing I knew, I was in cuffs and in the back of his squad car."

"And now you're being blackmailed into working for me."

"I take it you're the other owner of Stick Taps?"

He looks a little stricken that I'm asking. It's almost like he's shocked I'm not falling at his feet or something.

I suppose it's not surprising, given that if the rumors are true about the owners, he was once a big shot hockey player. I bet people used to worship him. Too bad for him that I'll never be included in that list.

"That's me," he confirms.

"Well, thanks for the sympathy hire and all, *Mr. Rawlings*, but I'm not interested."

He tips his head to the side, like he's studying me, and I shift under his gaze.

"Ezra," he says after several uncomfortable moments.

"What?"

"Ezra. My name is Ezra."

Ezra. I test his name in my head a few times. I'm not sure what I was expecting, but it wasn't that. It suits him, though.

"I'm Summer."

Okay, that was definitely *a twitch of his lips.*

"I know," he says. "Summer Anne Turner."

Great. Guess he didn't miss my dad's little speech earlier.

I bet Ezra thinks I need to grow up too.

I twist my lips to the side, crossing my arms over my chest as I narrow my eyes at my new boss. "Look, whatever preconceived notions you have about me, you're wrong. I—"

"I don't."

"Pardon?"

"I don't have any preconceived notions about you. How could I? I've spent all of five minutes with you, and most of those minutes included your father, who pulled me over *again*. If anything, I have preconceived notions about him."

"My father is a good man." I notch my chin higher.

"Tell that to my lawyer, who keeps having to handle all these tickets."

I snort out a laugh. "You say that like this is all his fault and not yours. You were the one behind the wheel. You were the one speeding."

"Because it feels good. I wasn't causing any trouble."

"Pretty sure doing over twice the speed limit invites trouble."

"Not if you're a good driver," he argues.

"Say that to the teenager who isn't paying attention or the single mother who takes her eyes off the road for one second."

"That sounds like a them problem."

"And you sound like an ass."

Both of Ezra's dark brows rise. *That's it, Summer. Insult your new boss before you've even started work. Good idea. This is definitely you growing up.*

Instead of yelling at me, he laughs, and it catches me off guard.

"Yeah, I guess I am." He runs a hand over his five o'clock shadow. "Look, Summer," he says, and I try hard to ignore how much I enjoy hearing my name roll off his tongue, "we really do need help at Stick Taps. While you're certainly not my first candidate, if you know how to pour a drink, then I guess you'll do."

"Gee, thanks. I feel so welcomed," I deadpan.

Another lip twitch.

I sigh. "Okay, fine."

"Fine," he echoes. "Monday?"

"Monday works."

"Great. Be there at eight."

I balk. "In the morning?"

"Yes . . ."

"Who the hell is hanging out at a cidery at eight in the morning?"

"I am." He pushes to his feet, and I have to tip my head back, back, back, just to look up at him. "See you then, Sunny."

Sunny? Why the hell would he call me that?

I certainly don't feel sunny knowing that as of tomorrow, I'll have to work with Ezra Rawlings.

And how I might like the idea of that a bit too much.

CHAPTER THREE

Ezra

If hockey taught me anything, it's that you can function on very little sleep if you put your mind to it.

It's a good thing, too, considering I didn't sleep for shit yet again last night. It's become a trend for me these days, and it's one I'd really wish would fade. But until then, I guess I'll continue to show up on just four hours of shut-eye and get my shit done.

I push my key into the door of Stick Taps, working as fast as I can to get inside to avoid the rain. Once in, I flick on the lights and move through the empty cidery to the employee break room, where there's a coffeepot calling my name. Not only do I need to warm up after dealing with the random summer downpour, but I am in desperate need of caffeine.

I tossed and turned all night. Some of it was because my hip was sore from the intense physical therapy session I had on Friday, and some because I stayed up way too late working on stuff for the cidery and the iceplex. But the rest? I couldn't stop thinking about the shitstorm that I managed to get myself into with Sheriff Turner.

He's blackmailing me. There's no doubt about that.

The worst part is that I don't entirely blame him for doing it. He's let me off easy too many times to count, and I guess it's only fair I finally have consequences for my actions.

I just wish he weren't forcing me to hire his daughter. His very *attractive* daughter. I didn't want to notice her shoulder-length brown hair, her bangs, or the dark freckle that sits just to the right of her nose. And I really didn't want to notice her chocolaty eyes that have little flecks of gold in them, or her ruby-red lips, and how perfectly pouty they were as she called me on my shit.

"And you sound like an ass."

I keep replaying Summer Turner's words on a loop. They were honest, and it was refreshing. I can't recall the last time someone called me out like that, other than Noah and Odette.

All my employees act like I'm some big bad wolf, and while I prefer that, I kind of like the challenge.

I think that's what having Summer work at Stick Taps will be, though—a challenge, and I'm not sure I have the time for that. I have too much going on as it is.

I make a fresh pot of coffee, noting the time on the clock hanging over the door, and frown.

8:05.

Summer is late.

If she were anyone else, I'd fire her on the spot, but I have a feeling Sheriff Turner wouldn't take too kindly to that.

It's fifteen after when I hear banging on the front door.

Instead of rushing out to rescue Summer from the rain that's only picked up since I've been inside, I take my time.

She made me wait. It's only fair I return the favor.

When I finally make my way out of the central area of the cidery, she's glaring at me through the large windows like *I'm* the one who has inconvenienced her.

"Hello?!" she shouts, gesturing to the door. "Let me in!"

I stroll casually toward her, still not bothering to pick up my pace, and when I finally unlock and pull open the door, she rushes inside with a hard stare.

"Seriously? I was knocking for five minutes."

That's a lie. It wasn't even two.

"And what's with that chicken out there? It was looking at me like it was about to attack me."

I look beyond her to see that—once again—Tootsie has escaped. I'll deal with her later. Right now I'm focused on Summer and the fact that she was late. Was it really that difficult to be on time when I'm doing her and her father a favor by letting her work here? I know the cidery isn't hard to find, which means she's clearly not taking this seriously.

"That's Tootsie. She's harmless."

"Okay," she says, stretching the word like she doesn't believe me as she wipes her feet on the floor mat. "I did not miss this rain when I was in Chicago."

Chicago? What the hell was she doing all the way out there?

Wait. No. I don't care about the why. She's my employee. Who cares about her personal life?

Summer shakes off the last bit of rain, running her hands through her bangs like she's trying to contain them, then stares up at me with brown eyes that nearly match the color of her hair. She shimmies off her dark-green rain jacket, revealing a pair of black shorts that are entirely too fucking short and a white T-shirt that hugs her far too well. Fuck, I've never been so glad for someone bundling up in a raincoat before. There's no way her shirt wouldn't be see-through if she hadn't been wearing one.

I look away. Not because I don't like what I see—I do—but I have no business looking at her at all.

I know that familiar stir in my pants is just because I haven't been with someone in a long, long time, but it still irritates me.

"You're late," I tell her to distract myself.

"That's because I sat in my driveway for fifteen minutes debating whether or not I even wanted to show up today." She shrugs. "But I'm here now, so let's get on with it, shall we?"

Her honesty shocks me, but I guess it shouldn't, considering she did call me an ass the first time she met me.

I smirk at the memory of how feisty she was sitting in that interrogation room.

She's scrappy, that much is clear, and I like that she doesn't take shit from anyone, least of all me.

"Follow me," I say, turning and heading back toward the break room to finish my coffee before we start the day.

Summer's shoes—black canvas ones—smack against the floor as she follows behind me. She sets her bag on an empty chair, sliding her dripping coat over the back of it.

I make a mental note to grab a mop later to clean the mess, then sidle up to the coffeepot, grab a second mug from the cabinet above, and pour her a cup.

"Thanks," she murmurs when I hand it to her. She curls her fingers around it, soaking up its warmth as she blows on the hot liquid.

I'm surprised when she takes a sip without adding anything to it. Most girls I know don't take their coffee black. They prefer something with a bit of cream or sugar.

Guess I shouldn't be too shocked, given her less-than-sweet disposition.

"This place looks nice," she remarks, taking in the upscale break room.

Even though we're just a cidery, Noah and I tried to provide the same sort of luxury we used to enjoy in our player lounges at the arenas. There's something about feeling at home while you're at work that makes you want to show up and do your job well.

"I like the floors."

"I picked them," I tell her.

She arches a brow at that. "Really?"

"What? A man can't know a little something about decor? That's not very feminist of you."

She rolls her eyes. "I'm not sure you get to lecture women on what's feminist and what isn't."

"Fair enough."

We're quiet for a few minutes, just enjoying our coffee in silence, and I try not to focus too much on the red lipstick she's leaving behind on her mug.

"So," she says, "what exactly is it I'll be doing here?"

"Well, you could work outside with the animals."

"Like the murder chicken out there?"

"I promise Tootsie is harmless."

"I don't know . . . she gave me those *Watch your back* eyes."

"She's just wary of new people sometimes." I can't believe I'm talking about a chicken like it's a person. "Anyway, if you don't want to work with them, you can work in here. The taproom is where we need help most, anyway."

She grimaces, and I can tell she hates the idea of it, but we need another reliable bartender. We're getting busier and busier each night, and there just aren't enough people to make it flow as smoothly as I'd like.

"Look, if you don't want to do this, just say the word."

"I don't want to do this," she says simply. "But I got myself into this mess, and you're clearly already doing my father a favor. So I'll . . ." She blows out a steadying breath. "I'll work in the taproom."

I don't know if she's that stubborn or just ready to tackle her fears, but I nod anyway. "Okay. Taproom it is."

Coffee cups in hand, we head out to the bar. Aware of Summer behind me, I do my best not to let my uneven gait show. It's not always prominent, and I like to think most people don't even notice it now, but I know it's there. Fuck, do I know it's there. This . . . weakness of mine.

I hate it, and not just because of the stares I get.

I hate it because it's a reminder of everything I lost. Everything I could have had and now don't.

Even though I'm thankful for the years I got on the ice, it wasn't enough. I wanted more, and now I'll never get it. So I have to settle for finding a thrill in other ways, like my slight speeding addiction. It's the only thing that makes me forget about my shit mobility.

Pushing those thoughts away, I step behind the bar and reach under the register for the stack of papers I stashed there a few weeks ago.

"First things first, you need to fill out an application."

"What? You were serious about that?" Summer asks, settling onto a stool, her coffee cup at her lips.

"Yes," I say, thrusting a piece of paper her way. "I'm a records guy, and we need to make this seem legit."

Mostly for Noah. I haven't exactly told him about our newest employee just yet, and I really don't want to hear *another* lecture on my speeding problem.

"You getting arrested would be a bad look for the business, Ezra." That's what he said after my last ticket. But I don't think *anything* we do would reflect poorly on the business. Noah is this town's golden child. He could probably set the local diner on fire and still be lifted on the people's shoulders as a hero.

It's great for us, but he's right. We're held to higher standards than others, and we need to act like it. Which means I really, *really* need to stop drawing the attention of the local law enforcement.

"Ugh. Fine. Do you have a pen?"

I grab one from the cup next to the register and hand it to her.

She hunches down, scanning over the paper before she starts filling out the little boxes.

She's quiet as she works, and I flick my attention between her answers and the way her brows cinch together the further along she goes.

"Do I really need to write down my last three jobs?" she asks, not looking up from her work.

"Fill it out entirely. Don't want to make anyone suspicious."

She groans but does as she's told.

When she's finished, I take the paper and look over everything closely. Under education, she put *Enough,* and in her previous jobs, she wrote *Does it matter? I'm here now.*

Part of me wants to call her on this, but can I really do that when I find them amusing? Besides, I'd bet she'd have a comeback, and it's too fucking early to be dealing with that now. My workload is maxed out today. I have much more important things to do than argue with Summer.

"Well?" she asks. "Did I pass your test?"

I glance back up at her. "You did."

"Good." She grins, and it almost looks like she's genuinely happy about that. "So, what's first, *boss*?"

The single word is so loaded, and it gives me the perfect idea for what I need her help with this morning, after I get her acquainted with the layout of the place.

"You've never been here before, right?"

"No. I was already in Chicago when this place opened."

There's that mention of Chicago again.

Just like the first time, I pretend I hear nothing, then motion for her to follow me. "Come on. I'll give you a tour."

We leave our now-empty coffees on the bar top, and I show her around the cidery. I stick to just giving her a tour of the place. No personal questions, no anecdotes. It's all very straightforward and cold.

Summer can tell.

"And I'm guessing this is where you stash the other victims of your thrilling tours?" she asks once we stop in front of a closed door with a plaque that reads EMPLOYEES ONLY.

"No. It's where you'll be spending the rest of your shift."

I push open the door, and I see the moment irritation fills her eyes.

"The stockroom?"

"Yep. The stockroom."

"And what, exactly, am I supposed to do in here?"

"Organize it."

"Organ—" She purses her lips, her brows pinching together tightly. "Are you serious?"

"Very."

"I thought I was working in the taproom."

I knock my fingers against the wall above the door. "This is the taproom."

"*This* is a room in the basement."

"In the taproom."

Her eyes fall to slits, and I just *know* she wants to keep arguing, but she doesn't. She just blows out a heavy breath and mutters "Fine" before brushing past me and into the storage room.

I'm a little disappointed. Even though I don't have time for it, I kind of wanted her to fight me. I want her to argue. I want to spar a bit longer.

Instead, she gets to work, and all it does is put me in a worse mood than I was already in.

With one last glance at her, while she's already pulling stuff off the shelves, I head back upstairs to my office and bury myself in my work, putting Summer out of my eyeline and my mind.

CHAPTER FOUR

Summer

Ezra Rawlings is ridiculously good looking, but that's all he is. Outside of that, he's a downright ass.

So I ignore him. I pretend he's not somewhere in the cidery. I act like he doesn't even exist as I work to rearrange the stockroom into something that actually makes sense.

I have no idea who they had do this before, but they did an awful job at it. I'm surprised, considering how nice the rest of the place is.

When I first pulled up to Stick Taps, I was annoyed because it was raining. Then I was even more irritated when Ezra took forever to open the door for me. And again when he made me fill out that pointless application.

But after I got over all that and he was giving me a tour, I couldn't believe how beautiful the place is. It's much bigger on the inside than it looks from the outside. An open-concept layout welcomes you when you walk through the doors with an incredible view of the Cascades in the background, thanks to the windows that take up the back side. A bar with a stunning wooden top to the right and more seating and tables to the left. Everything is clean and modern, and the vast amounts of hockey memorabilia could keep anyone busy for a few hours.

I can't believe I haven't made my way here before now. Sure, I've been busy taking care of my dad, but this is the exact kind of place where I could see myself grabbing a drink or two. Maybe I would have come sooner if I felt like I had people to hang out with. I've been so wrapped up in taking care of my dad that I didn't realize how lonely I've been feeling since coming back.

My stomach rumbling pulls me from my dreary thoughts, and I realize quickly it's because all I've had today is two cups of coffee.

Dropping what I'm working on, I go in search of food.

I pause as I approach the kitchen, and the urge to push open the swinging door is automatic. It's not that I haven't cooked since I quit the restaurant. I make my father dinner every night. I just haven't been in a *real* kitchen since then. One with people buzzing around, yelling requests, or that sweet melodic sound of vegetables being chopped. Hell, I haven't picked up a good set of knives or donned my chef's whites in over a month. Considering cooking was once my life, it's strange. It's weird not hearing people yell *"Yes, Chef," "Behind,"* or *"Corner"* every few moments.

I miss it more than I thought I would, especially since I was so damn miserable before I left Chicago.

Shaking myself from the thoughts of what once was, I bypass the door with the little window on it and head for the fancy break room that looked like it could be stocked with snacks.

My eyes catch the clock on the microwave as I walk in, and I see that it's nearly noon. Damn, I had no idea so much time had passed—no wonder I'm hungry.

I yank open cabinets until I find something worthwhile, and I nearly cry when I see a box of cheese crackers.

"Oh my god, yes," I say, practically tearing open the package.

I pour the contents straight into my mouth, chewing loudly, and my stomach finally begins to settle.

"Uh, can I help you?"

I snap my head up to find a guy—a very attractive guy, might I add—staring at me wide-eyed from the doorway.

"What?" I ask around a mouthful of food, trying not to stare too hard at his dark-blond hair or how tan he is for someone who lives in the Pacific Northwest.

"I said, 'Can I help you?' Do you, um, work here?" He pokes his head back out the door and looks down the hall like he's searching for something. What, I don't know.

"Oh, sorry." I run my hand across the back of my mouth. "Yes, I do. Work here, I mean."

He tips his head to the side like he's studying me, like he doesn't believe me. "Since when?"

"Today is my first day. I'm Summer."

I give him a small wave and instantly curse myself for doing so. It's awkward. This whole situation is. And I really just want to eat these crackers in peace so I can go back to my organizing.

His face relaxes, and a big grin stretches across his lips. "Cool. Hi, Summer. I'm Warner."

"Hi," I respond weakly.

Warner laughs, then finally comes into the break room with me. "So," he says as he pulls open the stainless-steel fridge. "How are my crackers? Hitting the spot?"

I blink a few times, his words settling in, and when they do, I realize my mistake. "Oh my god."

Neither of us misses the crumbs that fly out of my mouth.

I wipe at my messy face and rush to close the cracker box.

Another chuckle as he grabs a bottle of water. "It's fine. I don't mind."

"Are you—" I swallow the final handful. "Are you sure?"

"Yep. Totally sure." He nods, then hands me the water before turning to grab a new one.

"Thanks," I mutter, cracking open the top and taking a long drink. I didn't realize how dry my mouth was until just now. "And sorry. I had no idea they were your crackers. I thought it was like a communal thing."

"I guess it is now."

Then he winks and I feel . . . nothing.

Not that I *want* to feel anything—I'm certainly not interested in starting something with anyone, especially since this stint in Port Harbor is temporary—but aren't you supposed to get butterflies when a cute guy winks at you?

"So, first day, huh?" I nod. "Did you just get here?"

"Huh? Oh, no. I've been here since eight."

"Eight?" He wrinkles his nose. "But we don't open until one."

Then why the hell did Ezra have me come in at eight? Is this some sort of game he's playing? And furthermore, how long am I even working today? We didn't discuss any of this.

I shrug. "Don't ask me. Talk to the boss."

"Noah isn't here today."

"The *other* boss."

"Ah," he says, nodding. "You mean Grump Ass."

I laugh—it's loud and quick and thoroughly embarrassing. "Sorry. I just . . . you call him Grump Ass?"

"Yeah, but don't say that too loud. We—me and the others who work here—have this theory that if you say his name three times, he'll appear."

"Like Beetlejuice?"

"More like Bloody Mary."

"Is he really that scary?"

Warner weighs his answer for a moment before saying, "Nah. Ezra is a good guy. Really. He's just a bit . . ."

"Of an ass?"

His impossibly bright blue eyes sparkle as he laughs. "Yeah, that. But you get used to his grouchiness quickly and learn when to avoid him. And honestly, it's not that hard to do. He doesn't come out of his office very often. Out of the two of them, Noah is the one you'll see more, and while he can be a bit cantankerous, too, he's much easier to deal with."

Huh. I don't recall Noah being testy, but I suppose a lot can change when you haven't seen someone in years.

"So, Summer," he says, and I notice he does that a lot—starts a sentence with *So*. It's kind of endearing, almost like he's nervous. "Are you new in Port Harbor?"

I laugh. "Hardly. I grew up here."

He looks surprised by this. "No way?"

"Yep. I, uh, my father is . . ." I trail off. I don't know why I always get cagey when I talk about him. It's not like I'm not proud of him and what he does for this community. I am. But every time I mention that my father is the sheriff, people have two reactions: They clam up and start acting weird or ask if I can get them out of a ticket or something.

I guess that's what I'm doing here with Ezra as well. I'm getting him out of trouble. Myself too.

"My father is Sheriff Turner," I finally say.

Warner grins. "That's awesome. I bet you get away with a lot in this town, then."

If he only knew the reason I was working here.

"What about you?" I ask him. "Are you new in town?"

Port Harbor may be small, and I might have grown up here, but it doesn't mean I know *everyone*, despite what some people may think. And considering I've been in Chicago since I was nineteen, many people have come and gone. In a way, I feel like a newcomer in my own hometown.

"Sort of. I moved here about five years ago now. Followed a girl." He shrugs, a wistful smile on his lips. "It didn't work out, but I fell in love with the town. I like that it's close to Seattle but not so close that it doesn't feel like its own little world, you know?"

I do know what he means. Port Harbor truly has always felt like its own special place, even with all the sad memories I have here surrounding my mother and her cancer. It's a far cry from living in a big city, and all it took was twenty-four hours here to remind me how much I missed it.

Maybe that's why I'm still here, even though my dad is doing well after his "incident." I wanted comfort. I wanted somewhere familiar. I wanted to feel safe.

I wanted *home*.

"This is a magical place," I say, eating another handful of crackers.

"Exactly! You get it." He bumps his shoulder against mine, then takes a drink from his water. "Definitely not without its entertainment either. I heard someone got arrested at the Mid-Summer Fling. The first time that I actually wish I had attended it. I would have loved to see that."

I duck my head at his comments.

I guess word hasn't gotten out just *who* was detained at the event. God, I can't believe I did that. Don't get me wrong—I stand by my comments. But maybe my dad was right. Maybe I should have chosen a better time to let my feelings be heard.

That seems to be a pattern for me—picking the worst times to let everything I bottle up shake free.

It's what landed me in the unemployment line just six months after being appointed head chef, everything I had worked toward for years.

But I don't want to think about that. Right now I just want to get through this punishment of working at Stick Taps and figure everything else out later. It's not like my dad is going to kick me out of his place. I have time to . . . well, take my time.

And if I'm being honest, I'm not ready to leave yet either. I like being so close to my dad again. While being back in Port Harbor after so long might make me feel like a bit of a newbie, it still feels like being wrapped in a favorite old blanket, and that's just what I need right now.

"Warner."

We both snap to attention.

Ezra leans against the door in all his math teacher–like attire. He's rolled his sleeves up since I saw him last, maybe ran his hand through his black hair a bit.

He looks good. *Too good.*

"Don't you have a taproom to open?" he asks, not taking his hard eyes off the guy next to me.

I hear Warner swallow thickly. "Uh, yeah. Right. Sorry, boss. Lost track of time."

"We should have unlocked the door ten minutes ago."

"I—I'm sorry."

"Don't be sorry. Take action." Ezra's words are sharp, his jaw set tight.

Warner looks to me. "Uh, see you out there, I guess?"

"Sure," I tell him, even though I doubt it's true. I still have work to do in the storage room.

He gives me a small wave before rushing past Ezra, head down.

His boss watches him go, then turns that fiery stare to me.

My first instinct is to make myself smaller, hoping maybe he won't notice me. How could it not be with eyes like those boring into me? But I'm rarely the one to ever back down from a challenge, so I don't.

Instead, I tip my chin higher, meeting his heated glare. "What."

I don't even form it as a question.

"This isn't social hour. You're here to work."

"Do I not get breaks at work? Because if I don't, I'm pretty sure that's illegal or something."

His jaw tightens as he pushes off the door. Even from across the room, he looks impossibly tall. "Are you ever not a brat?"

"I guess you'll have to wait and see."

He looks like he wants to say something about that. Instead, he settles on, "You get breaks. We're not tyrants."

"Well, then I'm taking a break. I'm almost done with the stockroom."

"Seriously?"

"What? Didn't think I'm capable of organizing a few shelves?"

"I—" He snaps his mouth closed, then exhales heavily through his nose. "No. I was just hoping that would take you a little longer."

Interesting.

"Why?"

"Because I don't have the time to babysit you today. I have other shit to do."

"So much to do that you're in here bothering me on my break."

I'm pushing it. I know I am. I see it in the way the vein on his head is getting more prominent the longer we stand here in this little face-off.

He takes a step into the room, then another, and another. It's amazing how much space his long legs eat up, because I swear, he cut the room in half with just three steps.

"You're awfully bold for someone who is reaping the benefits of a favor."

"Favor?" I ask.

I push off the counter with a laugh, setting the box of crackers down. I approach until I'm just close enough to be suddenly hit with the scent of soap and laundry detergent. If this were any other moment, I might find it nice. But right now, I'm pissed.

My breaths are coming in sharp, and my lungs are burning like I've just run a marathon.

"You call this a *favor*? News flash: I didn't ask to work here, *Mr. Rawlings*. I'm being forced to, just like you're being forced to hire me. I assure you, neither of us is doing the other a *favor*."

His eyes narrow even farther, and he points a finger at me. I'm almost 100 percent certain he's about to tell me to get out. That he's about to fire me and risk losing his license.

But he doesn't.

He drops his arm finally, running a hand through his midnight hair before he says, "Go back to work, Summer."

Then he spins on his heel, walks out of the break room, and leaves me standing there with cracker crumbs on my fingers and a dry mouth.

I was right before—Ezra is an ass.

Yet despite all that, I haven't felt so alive in months.

CHAPTER FIVE

Ezra

I'm a dick.

I know it, Noah knows it, and now Summer knows it too.

I've gone out of my way to avoid her the last two days because I was an ass to her in the break room for no fucking reason.

Okay, fine. So maybe it wasn't for *no* reason.

It was Warner.

I grind my molars together just thinking of that pretty little fuckboy. He's a shameless flirt, and if he weren't so damn good at his job, I'd fire his ass.

Hell, I just might do it anyway because I can.

I hated watching him use his charms on Summer. I was standing there for several minutes before they even bothered looking my way, and it . . . well, it fucking pissed me off.

Not that I have any right, but still. It's her first day. She should be focusing on making a good impression, not getting laid.

I grip the pencil in my hand tighter, then go back to transferring the data on the screen to my ledger. It's silly and certainly creates double work for me, but I like having something physical for our records, just in case.

When I'm finished, I move on to my emails. I've been chatting with a few people about pinball machines and other games, trying to sort out the best ones to buy for the cidery.

I respond to the two new ones I have, then pull out my plans for the arcade and get to work on those.

Or I try to.

It's hard when I know Summer is out in the taproom with fucking Warner right now. With Noah at the iceplex to start the week, I haven't exactly had the chance to tell him about our newest hire, which means he can't be here to train Summer like he usually would.

Fuck, I hope he's not pissed about this. One thing we always said was we'd make hiring decisions together. These people are representing us and our business. It was too important to put on the shoulders of just one person.

"Oh my gosh! Summer!"

I lift my head at the sound of Odette's voice echoing through the taproom.

Shit. Speaking of Noah . . .

I set aside my work and rise from my chair. I barely suppress my groan as my hip screams at me for sitting in the same spot for so long.

Typically I set a timer to ensure I get up a few times throughout the day to prevent my hip from locking up, but that hasn't been the case with me hiding from Summer.

I make my way toward the bar, fully expecting to find Noah glowering at me from behind the counter.

But I don't.

No, he's *laughing*. Head tilted back and everything. Summer stands next to him, a smile on her face too.

Odette is hugging her like they're old friends, and something tugs at my chest. This place has come to feel like home so much over the last few years that I almost forget I haven't always lived here. That these people have a whole history I was never part of.

"I haven't seen you since . . . Gosh, when was it? Two Christmases ago now?" Odette laughs as she pulls away. "I still remember how potent that eggnog you made was." She pinches the ends of Summer's hair. "I love this cut for you."

Summer blushes, and it's so strange to see. She's been nothing but confident around me. Has had no problem calling me out. This is a different side to her.

"Thank you," she says. "You look amazing too. Being engaged suits you."

"It does, doesn't it?" Odette cups Noah's cheek, staring up at him. "Still can't believe this guy convinced me to say yes."

"And I can't believe you're marrying Izzy's brother! Everyone used to have the biggest crushes on you, Noah. *Especially* Odette." Noah grins, clearly proud of that. "Speaking of Izzy, where is she?"

Odette juts her bottom lip out. "France. She's abandoned me to go find herself after everything that happened."

I don't blame Izzy one bit for taking off. Anyone who finds their almost spouse cheating on them just before the wedding deserves time away.

"She didn't abandon you," Noah says, rubbing her back comfortingly. "She'll be back before the wedding."

"I know, I know. But it's not the same as having her here now, you know?" Odette shrugs. "Anyway, what are you doing here?"

"I, uh, I work here," Summer says.

Noah's brows inch closer together. "Since when?"

"My first day was Monday."

"Ezra!" Noah calls.

I sigh, then step out of the shadows and fully into the bar. "I'm right here. I heard Odette screeching from the back office."

The woman in question flips me off, and I almost chuckle.

I turn to Noah. "What's up?"

"When did you hire Summer?"

I flick my gaze to her briefly, and I'm surprised to find she's already looking back.

But I'm not surprised to see her glaring at me.

"It happened Saturday."

"What? When? You didn't even work on Saturday."

I shrug, shoving my hands into my pockets. "It was a . . . sudden decision."

"Blackmail. It was blackmail."

Noah snaps his head to Summer. "What?"

She jerks her thumb my way. "Ezra here was caught speeding by my dad, and I got into a little trouble myself, so my father cooked up this punishment for us both."

Noah glares over at me. "Speeding, man? Again?"

"It's my hip. My leg gets stiff, and the gas pedal gets stuck."

It's a crock of shit. He knows it as well as I do, but he's not about to chew me out in front of Odette and Summer.

Odette gasps. "Oh my gosh! You're the one who got arrested at the Mid-Summer Fling, aren't you?" She laughs loudly. "Oh, man. This is gold. You always were a troublemaker. Gave your dad the runaround, that's for sure."

Summer looks a little proud of that, and I bet she is. She loves being bratty far too much not to be.

"So, are you living here now? What happened to Chicago?" Odette asks.

I stand up a little straighter, entirely too interested in hearing her answer.

"It, uh, it just didn't work out. So I'm back in Port Harbor for a while."

To my surprise, she begins to fidget. She tucks her hair behind her ear, then pinches her earlobe before dropping her hand to her necklace and swinging it back and forth.

There's more to the story she's not sharing, and I'm dying to know what it is, but I let her have her secret.

"Anyway," she says, "if you want to fire me, you can. It won't even be Ezra's fault, so he can get out of whatever trouble he's in with my dad."

"I'm sorry, you think *I'm* going to get in the way of Sheriff Turner's punishment? Not a fucking chance. That man is *scary*! I still remember the time he busted me and a few guys for drinking down at the harbor when we were sixteen. He wasn't even on duty that night, but he was pissed. Your mother had to talk him off the ledge while he waited for backup. They were supposed to be going on a date night, but he followed us to the station and laid into us again while we were there."

"That sounds like my father." Summer smiles fondly. "And my mother."

"Mrs. Turner was the best. Still my favorite teacher."

Was. I don't miss Odette's use of the past tense, nor how Summer shifts uncomfortably.

She clears her throat. "Anyway, my dad isn't scary. You just have to know how to handle him."

"Apparently Ezra does if he's not under mountains of tickets and still has his license after all the shit he's pulled." I can feel Noah's scowl. "That's the third time you've been pulled over in, what, four months?"

"Three in three," I correct, and I know instantly it was the wrong thing to say.

"What the fuck, man?!" Noah explodes. *So much for thinking he'd keep his lips zipped in front of the girls.* "We're supposed to be role models. The kids are relying on you."

Shit. I hadn't even thought of the kids from the iceplex.

I glance at Summer, fully expecting her to be watching me with smug satisfaction that I'm getting yelled at, but no. She almost looks a little . . . sad for me.

I don't like it.

I return Noah's dirty look and tell him, "Later."

He opens his mouth to argue but thinks better of it when Odette squeezes his arm.

"Sure. Later."

His words are clipped, and fuck if they don't cut me because he's right. I should have thought more about the kids. I should have thought about the example I'm setting for them, especially since I've been in their position before.

Unlike Noah, I didn't just want to build the iceplex because I missed the game. This was more personal to me. I didn't have the same picture-perfect family dynamic he grew up with. Far fucking from it, actually. My local rink was the only thing I had. It's what gave me the game I love so damn much.

I'm supposed to be there for these kids like my earliest coach was there for me.

"Summer, we *must* have dinner together sometime soon," Odette says in an attempt to change the subject.

"I would love that."

"And, Ezra, you can come too! We can play cards or something after. It'll be fun."

You never come out with us when we invite you.

Odette's words from before echo through my mind. While the urge to still tell her no sits at the tip of my tongue, I find myself nodding.

"Sure."

She's as shocked by my answer as I am, her mouth dropping open. "Seriously?"

"Do you want me to change my mind?"

She pretends to zip her lips closed and does a little shoulder shake before turning to Summer. "Let's coordinate something. You still have my number, right?"

"I should," Summer says as she drags her phone out of her back pocket to check.

"No phones on the floor."

She narrows her eyes at me. "Sorry, *boss*. Won't happen again."

Boss.

Every damn time she says that to me, my jaw tics. I want to reprimand her for her smart mouth, but I keep quiet.

"Oh, I like you," Odette says with a grin. "You aren't afraid to get sassy with this guy, who is, like, a total ass seventy percent of the time."

"Seventy?" Summer laughs. "I think your calculations are off."

I'd defend myself, but she's right.

I know I'm a jerk, which reminds me that I need to apologize for being one the other day.

But not now. Not in front of Odette and Noah. Later.

"Speaking of numbers, I should get back to work. You too, Summer."

Her eyes fall to slits once more, but this time, instead of arguing, she nods.

"Probably. Warner was just about to show me how to load a new keg." She turns to Odette and Noah. "It was so good seeing you guys again."

"You too! And text me," Odette instructs her.

She gives them one last smile before hurrying away to find Warner, not bothering to spare me another glance.

For some reason my hands curl into fists as I watch her go.

Fucking Warner.

"What are you still doing here?"

Summer jumps at the sound of my voice, her hand going to her chest.

It's late. The cidery closes in less than sixty minutes. She should have been gone hours ago.

"Uh, Warner had a thing come up. Something about his grandma, so I said I'd close tonight."

"Warner's grandma who died last year?"

Summer's mouth drops open at the news, then she shrugs, shaking off her shock. "He could have more than one grandmother. You don't know."

I do know, because he lost the other one the year before.

He just wanted to cut out early so he could go to Hank's for two-for-one tequila shots tonight. The money they raise is supposed to go toward the community center, but I know Warner isn't there for that. He's there to drink and have fun while someone else does his work for him.

Fucking Warner.

"Do you even know how to close the cidery?"

"Uh, what does it look like I'm doing?" She holds up the glass she's drying. "Think I can handle closing out the register and putting the chairs on the tables. It's not that difficult."

"And do you know the code to secure the doors when you leave?"

"I—" She doesn't. The way her face falls makes that clear. "I could have texted Warner for the code."

She has his fucking number?

"Just go. I can lock up."

She scrunches her nose. "No. I'm not leaving until we're closed."

"Summer, I'm telling you—"

"And I'm telling *you* that I'm staying. I'm not an idiot, *Ezra.* I can do this simple task."

"I never said you were an idiot."

"No, but you sure as shit implied it," she snaps right back. She huffs. "I'm staying, okay? You need to stop treating me like you're my babysitter. You're not. I'm just another employee."

"Good. Then you're fired."

"Really? Are you going to be the one to tell my father that?"

Fuck. She has me there.

"Fine. You're not fired. But you're also not—"

"I'm staying."

My teeth gnash together for what feels like the fiftieth time since I met her. She's infuriatingly stubborn.

"Fine. Stay. I don't care."

I turn on my heel, making my way to the break room to grab a cup of coffee. It's later than I'd usually drink it, but I'm going to be here for at least another hour or two. I need it.

Coffee in hand, I make my way to my office and lock back into work.

Or at least I try to.

I can still hear her moving around in the taproom, and it's distracting as hell.

It's not that I don't trust her to close. I have no doubt Warner taught her how to do it the right way, because, while he's a shithead, he does know what he's doing. I just . . . fuck, I don't know. I'm on edge, and I have no idea why. Maybe it's from the lack of sleep I've been getting or the fact that I don't even remember if I had breakfast this morning, and I'm just hangry. Whatever it is, I need to get it together.

I take three deep breaths, then swear to myself I'm actually going to get some work done so I can get out of here and head home. I could use a good seven hours of sleep for a change.

But forty-five minutes later, when I've barely moved my pencil or touched my laptop, I rise from my chair and make my way back to the bar.

And there she is, resting against it, her chin in her hand as she stares at the door.

She's wearing another pair of shorts today, these frayed a little at the ends, and a simple black T-shirt that's been threatening to show off her stomach all day. We don't exactly have a uniform here at the cidery—just whatever everyone is comfortable in.

I guess this is what's comfortable for her. Those tiny shorts, a shirt that hugs her curves, and that damn red lipstick that I find myself liking way too much.

"Can I flip the sign?"

I force my gaze from her lips to her eyes. "What?"

"Can I flip the sign from *Open* to *Closed*. Nobody has been in for an hour, at least."

She's right. We're unusually slow tonight, though I suspect that has to do with the event at Hank's.

"Yes, then you can go."

She huffs, pushing off the counter and heading for the door. "Still not happening. I have more work to do."

"I can take care of it."

"Not a chance." She spins the sign around, then dead bolts the door, the sound loud in the otherwise quiet cidery. "Just go back to your office."

"Are you always this obstinate? Is that why your boyfriend broke up with you, and you moved back here?"

Fuck. Why did I say that? I don't even care.

"I don't have and haven't had a boyfriend for a long time."

"No surprise there, given your attitude."

"Yes, because yours is *so* charming. I'm sure your girlfriend loves it."

I snort. "Oh, sweetheart, I don't do girlfriends or love. Not even a little bit."

"No surprise there, given your attitude." She tosses my words back at me.

She makes her way behind the bar and starts pressing buttons on the payment system. Her brows tighten, a little crease forming between them, and I can tell right away that she doesn't know what she's doing, despite her claims.

With a sigh, I step up behind her, watching as her fingers press all the wrong buttons.

"You're doing it wrong."

She jumps, glaring at me over her shoulder. "Jesus. You're like a cat, you know that?"

"A cat?"

"Yeah, an orange one. All stealthy and shit but also mean."

I barely resist a smile. "Move. I'll close the register."

I expect her to argue again, but to my surprise, she doesn't.

She moves aside silently, and I step up beside her.

"This is how you do it," I say, going through the steps slowly. "See?"

"No." She pushes closer, and I freeze.

Vanilla. She smells like a damn vanilla cupcake, and fuck if it doesn't make my stomach rumble.

"Um, was that your stomach?" she asks with a laugh.

"No," I lie.

She huffs. "Have you even eaten today? I haven't seen you since Odette and Noah were here earlier, and I didn't see you eat then. Unless you keep something stashed in that cave of yours."

"Cave?"

She ignores my question. "I can make something. You guys keep the kitchen stocked, right? I'm sure I can whip something up."

She's already walking toward it before I even realize what's happening.

"Wait, what? Where are you going?"

"The kitchen!" she calls over her shoulder, almost out of sight already.

She's moving fast, like she can't wait to get in there, and I'm sure it's just because she's desperate to get away from me. I don't blame her. I still haven't apologized.

But that's the last thing on my mind. What the hell is she talking about, making me food?

"We're supposed to be closing the cidery!"

"Then you close it! You were so eager to do so just a few minutes ago!"

So were you, I want to say, but I don't.

She's gone. Disappearing around the corner and into the kitchen.

What the fuck is happening?

CHAPTER SIX

Summer

Chefs love to feed people. That's a given.

When I heard Ezra's stomach rumble, my instincts kicked in, and I went for the nearest kitchen.

Now that I'm standing in it, I'm trying to figure out just what the hell it is I'm doing, and not just because this place is depressing.

They have the basics, like bowls and pans, and not nearly enough seasoning from the looks of it, but that's it. It's evident that Stick Taps doesn't spend a lot of time and effort on their kitchen, and I guess I get it. After glancing over the menu earlier, which primarily features simple dishes like Seattle-style hot dogs, chicken tenders, and mac and cheese bites, it's clear they aren't trying to impress people with their culinary skills.

It's such a shame, because I think they might draw even *more* of a crowd than they already do. They need an overhaul. They need someone to come in and make this place a go-to for drinks *and* dinner. They need— *No.*

I banish my thoughts right there. I am *not* here to work in another kitchen. I'm here to pay off a debt to my father, and that's it. Besides, I'm not even sure if I still want to be a chef. There's no reason for me to get involved with another kitchen when I'm so uncertain.

Still, Ezra needs to eat, and this place is so lacking that it's basically like cooking dinner for my father. No harm in making a *little* something, right?

I move toward the industrial-size fridge they have—their one saving grace—and take inventory of what I'm working with.

It's not much. In fact, it's barely even stocked with . . . well, anything. Where are the fresh herbs? Where are the ingredients for the salsa served with the chips? Where are all the eggs for their batter for the chicken tenders?

I slide my eyes to the freezer.

Ugh. It's all frozen, isn't it?

The door swings open behind me so hard that it nearly bounces off the wall. "What the hell are you doing?"

I turn to Ezra, who has taken up his usual stance—arms crossed over his impossibly big chest, his veins popping on his forearms, and his legs spread just a few inches apart. His dark brows are slashed together, his pouty lips flat, his strong jaw set. It's all very authoritarian-like, as if he's about to yell at me. Or take control of the situation.

A shiver rolls down my spine at the thought, and I quickly push it away before it can spread into something it shouldn't.

"Where are your ingredients?"

He flinches at the question, like it was the last thing he expected. "What?"

"I thought this was a kitchen, so where is all the food?"

"Uh, I don't know. The freezer? I don't exactly come in here often."

"Is that because nobody ever even orders food?"

He opens his mouth—I assume to argue—then he snaps it shut. He knows I'm right. I've worked here for only three days, but I think we've had fewer than twenty people actually place an order for food. They don't even have someone who works the kitchen full-time, unless it's for big events or weekends, according to Warner.

"Most people are here to drink, not to eat."

"Yet you're still smart enough to know that you need a menu."

"A lot of cideries and breweries around here allow people to bring their own food. We don't discourage that."

"You would if you actually believed in your menu. I'm surprised this is what you have to offer, especially when you're hosting so many weddings here now. Caterers want a usable kitchen, too, you know."

Somehow his perpetual frown deepens, but I don't care. I turn from him, looking for something to make.

I find some noodles, a couple of blocks of cheese that look like they've been destroyed by a toddler, and a few spices that will have to do.

I grab a pot and fill it with water, then set it on the stove, which I'm thankful is gas. There's nothing worse than trying to cook without a flame.

I take the cheese to the cutting board, flipping through a few cabinets before I find a grater. It's cheap, but it'll do.

"What are you doing?" Ezra asks again.

I don't spare him a glance. "I already told you, I'm making food."

"I can make my own food."

"I'm sure you can, just like I'm sure you're going to be here late tonight, and it's clear you're hungry. So just shut up and let me do this, will you?"

Oh my god. I just told my boss to shut up.

I dare a peek over my shoulder, and I'm surprised to find that he's now resting against a table, watching me as I work.

I ignore just how much I like that.

"Anything else?"

His lips twitch so quickly, it's a blink-and-you'll-miss-it moment.

He shakes his head. "No. It's obvious you're going to be stubborn about this, too, so do whatever you want. I'd *love* to see what you're going to make that I can't make for myself."

All his words do is give me motivation to make him the best damn macaroni and cheese he's ever had. It'll be hard, since I'm working with so little, but I'm determined.

I work silently, acutely aware of Ezra's eyes on me the whole time. I feel it when I salt the water for the pasta, when I grate the cheese, and when I chop the parsley left in the fridge. In every shake of onion and garlic powder. And especially when I add the dash of cayenne for an extra kick.

It's exhilarating, and not just because he's watching me so closely. No, it's being in a kitchen again. Sure, I'm making something simple, and this kitchen kind of sucks, but that's not the point. The point is that I'm cooking for someone other than myself and my father again.

It feels good. It feels like it used to, before everything blew up and I took off my chef's whites for the last time.

Sometimes I wonder if I made a mistake, walking away from Lore. I wonder if I was too rash and stressed with trying to keep up and prove myself capable of running my own crew. Would things be different if I hadn't started to feel stagnant so soon after *finally* getting what I had been working toward? Would I still be here in Washington, or would I be back in Chicago, bossing everyone around? Would I have still folded under all the pressure, or would I have made it through the rough patch?

I don't know the answer to any of it, so I pack those thoughts away for another time and refocus on the task at hand—the dish. When it's finished, I scrounge for bowls and portion us each a healthy helping, then top it with the parsley and a little crack of pepper.

He lifts his brows as I hand him the final product. "Mac and cheese, really?"

I glower at him. "Just try it, you big baby."

His eyes darken as he takes the bowl, his fingers brushing over mine just slightly. He's warm, which is a stark contrast to how cold he comes across.

I ignore that, then stab my fork into the noodles, taking a bite so I don't do something silly like speak my inner thoughts out loud.

Ezra does the same, although much more tentatively, and I watch him closely for his reaction.

I see the moment he decides it's good, and that's because it is. It's *really* fucking good, all things considered.

"Holy shit," he says, going for another bite. "This is . . . actually good."

I'm too glad he likes it to be bothered by his insinuation that he expected it not to be. "I told you."

"This is way better than whatever we put in our mac and cheese bites." He shovels another forkful into his mouth, chews, then swallows. "How do you know how to cook?"

"I wasn't in Chicago for a guy. I was there for culinary school."

He pauses, his fork hanging in the air between us, the gooey mac and cheese slipping off his utensil and back into the bowl. "What?"

I shrug, moving to stand next to him, crossing one leg over the other as I hide behind my dinner. "I've been working in a kitchen for years. I was an executive chef at a restaurant called Lore before I moved back here."

"Are you being serious right now?"

"Um, yes?"

When he doesn't say anything else, I glance up at him, and I'm surprised by how he's staring down at me. His eyes are hard and narrowed, and . . . *Holy shit, is he* mad?

"What?" I ask.

He shakes his head once. "I just . . ." A scoff. "What the fuck are you doing here, Summer?"

"Um, eating dinner?"

"No. That's not what I mean, and you know it. I mean, what the hell are you doing here in Port Harbor and not back in Chicago? Why aren't you working in a restaurant? Why are you tending bar at a cidery?"

"Because my dad hates me."

"That's not true at all."

I sigh, setting my bowl to the side. "I came back because my dad had a heart scare last month. It wasn't a big deal. He had a minor procedure and should be just fine now, but that's why I'm here. I came back for him."

It's not entirely a lie, but I've certainly left out the rest of the story, about how I had a major blowup at work and screamed at my staff, my boss, and even the damn owner of the restaurant before quitting.

But considering he's just my current boss, Ezra doesn't need to know all that.

His features soften just a little. "I didn't know that about Sheriff Turner."

I shrug. "He didn't want to make a big deal about it. He's up for reelection this fall, and he felt a medical episode wouldn't be very good press for his campaign."

"That's fair. I just wish he'd said something."

"And what? You would have driven ten miles per hour slower?"

For the first time, Ezra smiles. Like *really* smiles.

And it's . . . well, it's fucking beautiful. His whole face lights up in a way I'd never seen before. I swear his eyes brighten by at least two shades, crinkles forming around both of them.

It's officially my favorite look on him.

When I don't say anything for several moments, he tips his head to the side, that grin still stretched across his lips. "What?"

I shake my head, unable to stop myself from smiling right back. "Nothing. It's just . . . you have a nice smile, you know that?"

Then just like that, it's gone, and I miss it instantly. I want to make it come back. I want to see his face glow. I want that easygoing guy I have a feeling is hiding behind every frown.

I don't have much room to talk. I'm not exactly the sunniest person around, either, but I get the feeling I have more fun than he does.

"I'm sorry for being an ass the other day. I—I had no right to be one. You didn't deserve that."

His words surprise me. An apology is the last thing I ever expected from him. I get the feeling it's not something Ezra does very often either.

"You're right. I didn't."

He almost looks taken aback by my words, like he was expecting me to tell him it was okay or that it wasn't a big deal.

It *was* a big deal. He had no reason to treat me that way, but I appreciate him copping to his fuckup and apologizing. And I tell him that.

He nods in response, and that's that.

We finish our dinner in silence, then he grabs our bowls and takes them over to the sink. I don't argue with him as he pulls off his watch and sets it aside, then begins to do the dishes.

Instead, I hop onto the counter next to him, keeping him company as he hands me a dish to dry. It's annoying whenever the water drips onto my thighs, but I can't be bothered to move. I'm not quite ready to leave the kitchen just yet.

Or Ezra, truth be told.

He's intriguing. Grumpy, that's for damn sure, but intriguing. I get the sense he's hiding a lot under his gruff exterior, and I want to find out just what that is.

"So why aren't you working in a restaurant now?" he says after a while.

"I told you. My dad."

"Yeah, but there are plenty of places here in Port Harbor you could be working instead of here."

I wrinkle my nose. "Not really. They're kind of lacking in restaurants here. We have, what, like five good ones?"

"Depends on your definition of good, but yeah, somewhere around there. Why not work at one of those?"

"I'm not sure I want to work for anyone else anymore."

"You want your own restaurant?"

I laugh lightly. "I would kill for my own kitchen—one that's truly mine—but it's not in the cards right now."

Besides, I'm back in Washington for my father, not my own self-serving reasons.

Ezra stares at me a moment before nodding like he understands, and maybe he does.

Still, I'm grateful when he moves on and asks, "Why Chicago?"

"Because it wasn't Port Harbor. I'd spent my entire life here up until that point, and something new felt like what I needed at the time. I hated leaving my father, but I'm still glad I did it."

"And your mom?"

That familiar tug I always feel when I talk about her pulls at me. "She passed away when I was eight. Breast cancer."

He nods. "That sucks."

I laugh at his response.

"What? Was that not the right thing to say?"

"No, it was perfect. Most people say how sorry they are—which I do appreciate—but they never state the obvious that, yeah, it does *suck*."

"I lost both of my parents pretty young, so I understand."

My heart races at the thought of just how close I came to being in his same position a month ago. *Almost* losing my father was bad enough. I can't imagine how hard actually losing him would be. "That had to have been tough."

"Honestly, I don't remember much. I was only six, so it's not as if that time in my life is full of memories, you know? There are flashes, sure, but nothing concrete." Something flickers in his eyes, and it's clear it bothers him that he doesn't recall things clearly, but he tries not to show it. "I barely even remember the night they passed. It was a multicar wreck where I grew up in Minnesota. Bad weather, too much snow and ice. That kind of thing. I just remember the cops pulling up to the house with their lights on and telling my uncle Paul, who was watching me at the time, what happened. After that, I was just with him. He raised me like I was his own, and I don't think I fully comprehended what I had lost until later. In more ways than one."

He says that last part so quietly that I almost don't hear him.

The urge to reach over and hug him is so strong that I actually do it.

At first he's stiff. It's like hugging a board. A really big, broad board, but still rigid.

Then he yields, giving in to it, and he sinks against me, his arms going around me just as tight as I'm squeezing him.

I don't know what I expected tonight, but it certainly wasn't this. The scent of rain-like soap fills my senses as I hold Ezra in my arms, and he nuzzles his nose against my neck.

Wait, what the hell?

His touch is soft, almost imperceptible, but it's there, and my pulse begins to thrum under it. There's no way he doesn't feel it. There's no way he doesn't know that my heart is thundering in my chest like it never has before.

There is no damn way that Ezra Rawlings doesn't know what he's doing to me right now.

He pulls away slowly, his eyes meeting mine, and *fuck*. They're dark in a way that I haven't seen before. The kind of dark that says *I'm going to kiss you now*.

And I'm okay with that. Hell, I *want* him to kiss me. I want to kiss him too.

His gaze flicks to my lips, then back to my eyes. Over and over as he inches closer.

Holy shit, this is happening!

I hold my breath and close my eyes, anticipating the moment his lips meet mine.

Except, they never do.

No, when I open my eyes, Ezra is now standing several feet away, and I wonder when that happened. I was so caught up in the moment that I missed him moving.

Though his eyes are still dark, it's different now. He's not looking at me like he wants to kiss me. He's looking at me like he wants to be anywhere else in the world.

And it's fucking embarrassing. Did I misread the entire situation? Was he not just looking at me like he was a starving man?

"I should go," he says, ramming his hands into his pockets.

Okay then.

"Sure." I don't know what else to say.

"Good night, Sunny."

Then he disappears through the kitchen door like nothing ever happened, leaving me sitting there trying to figure out what the fuck just occurred.

CHAPTER SEVEN

Ezra

I almost kissed Summer.

And I don't mean a spur-of-the-moment kind of kiss. I mean, I *consciously* decided to kiss her. I was *this fucking close*, could smell her vanilla cupcake perfume, could see the look in her eyes like she wanted it too.

But I didn't. I came to my senses before I could fuck this thing up even more and got the hell out of there.

That was two days ago, and I haven't spoken to her since. I was shocked when I stopped by the cidery yesterday to find my watch sitting on my desk. She must have put it there before she left. I had completely forgotten about it, which is surprising, because it's one of the only things I have left of my father.

Fuck, I can't believe I told her about my parents. Almost nobody knows what happened to them. It's not something I like to advertise, mostly because I hate the pity that fills their eyes. But she told me about her mother and now what's going on with her dad and . . . shit, I don't know. I wanted to share my scars too.

I had no idea that Daniel Turner was having heart problems. I get why he didn't announce it to the town—this place is full of busybodies—but I wish I'd known. Maybe I'd have been a bit less of a jerk to him or would have accepted this arrangement with Summer a little easier.

Or maybe not.

Either way, I shouldn't be kissing his daughter, that's for damn sure. Not just because Sheriff Turner is doing me a favor either. She's my *employee* for fuck's sake. I don't care if this deal was done under the table or not. I'm still the one signing her paychecks.

It's wrong, no matter how wrong it didn't feel.

I push that thought aside and try to refocus.

A kid—Joel—skates by, his blades swishing across the ice with that sound that's so damn familiar to me at this point that I swear it's embedded in my brain.

"Doing good," I say to him as he holds the puck on his stick.

We're doing simple drills today at Stick Taps Community Iceplex, and I'm thankful as fuck to be away from the cidery for a few hours. I don't need the memories of the way Summer looked at me on that kitchen counter at every turn.

And it wasn't just the almost kiss either. It was more than that. It was how she looked at me when she was talking about owning a restaurant one day. It was obvious watching her work that she loves cooking and that it's her passion. It saddens me she's not following it.

It did get me thinking . . . she was right that the Stick Taps kitchen is lacking. We don't sell a lot of food, and I've always told myself that was okay because it wasn't what drew people to the cidery anyway. They came for the drinks, the entertainment, and that beautiful fucking view. If they could grab a bite to eat, that would be great. And yeah, we've had some caterers bitch about the lack of kitchen space, but we've always handled that.

But what if we *did* have a real kitchen? And a better menu? My gut tells me that more patrons, better profit, less space going to waste, and stronger relationships with the catering companies are all possible. It would be a win-win all around.

And even better, we *have* a wedding coming up—Noah's. It's only ten weeks away, so we'd have to get started now if we were going to overhaul things, but if I play my cards right, we could complete the renovation before then and use it as a test run. It would be perfect, especially if Summer ran the kitchen for us.

I know it's a stretch, and asking her to take that on when she's already being forced to work at the cidery is a lot. Still, if she was able to create something like that mac and cheese I had the other night on a whim, I can only imagine what else she can do with the proper equipment and ingredients. I could bring her on as a consultant for the renovation too. It would make sense. She has more experience in that area than I do. Hell, she could even make the menu. It might not be her own restaurant, but it would be damn close.

The thought gets my heart racing in a way it hasn't since . . . since I almost kissed her two nights ago.

I scratch at the scruff lining my face—something I desperately need to shave off—then run a hand through my hair.

Shit. This could never work. She's never going to help me. Not after that. What the hell was I thinking? I wasn't, that much is obvious. Thank fuck I caught myself at the last moment, or that could have been an even bigger disaster.

"Coach Rawlings! Did you see that goal?"

I snap out of my thoughts and give Jensen a thumbs-up. "Looked good, buddy. Nice technique."

I was only half-ass paying attention, but the kid doesn't need to know that.

"I'm going to do it again!"

He does, and this time I watch every second of it, which is why I notice the goalie is out of position.

Though my strides are choppy compared to how they used to be when I was playing, I skate over to Marshall, who has his head hung low with disappointment from getting scored on twice in a row from the same move.

"Hey, man," I say to him. "You good?"

"No. I suck. I don't . . . I don't know if I want to play anymore, Coach."

His voice is so dejected, and I hate hearing him talk about himself like that and giving up on the game so quickly.

"You think if I had given up every time something didn't go my way, that I would have been in the NHL?"

He sniffles a little. "No."

"And that's what you want, isn't it? You want to play in the NHL?"

"Yeah, I want to be the next Arthur Fox. That guy is amazing."

I grin. "Yeah, the Seattle Serpents goalie is pretty dang good, isn't he? Do you think *he* was ready to give up after a few missed saves?"

"No, Coach."

"Exactly, so you shouldn't be either. Especially not when we can fix this really easily."

He looks up at me, his eyes filling with hope. "We can?"

"Yep. Here, let me show you."

I drop down next to him, my hip stretching uncomfortably. I disregard the twinge of pain and show him how he should hold himself if he wants a better chance of stopping the puck.

"Makes sense?" I ask.

"A lot. Thanks, Coach Rawlings. You're the best."

That swell of pride I get every time something clicks with one of these kids hits me again, and I give him a small smile. "No problem. Now get out there and stop the next one, yeah?"

He skates back into his crease, ready to go, and I make my way to the center of the ice, where the other kids are lined up to practice their one-on-one shots. I blow the whistle and watch closely as the eight-year-old beside me takes off full speed—or as fast as a kid can at that age—and charges in for the shot. He's going for the same move the kid before him just did, probably because he saw how successful it was.

Marshall is prepared this time.

He drops at the exact right moment, and the puck soars through the air and straight into his glove.

"Yes!" I shout, clapping for him. "Well done, Marshall!"

Much like his idol, Arthur Fox, he nods in response, then gets set to go again. I love the dedication and that he doesn't let it go to his head, especially considering his young age.

He plays well the rest of the session, and when I finally call time on it, he's in a much better mood than earlier.

"Still want to quit?" I ask him when he skates to the open door.

He shakes his head, his grin wide and damn near contagious. "Not a chance in hell, Coach."

I should probably say something about him saying *hell*, but I can't find it in me, given how happy he is.

So instead I pat him on the helmet and tell him to get out of here.

I help the other coaches clean up the equipment, and we prepare for the next set of kids to arrive.

By the time I make it back to the cidery hours later, I'm beat, and my hip is aching in a way it hasn't in a long while. I spent a lot of time getting up and down on the ice today, and I know I shouldn't have done it, but dammit, I'm supposed to be teaching these kids. I need to be able to *show*, not just *tell*, them how to play. I'm just going to have to push through and keep up on my meds.

I head to my desk first, waving at some of our regular customers on my way. I pop a few ibuprofens before things get too out of hand and I'm back at the doctor's office, begging for another cortisone shot.

"Hey, man."

I lift my head to find Noah standing in my doorway. We haven't really had a chance to talk much this week, so we still haven't cleared the air about the whole Summer thing.

Summer.

I know she's here somewhere. There's no way she isn't, seeing as it's a Friday night, and all hands are on deck.

Besides, I'm like 95 percent certain I smelled vanilla cupcake on my way in here.

I also swear I can still taste that incredible mac and cheese she made, which only makes me wish I could bring her on as our new kitchen lead even more.

"Can I?" Noah asks, pointing to the chair across from my desk.

I wave him in, and he closes the door behind him. "Sure."

I take a seat opposite him, forcing myself not to grimace as I do.

Fuck, I really overdid it today. Maybe I can talk to one of the other coaches tomorrow and see if they can handle it on their own so I can take an actual day off.

Maybe.

"So," he starts, folding his hands together behind his head and reclining. Something about the relaxed position puts me on edge, which is funny. But that's Noah for you. He acts like everything is good, then he hits you with the real shit. I have a feeling this will be one of those *real shit* conversations.

"So," I repeat in the same calm tone.

"You got another ticket, huh?"

And there it is.

"In the end, no. I was threatened with one, and the idea of taking it to court because there's no way it wouldn't land there. So I chose the lesser of two evils and hired Summer. Are you mad?"

Noah sighs. "I think if it were anyone else, I might be, but Summer is cool. I mean, it's not like we ever hung out a lot or anything, but she was around a bit when Izzy was still in high school, since they all used to hang out. I always liked her. She didn't annoy me as much as the other girls did."

"Even Odette?"

He smirks. "*Especially* Odette."

I chuckle. *If* I were to believe in love, then I could get behind something like what Noah and Odette have. It seems kind of . . . fun.

But I don't believe in it. It's never felt like something that's been in the cards for me, and even less so now that I have this screwed-up hip. I don't want to burden anyone else with it. Who would want to deal with the endless doctors' appointments, physical therapy, and someone in pain every day for the rest of their life? Nobody. Hell, I don't even want to deal with all that shit, but it's my life now, so I guess I have to.

"But Odette isn't who we're talking about now. We're talking about you and that damn lead foot of yours." He shakes his head. "I can't believe you got pulled over again."

I lift my brows in a silent *Really? This is what you can't believe?* sort of way.

He laughs. "All right, I retract that statement. I definitely can believe it. I just wish . . . fuck, man. I don't know. I get it. I do. It makes you feel alive, gives you back that rush you got from hockey. But it doesn't mean that I like it, and I don't just mean for our reputation. It's dangerous. Something could happen."

He's wrong. He doesn't get it. Unless you've had the thing you love ripped away from you on a moment's notice, then you don't know.

If only I had turned just slightly when I took that hit. Or if I hadn't gone so hard after the puck. Everything would be different.

But it's not.

"Something could happen to anyone at any time. What's the harm in having a little fun until it does?"

Noah levels me with a look, and it has me sitting up a little straighter in my chair.

I nod once. "All right. I'll cool off. You happy?"

"Very. Now," he says, sitting forward, folding his hands together over his knees, "let's address the other elephant in the room . . ."

I tip my head to the side, because I'm not aware we had another one. "What's that?"

"The pinball machines!"

I grin. "I have eight ordered so far. Trying to find at least a few more to start things over, gauge interest, you know? Figured we'd go from there."

"Solid. I approve of this."

"Good. And things are going well over at the iceplex? Looked good to me today, but they could have been putting on a front."

"That's because everyone's scared of you."

I open my mouth to argue before I realize he's not wrong. I'm well aware that my employees call me Grump Ass behind my back, and I'm perfectly fine with it. If it means they're doing what they're hired to do, then so be it.

Is that what Summer calls me too?

I don't know where the thought comes from or why it matters, so I shove it away.

"But you'd be correct," Noah continues. "Things are great there. Don't have a single complaint."

"The kids were really happy today."

"Good, and that's all that matters. As long as the kids are happy and have a place, then I'm good."

I nod in agreement. It's the whole reason we're doing the iceplex. I'll drain whatever resources we have to keep it going for as long as possible. I don't care what it costs to give the game to someone else, the way it was given to me. It changed my life too much not to do it.

We're quiet for a moment, and that one thing that's been sitting in the back of my mind all day rears its head.

I clear my throat, trying to bring it up as casually as possible.

"Did you know Summer is a chef?"

Noah's eyes narrow for only a moment before he says, "Yes, I did. It's why I was so surprised to see her working here. She has to have better places to be than slinging cider for us. There's no way we're the only place that would hire her."

"I don't think we are."

Not by a long shot, actually. But she claims she's here for her father, and while I do believe that, I think there's another reason for her coming back to Port Harbor.

"So what's she doing here then? I mean, besides Sheriff Turner forcing you to hire her?"

"No clue, but it doesn't mean we can't take advantage of it, no?"

Noah looks at me skeptically. "What exactly are you proposing, Ez?"

I sit forward, resting my hands on the desk. "I think we should overhaul the kitchen."

"Ha. Very funny. Clever joke, Ez."

When I say nothing, he takes it as a sign that I most definitely am *not* joking.

"Holy shit, you're not joking." He runs a hand through his hair, blowing out a puff of air. "You mean after the wedding, right? *My* wedding that we're holding here in ten weeks?"

When I say nothing, Noah barks out a laugh.

"You mean now, don't you?"

"Yes, but only because I think it's the best time. It could be a trial run." He opens his mouth to say something, but I point at him and keep going. "You and I both know that Odette has everything planned to the very last detail, including several backup options just in case." Noah agrees with a nod, then motions for me to continue. "If something went wrong, we'd be set. But it won't go wrong. I bet we could have this place turned around in a month, which leaves us plenty of time to work out the kinks for the big day."

He looks apprehensive, and I get it. It's a big undertaking. I keep swearing I'm not taking on new projects, but this just seems like too good an opportunity to pass up. Besides, the arcade is nearly finished, so that's a major task off my list. I can shift my focus to the kitchen.

"Not having a proper kitchen has been our number one issue with the wedding venue side of things since the beginning," Noah remarks, and I know I've got him on board. "Most people either cater their own food or have food trucks. We could bring that back in-house. Charge more. It would be a win-win."

"Exactly my thinking. And I've already run the numbers. We'd break even within six months, maybe less, especially if we have a killer menu. And we have someone right under our noses that could make it."

"Which is why you brought up Summer being a chef." He laughs, shaking his head. "Fuck, man. You're good. I'll give you that."

He contemplates the proposition for a moment, turning it over in his mind.

Finally, after a few quiet minutes, he says, "Honestly, it's a good idea. Probably something we should have done sooner, considering *I* don't even grab food off our menu. That's likely a sign we should be doing something else. While the timeline scares the shit out of me, if we could get it done, then I think it'd take a lot of stress off Odette's shoulders. We'd just need Summer on board."

"That'll be easy. She, uh, she made some food the other night when I was working late, and fuck, dude. It was good. Like some of the best I've ever had. I don't think we'll have any issue convincing her to get on board."

His brows lift. "She cooked for you?"

Images of Summer sitting up on that counter with me between her legs run through my mind on fast-forward.

I blink them away. "Yeah. So? She's a chef. That's what she does."

"Hmm."

"Hmm? What does that mean?"

"Nothing," he says, but it doesn't *feel* like nothing. It feels like a whole lot of something, and I want to ask him just what he means, but he speaks before I can. "Look, do you need me to stick around tonight?"

"Nah, man. It's Friday. I'm sure you have something better to be doing than worrying about the cidery. Go home to your girl."

He sags back in relief, then grins. "Thanks, Ez. You're a nice guy, you know that?"

"Don't mention it. Seriously."

He laughs, then rises from the chair and makes his way to the door.

With his hand on the knob, he turns. I stare up at him, waiting for whatever it is that he's going to say.

I have a feeling I'm not going to like it one bit, so I brace myself as best I can.

"Summer's really nice, isn't she?"

Fuck. Here we go.

"She's . . . fine."

I hate how I notice that Noah's lips slowly pull into a grin and how his eyes get that obnoxious *knowing* look in them.

I hate that he's looking at me at all.

"Get the fuck out of here," I grumble.

He laughs, shaking his head. "Oh boy. This is going to be fun."

"What's going to be fun? What are you talking about?"

He just laughs harder as he pulls open the door, and all it does is piss me off.

"Noah!" I call to him as he exits my office. "What's going to be fun?!"

But he doesn't answer. His shoulders shake as he disappears down the hall and back into the taproom, leaving me sitting at my desk and wondering just what the hell it is that I might have gotten myself into.

And why do I have a bad feeling about it?

CHAPTER EIGHT

Summer

"Do you have a minute?"

The glass I'm holding slips right from my fingers, and I barely catch it in time before it smacks against the counter.

Ezra stands in the hallway entrance. He's wearing a crisp navy dress shirt that makes his green eyes pop even from here and gray slacks that *really* shouldn't look so damn good but do. With his sleeves rolled up and showing off his taut forearms, his watch is also on display. I've never given much thought to a man wearing a timepiece before, but now I can't seem to take my eyes off it.

After he walked away the other night—after he almost kissed me—I held on to it for I'm not even sure how long. I just turned it over and over in my hands, memorizing every inch of it before finally convincing myself to put it on his desk.

I still can't believe that happened. I can't believe Ezra almost kissed me, and I can't believe I almost let him do it.

And I really can't believe I still want him to.

"Uh, sure," I manage to say, my throat now suddenly dry.

I set the glass I'm holding under the nearest cider tap, pour, then chug it back.

"What?" I ask when Ezra's eyes sharpen. "We're closed."

"Where's Warner?" he asks, walking into the taproom. His limp is noticeably more pronounced today. I force myself not to react, even though I want to ask him about it.

"I think he's in the basement or cleaning the bathrooms." I know he told me, but I can't remember. I was just glad to get a break from his constant flirting. He's nice and I'm sure it's harmless, but I'm not interested in him.

I don't say any of that to Ezra, though.

"So," I say as he climbs onto a stool, and I lean against the counter in front of him, setting the glass that I now have to clean again to the side. "What's up?"

His watch glints off the overhead lights as he folds his hands together in front of him. "I have a proposition for you."

I lift my brows. "Excuse me?"

His lips turn up just the slightest. "Not a sexual one, though I find it interesting that's where your mind went."

I roll my eyes. "I wasn't thinking pervy things, for your information." *I totally was.* "I was just surprised you think we can mutually benefit one another."

Now *he's* the one who raises his brows, and my cheeks heat when I realize just how suggestive that sounded.

"I—I didn't . . . I meant . . . I—" I huff. "Can you please throw me a lifeline?"

He chuckles lightly, then clears his throat, and something tells me that whatever he's about to say, he's serious about it. My heart rate picks up, my blood pounding in my ears. What is this? What's about to happen? Is . . . is he about to fire me because of the almost kiss?

"We're remodeling the kitchen."

My senses go on high alert immediately.

"Good. It needs it," I say. When I was in there the other night, I spent a good portion of the time mentally rearranging everything and planning how I would do it if it were my kitchen. I quickly squashed those thoughts, though, because it's *not* my kitchen and never will be.

"It does. You made me realize that, actually. You also made me realize we're wasting a ton of space by not using it to our fullest potential."

"You are." They could be doing so much more with it and their menu, like taking off all that frozen crap and replacing it with *real* food. Something like—*no*.

There I go again, acting like it's mine.

"Right," Ezra says, pulling my attention back to him. "So, we're remodeling it. Before Noah's wedding, actually."

"That's brave of you."

He sighs. "I'm asking you to be our chef, Summer."

I blink once. Then twice. Then a third time, because there is no way he said what I think he said.

"What?"

"Be our chef. I spoke with Noah about this earlier, and he's on board as well. He—"

"No."

He whips his head back like I've just struck him. "What?"

"No."

His face hardens. "Why not?"

Because if I do, I'll fall in love with running a kitchen, and I can't risk losing it again.

"Because I don't want to," I say instead.

I grab the cup I used, then set it in the dirty dish bucket. That's a problem for tomorrow. I take another glass from the clean rack and begin polishing it, and it takes me right back to my first year in a real kitchen and just how much even doing mundane tasks like this made me fall in love with being in a restaurant.

"Bullshit."

I drag myself out of the past and turn back to Ezra. "Pardon?"

"You heard me. You're being bullshit right now."

"I am *not* being bullshit. I don't want to be in the kitchen. I—"

"Bullshit."

"Stop saying bullshit!" I launch the towel at him before I can think twice about it, and I'm surprised when he catches it out of midair.

I don't know why. The guy used to be a professional hockey player. I'm sure his hand-eye coordination skills are incredible.

He sets the towel down next to him, not once taking his eyes off me. "Then stop being bullshit."

I huff. "You can't *be* bullshit."

"Can too, and that's exactly what you are right now. You're acting like being in the kitchen the other night wasn't the happiest you've been since you started working here."

"That's not true." It is true, though. It's completely true, and I wasn't expecting him to notice that.

What else does he notice?

He scoffs. "Keep telling yourself that, if that's what you need to do, but I know what I saw. I know what the look on your face said. You looked like I did when I was out on the ice. It was your happy place. It was your escape. It was your fucking refuge, and you're casting it aside like it means nothing."

I want to argue with him more. All the words are sitting on the tip of my tongue, but they never tumble free. How could they when he's right about everything? How can I stand here and pretend I don't want to be back in a kitchen more than anything else in this world?

And how can I tell him that's the exact reason I can't say yes?

"Look," he says, "we're doing this. We're buying new equipment and upgrading the appliances. And we're going to change the menu. We're going to serve actual food. Not just frozen shit we slap together now. It's all going to be new. We want you, Summer. We want you to help us with this project. We're not asking you to stay in Port Harbor forever, but we want you for the interim. We need someone who can get the place running like it needs to, and after that little show the other night—that fucking mac and cheese I'm *still* thinking about—I want that person to be you."

He's still thinking of my food? God, I hate how that makes me vibrate from head to toe. I've been complimented on my plates before—by people with more refined palates too—but it still feels so damn good to hear, especially after taking this time away.

Do I . . . do I want to run a kitchen again? *Can* I? *Should* I? I failed so spectacularly last time. Fell right on my face when I was given such a grand opportunity. Am I ready to try again so soon?

I can't deny that it hasn't crossed my mind since being back here. The other night, when Ezra asked me why I wasn't working at a restaurant in Port Harbor, I told him it was because there weren't any good ones here. I stand by that. But that doesn't mean there *couldn't* be good ones here.

I could . . . I could make one. I could have my own place. I could make all my dreams come true. Be in charge of the menu and have a say over who gets hired and fired. Be close to home and to my father again. I could make it mine in a way Lore never was.

I could, but I won't. I can't gamble on myself like that, not when I know what the results will be.

And I can't let Ezra do it either. If I were to do this again, I'd need to be damn sure I could, and right now . . . right now, I'm just not sure if that's where I'm at.

"I appreciate the offer, but I don't think that's a good idea."

Ezra sighs, shaking his head and closing his eyes momentarily, and I fucking hate it. I cannot stand how disappointed he seems right now.

When he looks at me again, I want to run and hide from what I see.

It's not just disappointment. It's pity.

I fucking hate pity.

"No," he says, rising from the stool.

"No?"

"Yeah, no. You're not the only one who gets to say that. Now it's my turn, and I'm telling you *no*. I'm not taking that as your answer. I'll ask you again later, then again and again until I wear you down."

"I'm pretty sure that's called coercion."

"I prefer peer pressure."

"Ezra . . ." I warn with gritted teeth, but he doesn't seem to care.

He grabs the towel I threw at him earlier, then tosses it back my way. I catch it with much less finesse than he did.

Then he spins on his heel and heads back toward his office.

He's gone for a moment, leaving me with all my whirling thoughts, then he reappears as if he didn't just shock me to my core.

"I'll ask again tomorrow, Sunny."

"Ezra!" I call his name, but he doesn't stop.

He just keeps walking, and while I know I could follow him, I don't.

Some people's childhood homes smell like fresh-baked cookies or flowers. Some smell like freshly washed laundry or a nice, plump roast simmering in the Crock-Pot all afternoon.

Even after all these years, mine still smells like my mother—like honeysuckle. It has everything to do with the bushes that surround the front door. The same ones my mother planted when she was pregnant with me and tended to until she couldn't anymore.

The same ones my father has maintained all these years.

It's the first thing that greets me when I wake up, and that's solely because I keep my windows open nearly all year long when I'm in Washington. Even when it gets unbearably chilly out, I still can't bring myself to close them. I like the smell of the Pacific Northwest too much.

I peel my eyes open and take in my childhood bedroom. It still looks the same in so many ways, but a lot less childish than it once did. There are no longer posters of my favorite boy bands and celebrity crushes of the month covering the walls, and I've long since boxed up my old trophies and photos.

But everything else is the same. The same floral wallpaper that I picked out with my mother on my seventh birthday. The same bed and dresser my father got me for my sixteenth birthday. And the same full-length mirror hanging off the back of my closet.

It's how I know I look like a complete wreck.

My bangs are pushed up from sleeping on my face and not pinning them back last night, and my eyes are tired from tossing and turning at all hours.

I want that person to be you.

Ezra's offer replayed in my mind on a loop. I even put on a show on my iPad to help quiet it, but it didn't work. All I did was end up missing three episodes of *Gilmore Girls*.

I both love and hate that he offered, just like I feel the same about telling him no last night.

I'm proud that I didn't put myself back in that position again, especially when the wound from losing my last kitchen is still so fresh.

But, truthfully, I'm also sad that I said no.

It would be the perfect chance to finally make something of my own. That's what I was trying to do with Lore, but the owners weren't having it. They wouldn't listen to me about the menu. They wouldn't take into account my years of schooling, real-world experience, or advice on anything. They just wanted what they wanted.

The worst part is that I get it. I would be the same way with my kitchen. If I had the chance to create the menu at Stick Taps, I would feel sick if someone came in and tried to change it.

You could stay.

That little voice in the back of my head makes itself known. I could lie and say it means nothing, but it does, and it's been there since I set foot back in Port Harbor.

I love this little town. It has my dad, who has been my hero my whole life. It has memories of my mother and the years I had with her. It has friends I've known since childhood. And I love the people because, even when everyone is all in one another's business, they're still respectful. It has everything I could ever need except for the opportunities Chicago gave me.

Opportunities I squandered, but still opportunities.

I'm just not sure if that's enough to go back. I have a friend who is taking over my lease while I stay here to figure things out, but maybe that doesn't have to be temporary. Maybe I could move back here.

I want that person to be you.

Ezra's words rattle around in my head again, and the more I hear them, the more I like them.

Still, I'm scared. I can't say yes, because what if I fail? What if what I create for them *doesn't* work like Ezra thinks it will? What if nobody orders from the new menu? What if they say what I make sucks?

There are too many "what-ifs," and I can't deal with them right now, so I tuck all the thoughts away and peel myself out of bed.

I get dressed for the day—which I thankfully have off from the cidery—and make my way to the living room, where I'm unsurprised to find my father enjoying a cup of coffee.

"Morning, kiddo," he says, taking a loud sip from his mug.

"Hey, Dad. Hungry?"

He pats his stomach. "Always."

I chuckle. "I'll make breakfast."

"French toast?"

"You're supposed to be eating more heart-conscious things, which I'm pretty sure means not drowning your breakfast in sugary syrup."

"I'm an old man, Summer. Cut me a break, will you?"

I roll my eyes. "I'll see what I can do."

I move around the kitchen, frying up some turkey bacon—which my father hates but eats anyway—egg-white scramble, and a stuffed French toast that I'm hoping will help curb his sweets craving so he can forgo the syrup.

By the time it's done, he's already pouring another cup of coffee and setting the table.

I like this. It reminds me of old times when I was a teenager and we'd do this every Saturday morning. It was the only time of the week he'd block off. He wouldn't allow anyone to bother him until at least noon, and never a second before.

"This looks great," he says, stabbing his fork into his hot-sauce-covered eggs. "I mean, I'd prefer real bacon, but you know I'll eat anything you make."

"You heard your doctor, Dad. Small changes lead to big results."

"Yeah, yeah," he grumbles, then takes a bite of the bacon. I don't miss his wince as he chews and swallows.

I wonder briefly what it would be like if my mother were still here. Would she make him eat healthier too? Or would she fry him up "real bacon" because that's what he wanted?

I don't know, but I do know that I'm doing the best I can to keep my dad around as long as possible, so if that means having to hear him bitch about the turkey bacon, then that's what I'll do.

"So, I was driving through Port Harbor the other day, and I noticed that Mr. Looper—you remember him, right?"

I nod. "He used to give out full bars of candy on Halloween. It was the good stuff too. Of course I remember him."

Dad chuckles. "Well, he's moving to Arizona to be closer to his grandkids and is putting his house up for rent. Just, uh, just something I noticed. You know, if you decided to stay."

I peek up at my father. This isn't the first time he's made a comment like this since I've been back. I know he loves me and wants me to do whatever makes me happy, even if that does include going back to Chicago.

But it is the first time I've truly heard his words, and that's all thanks to Ezra putting ideas in my head.

Moving back here wouldn't be the worst thing. I could see myself here easily. Having breakfast with my dad every Saturday morning. Walking along the harbor, hiking the nearby trails on my days off. Having my own restaurant.

I could see it all. But is that what I want? I know nothing would make my dad happier than to have me close again. He let me go the first time all those years ago, but I know it wasn't easy for him to do, especially not since I'm all he has left.

My heart aches at the thought of my father here alone, navigating all this medical stuff by himself. What if something else happens? Could I live with myself if I left again and I got another—a worse—call in the middle of the night?

No. I couldn't.

But could I live with myself if I gave up my dream of having my own kitchen entirely?

Also no.

"Ezra told me he's going to overhaul the menu at Stick Taps and asked me to be their head chef."

The words come out quickly, almost like I'm afraid to say them, and maybe I am.

Honestly, I don't even know *why* I said them. I already told Ezra no.

Even still, I watch my father carefully, gauging his reaction.

His next bite hovers in the air as he raises his brows at me. "Oh? And?"

"And that's it. I told him no."

His eyes—the same brown as my own—fall to slits for only a moment before he says, "Okay."

Okay.

That's it, but it sounds like so much more than just that.

It sounds like *What the hell were you thinking?* and *You should have told him yes.*

I hate that he doesn't say the words out loud. It would be better if he did. It's worse just being stared at like this.

He takes another bite, chews, then swallows.

"Do you have anything else to add?" I finally ask.

"Sure don't, kiddo."

"Oh, come on. You clearly have an opinion about this. You ate that piece of turkey bacon without making a face, so this must be bothering you more than that. If you have something to say, then say it, old man."

He sets his fork down, then rests back against his chair. He folds his hands over his belly, which he got from eating way too many sweets. "Well, I guess I'm just trying to figure out why you told him no."

"Because I don't want to."

"Bullshit."

My head whips back at the word. It's the same one that Ezra used. Repeatedly, actually.

What is it with the men I know and that word?

"It's really not. I used to run a five-star restaurant. Running a kitchen in a cidery is a bit of a step down, isn't it?"

"If it's something you love, then no. Nothing is a step down if you're happy."

"I . . ."

But nothing else comes out, because he has a point.

Still, I shake my head. "No, it's not what I want."

I don't want to be under anyone's thumb when it comes to being in the kitchen. That was my biggest problem at Lore. I could never truly do what I wanted, and if I helped build the kitchen at Stick Taps, it would be the same thing. Perhaps not immediately, but eventually it would. I would itch to spread my wings and do something else. I'd be in the same limbo I'm in now, and I'd hate it.

Just like I hate how I don't know what I want, and I hate how I'm afraid to make a decision. If I go back to Chicago, I'm risking having the same breakdown I did before. And if I stay and work at Stick Taps, would I just be sidelining myself and working for someone else forever?

I don't know, but what I do know is that I'm not happy. And I really, really want to be. I'm just not sure what the right call is here.

"Listen, Summer," Dad says, leaning closer, "all I want is for you to do something that makes you feel good. I don't give a flying hoot what that is. You could move back to Chicago and be a damn street musician for all I care. I just want whatever you want. So if you want to run the kitchen at Stick Taps, then do it. But do it for you. Don't do it for me or for Ezra Rawlings or for anyone else. *You*. And remember that whatever you decide to do, I'll be proud of you and I'll be cheering you on every step of the way. But . . ." He pauses, then sighs. "But for what it's worth, I think you *do* want this. Or some version of it. Sure, it might not be your greatest dream right now, but it's your chance to try again. It's your chance to get it right. So why not seize it?"

He gives me one last meaningful look before picking up his plate and walking into the kitchen to do the dishes.

That's how it works—I cook, he cleans. Those are the rules.

And right now I'm thankful for it, because I don't want to be here right now with his words hanging between us. His very, very poignant words.

I grab my own plate with the half-eaten breakfast on it, then scrape the food into the trash before setting it on the counter beside him.

"I'm running to the grocery store. Need anything specific?"

"Real bacon would be nice."

"Dad . . ." I warn him.

He sighs, then shakes his head. "Nah, nothing specific. Just whatever you think is best, Doc."

I roll my eyes, then press a kiss to his cheek with a loud smack. "See you tonight, Sheriff."

He grunts in response, and I laugh, grabbing my purse from the hook near the door and slipping it over my head.

I turn right out of our driveway, taking in the gorgeous views as I stroll along Harborview Boulevard, the waterfront to my left, and the Cascades silhouetted in the background.

This has always been my favorite part of living here—cool early mornings, the smell of salt in the air, and the postcard-esque backdrop. It's heaven on earth, and sometimes I wonder why I ever moved away.

Oh, right. Culinary school.

I don't remember exactly when I fell in love with cooking. Maybe it was all those hours after school I spent with my mom, mixing up cookies and bread and helping with dinner. Or maybe it was before then, when I would just watch her. Either way, it's always been part of me, so when it came time to figure out what I wanted to do with my life, it made sense. Going away to school made me love it even more.

Maybe that's why I'm so scared of saying yes to Ezra. I love it so much, I'm afraid of failing again, because that'll make me hate it, and I never want to do that.

But maybe my dad is right. Maybe this is my chance for a do-over. Maybe this is my shot to make it right. To do it better.

Maybe . . . maybe I should seize it.

CHAPTER NINE

Ezra

I haven't seen Summer in five days now, with me running back and forth between the iceplex and trying to sort out our new arcade going in.

We're up to ten different games, and based on the social media response to the announcement, that's not going to be enough. We need more, and selfishly, I want more. I've been test-driving the pinball machines every night after work for far too many hours. I was right in thinking it would be a stress reliever. I think it's the only thing that has kept me from going entirely off the rails while we get this off the ground and start planning for the new kitchen, which we now have just nine weeks to complete.

I watch the ball roll closer, then hit the button on the right side just in time, sending the silver sphere soaring up the playfield. The machine makes a bunch of noise, lights flash, and my score goes up, up, up on the little screen in the middle.

It's annoying how elated it makes me, especially since none of this matters at all.

"Are you enjoying yourself?"

I jump at the intrusion and turn to find Summer leaning against the doorway to the new arcade. The area used to be semiprivate and quieter, with seating, but not many people came back here, so I figured this would be a great place to convert into something more engaging for customers.

"What are you doing here? Here to say you've come to your senses and will help us with the kitchen?"

Her eyes narrow for a moment. "My senses . . ." she repeats disdainfully. "My answer is still no, if that's what you're asking."

I try not to show how disappointed I am by that. I've spent the last five days trying to sort out what exactly we all need to make the kitchen better, but since my skills are more of the "poorly fry protein, put noodles in pot, open jar" caliber, I have no idea what I'm doing. I could use her help more than she realizes.

"Then what are you doing here?" I ask again.

"Uh, closing?" Sarcasm drips from each word. It's maddening how attractive I find it.

I draw my eyes away from the peachy strip of skin that's peeking out between her jeans and cropped top and right up to the ruby-red lipstick she's always wearing.

No, not her lips, dammit.

I clear my throat. "Since when? You weren't supposed to be working tonight."

She looks surprised by that. "Do you have my schedule memorized or something?"

"What? No."

But I say the words far too quickly for them to be believable.

I *do* have her schedule memorized, and I hate myself for it. I don't know why I care, other than to be able to ask her about the kitchen again. Still, I shouldn't know it. I should just wait to run into her, and that's it.

"I'm covering for Warner," she explains, letting me have my crappy lie. "He said he had a thing again with his grandmother."

"His other *other* grandmother?"

She wrinkles her nose. "He's totally lying, isn't he?"

"Big-time." I make a mental note to have a chat with him about that. If he doesn't want the hours, I'll happily give them to someone else.

"Well, whatever," she says, coming into the arcade and standing at the machine next to me. I dig into my pocket, then pop a few quarters into the change slot for her. "I knew the place could use the extra hands with trivia night. Not like I had anything else going on anyway."

There's no missing the bitterness in her words. I bet Port Harbor is nothing compared to the fun she was used to having in Chicago.

"I mean, it's not like I used to go out a lot before coming back here," she says, pulling back the plunger and letting the ball fly. "But at least I had a few friends to hang out with. Here, all I have is Odette and Noah, and no offense to them, but I have no desire to be their third wheel."

"That's what I tell them every time Odette is on my ass about not hanging out with them. Right."

"Huh?"

She looks over at me just as her ball goes soaring right between the flippers.

She frowns, and I chuckle.

"Shut up," she practically growls. "That was your fault."

"Was not. And you get another, so suck it up and do better."

Summer shoots me a dirty look before launching the ball again. She doesn't miss it the first few times it comes toward her, but she doesn't do a good job of hitting it either. It goes nowhere near where it should.

"Left," I say, and she hits the button a second too late. "Faster."

"Faster? What do you mean?"

"I mean, press the button faster. Sooner. Right."

"Stop telling me what to do!" she yells as she hits the left button.

"Right, right."

"Shut up!"

"Left."

"I swear—"

"Right."

"Ezra!"

She panics and smashes both buttons repeatedly. The ball flies all over the playfield, hitting bumpers and spinners, and I laugh at the absolute terror on her face as she tries to keep it in play.

Honestly, it's not the worst strategy I've seen, but I'm not shocked when she loses again.

"Ugh, this is all your fault!" She points an accusatory finger at me. "You made me suck."

"I did not."

"Did too. *Right, left, right, right,*" she says with a low voice, that I assume is supposed to sound like me but isn't even close.

"Are you . . . mocking me?"

"Yes."

She says it so quickly and defiantly that I can't help but laugh. And I don't mean a quick one this time. It's deep and rich and right from my belly.

Which is why it takes me so long to realize she's staring at me with the goofiest grin.

"What?" I ask after sobering up.

She shakes her head. "It's just . . . you just have a really nice laugh, you know that?"

Suddenly my cheeks feel warm, and I know it has nothing to do with my laughing.

Am I . . . *embarrassed?* Holy fuck, I can't remember the last time that happened.

"I can say with certainty that nobody has ever said that to me before."

"Is that because you rarely laugh?"

"I laugh."

She points at the spot between my eyebrows. "You scowl more often than laugh."

"Well, nobody ever gives me anything to laugh about. Which is other people's problem, not mine. Oh, sorry. I'm sure that makes me 'sound like an ass,' doesn't it?"

"Yes, it does. But it's still funny."

Her perfectly shaded brown eyes sparkle with humor, and her lips turn up in the corners like she's about to laugh. It's so fucking cute. *She's* so cute.

It feels like I'm standing in the kitchen all over again, and the urge to kiss her strikes me so fast that I nearly stumble backward.

Don't do it, Ezra. Don't fucking do it.

Still, I find myself moving closer. Then again.

I can't stop myself even though I know I should. Her eyes flick to my lips, then back again, and fuck. I'm barely holding on right now.

I want to kiss her more than I've ever wanted to kiss anyone before.

"Ezra, what are you doing?"

Though her words come out in a whisper, they're the loudest thing I've ever heard, and it's enough to snap me out of my stupor.

I shove my shaking hands into my pockets, then nod toward the pinball machine she's practically pressed against. "I'm teaching you how to play pinball."

She swallows roughly, then spins around, and I exhale for what feels like the first time in minutes.

"Then get on with it, Mr. Rawlings."

And that's how we spend the next thirty minutes—her pressed against the machine, me standing over her shoulder, instructing her when to hit the buttons.

She's terrible at it, but I don't care.

It's still the best thirty minutes I've had all day.

I'm not playing fair, but I can't find it in me to care.

I take all calls about the kitchen remodel in the taproom within earshot of her. I purposefully ask absurd questions, just to see her reaction.

Yesterday she had to walk out of the room twice, then she went on a five-minute rant about the different kinds of gas stoves, which is the best to buy, and why.

I think I smiled the whole way through it, then asked her to be our chef again.

She threw a towel at me and stomped away.

If she were anyone else, I'd have fired her on the spot, but I can't seem to make myself do it when it comes to her, because, for the first time in a really long damn time, I'm actually having fun.

Maybe Odette was right before, because this feels nothing like all the other "fun" I was claiming to have.

"Are you serious?"

I barely hold my laugh in as I look up from the stack of invoices I'm shuffling through. "What can I help you with, Ms. Turner?"

Her glower would scare lesser men, but not me.

"An Easy-Bake Oven?" she practically yells as she marches into the small space.

She shuts the door behind her, and while part of me is grateful for it since we have a room full of customers who don't need to witness this, I wish she had left it open. Maybe I'd trust myself to behave a little more if that were the case.

I've almost kissed her twice now, and I'm not so sure I'll be able to hold back if there's a third time.

"What's the problem?" I ask.

"You know damn well what the problem is. You're doing this to get my attention, Ezra."

Summer stands over me, her hands on her hips. She's referring to me ordering an Easy-Bake Oven and placing it in the kitchen with a note that says *Our New Oven*. It was ridiculous, but it worked.

"I know you're tormenting me so that I'll give you what you want," she continues. "Despite knowing that, I hate myself because . . . because . . ."

"Because it's working?"

"Yes!" She tosses her hands into the air. "Yes, it's fucking working, and I don't want it to work. Or maybe I do. I don't know."

She's pacing back and forth in front of my desk now, and I watch her as she goes from left to right.

Left. Right.

Left. Right.

It *almost* makes me feel bad for messing with her.

Then I remember that delicious mac and cheese she made me, and the remorse goes right out the window. I don't feel bad at all. This is clearly her calling, and it's also obvious she misses it. The kitchen here might not be as extravagant as she's used to in Chicago, but at least it's better than slinging drinks. Not that there's anything wrong with tending bar, but there is a problem with it when you're as talented as Summer is.

There's no reason to waste that kind of magic, especially when you have an opportunity like this lying at your feet.

"Does that mean you're accepting my offer?"

"You're not really leaving me a choice, are you?"

I rise from my chair, moving around the desk until I'm seated on the edge. The position causes my hip to pinch with pain, but I do it anyway, just to be closer to her. It's clear this is stressing her out, and that's the last thing I wanted. "Of course I am, Summer. This choice was always yours."

"It doesn't feel that way," she mutters, turning once more to go back the other way.

"I'm sorry. I was just messing with you."

"You were pushing me."

I nod. "I was."

"And it was mean."

"It was," I agree, and as she passes by me again, I grab her wrist, stopping her.

She's soft beneath my fingers, her skin like velvet. Warm too.

She looks down at where my hand is curled around her, then back up at me, but she doesn't pull away, and I don't either.

Stop touching her, Ezra. She's your employee.

I ignore myself.

"I'm sorry," I tell her again. "I shouldn't have done that, but Summer . . . you're incredible in the kitchen, you know that, right?"

She looks anywhere but at me as she shrugs. "I guess."

"You guess?" I tug on her until she looks up at me because I *need* her to hear this next part. "There is no guessing, and you know it. Just like I know you know how much you enjoyed being in there. I have no idea what happened at your last job, but it's obvious that whatever it was, it has you scared to try again, and that's fucking heartbreaking. You're too damn talented to let your passion fizzle out over one bad thing, and you're too young to give up now."

"I'm not that young."

"You're twenty-six. Talk to me when you're thirty-four and your dream is nothing but a distant memory."

As if I need the reminder, my hip throbs, and I swallow down the pain—the physical and the emotional.

"Anyway, you can't just give up. I know you want to, but don't."

"I . . ." She runs her tongue along her bottom lip, her lipstick not moving an inch. "I don't want to give up. I just don't know if I'm ready. What if I let you down?" Then, quieter, she says, "What if I let myself down?"

"You won't. I promise that you won't. And if at any time it's not what you want, you tell me, and I'll let you out. You can walk away. No harm, no foul."

She weighs my words carefully, letting them hang between us.

Say yes, I beg silently. *Say yes, and not just for me, but for you too.*

Then finally—*fucking finally*—she utters a single word. "Yes."

"Seriously?"

She sighs, then nods. "Yes, seriously. But I have . . . requests."

"Whatever you want. I'm not an expert in this area. You are."

"Pfft. Please. I'm not. An expert wouldn't have lost their kitchen so quickly," she says softly.

I know I should have more questions about that—and I do, and I will ask them later—but right now, I'm fucking elated, and it's not solely because I *know* that the cidery is going to benefit from this.

I'm happy for *her*. I'm glad she's getting her passion back. I know all too well what it feels like to lose the thing you love the most. I wouldn't wish it on anyone, least of all Summer.

I don't know what it is about her, but . . . fuck, I don't know. I just want the best for her. I want her to get everything she's ever wanted, and I can't remember the last time I felt that way about anyone.

I run my thumb over the inside of her wrist, and her pulse intensifies. I can feel it thrumming against me. And fuck if it doesn't make mine ramp up too.

Her brown eyes darken until they're nearly black, her mouth dropping open just slightly, and once again I find myself leaning into her.

Stop this, Ezra. Stop it right now.

But I don't.

And neither does she.

Closer and closer, and I know I should stop. I know it, yet I can't make myself do it.

"Ezra . . ."

She says my name in a whisper just before our lips connect, and *fuck*. *Fuck, fuck, fuck.*

She's sweet. She's soft. She's everything I thought she would be as I tug her closer. I drop her wrist, instead cupping her face as her mouth works against mine.

There's a tiny voice in the back of my mind that's telling me what a bad idea this is, but how can that be when she feels as good as she does? When she tastes so fucking heavenly. When she lets out the softest whimpers as my tongue brushes against hers.

This can't be a bad idea. It's not possible.

Summer steps closer, and it's not enough, so I tug on her, her weight resting on me.

That's when I feel it—a jolt through my right hip and down, and I nearly crumble.

I snap back from her in a flash, and I know instantly it's a mistake.

Regret and shame and utter fucking embarrassment swirl in her gaze, her face falling right in front of me.

"Oh my god!" Her hand goes to her mouth, her eyes wide as she stares at me with horror. "I'm sorry. I'm . . . I didn't . . . I . . ."

"Summer, wait." I push off the desk, and my hip screams at me so fucking loud, I sit right back down. I gnash my teeth together, trying to fight the ache, but it's too much. My leg is completely stiff, my body coursing with pain. "Fuck, I—"

She shakes her head. "No, I . . . I . . ."

It's the last thing she says before she turns and runs out of my office.

CHAPTER TEN

Summer

My role at the cidery has significantly changed in the last couple of days.

I've gone from working closely with Warner to now working beside Ezra, and that would be fine if I hadn't kissed him.

I kissed him!

He's *my boss*, and I fucking kissed him.

What the hell was I thinking? I wasn't, clearly. How could I? He had just said all those nice things to me, and every single intelligent thought I'd ever had flew right out the window. How pathetic is that? A man says something nice, and I fold completely.

God, the look of pure torture on his face when he pulled away is something that's haunted me ever since.

Now everything is awkward, and it's all my fault.

I've done a good job of not looking him in the eyes since it happened, which is a damn miracle, if you ask me.

Together we've ordered an appropriately sized stove and oven, actual storage, a new light for the fridge, and three prep tables that they were in desperate need of. Next up is replacing all the other odds and ends, including those horrid mixing bowls they had that were cracked in at least two spots.

It's only just scratching the surface, but it's a good start.

"What about brussels sprouts?"

He curls his lip up. "Does anyone even like those?"

"Um, yes. They were a huge hit at Lore, and they're easy to make in bulk. We can dress them up with bacon, balsamic, and seasoning."

"Whatever," he says. "This is your gig, not mine."

I huff. It's not the first time he's said this, and it irritates me more and more each time because this *isn't* my gig. This is his business. I'm just helping him make the kitchen something . . . well, way better than what they currently have.

It's telling that we've never had to say to customers the kitchen is closed, because nobody has tried to order anything in days. Truthfully, they probably should have done this years ago. It's been a missed opportunity for them, and it makes me all the more nervous to reveal the new and improved menu to patrons. While the bar might be low, I still want to wow them.

"What?" Ezra asks, not looking at me.

He can't do it, either, and even though *I'm* avoiding him, I'm annoyed he's avoiding me too.

We're adults, for crying out loud. Surely we can move on from one little mistake.

I throw my pencil down, then spin my chair to face him.

He pauses for only a moment before he continues on with whatever it is he's doing. I'm honestly not sure it's even anything. He hasn't moved in what feels like hours. An alarm on his phone has gone off a few times, but he silences it each time and keeps pretending to work.

That's how we sit for several moments—me staring at him and Ezra acting as if I'm not.

Then finally, he drops his pen and turns to me. His face is hard, but if I look close enough, I can see the worry in his green gaze.

"What can I do for you, Sunny?"

These are obviously not the first words he's spoken to me today, though it certainly feels like it, because they just might be the realest. Everything else has been strictly business. This is personal.

"Why do you call me that?"

"Call you what?"

"Sunny. I'm not a ray of sunshine. I know that. I'm stubborn to a fault most of the time. There's not much that's 'sunny' about me."

The corners of his lips twitch. "Maybe, but you're . . ." He lifts a shoulder. "I don't know. You're something."

"*Something?* What the hell does that mean?"

He sighs. "I don't know. You, Summer. You're *you*. And I think you're sunny."

It *almost* sounds like a compliment, and I want to ask him to elaborate, but I'm too afraid he's going to clam up and stop talking to me again, so I don't.

"Was that all you needed?"

"No."

I want to know why you freaked out after I kissed you.

But I can't bring myself to say the words out loud.

So much for acting like an adult in this situation.

"I want your opinion on the menu."

"But that's your area. That's the reason we're bringing you on for this project."

"Right. I know. But these are your customers. You're the one who knows them. What do you think they'll like?"

He sighs, and I roll my eyes, spinning my chair back around.

"Never mind. I'll just figure it out myself. I'll just—"

"Hey." He grabs my chair, turning me to him. "I didn't say I wasn't helping. I was thinking."

"Oh."

"Yeah. Oh." Another lip twitch. He picks his pen up and begins flipping it through his fingers, and it's as obnoxious as it is attractive.

God, get a grip, Summer. They're hands. *You have them too.*

I do, but they're so different from his with his long fingers that I bet would feel really, really good between my— *No.*

I cut that thought off right there.

I do absolutely *not* need to go there, especially after what happened the other day.

"What's up?"

I lift my gaze to his. "Huh?"

"Your face. It just got all red." He frowns. "You okay?"

Oh god. Am I blushing?

I nod, rubbing at my cheeks, trying to chase away the flush. "Yeah, I'm fine. Just hot."

"Take your shirt off."

I don't know whose eyes widen first, but I do know we're mirroring each other.

"Shit." Ezra laughs, shifting uncomfortably as he scratches at the stubble lining his chin, the same scruff that felt so good against me the other day. "Uh, I definitely did not mean to say that. I meant your sweater. Take your sweater off."

"Cardigan."

"What?"

"It's called a cardigan. And I'm okay, but thank you."

He rises from his chair and walks over to the thermostat on the wall. He presses a few buttons, then resumes his spot, and I notice the wince as he settles back down.

Ezra must sense that I have questions, because he says, "You can ask."

"Ask what?"

He tips his head to the side in a silent *Come on* sort of way.

"Okay." I clear my throat and settle back in the chair, crossing my arms over my chest. "What happened?"

"Hockey happened." He grabs the pen once more, flipping it through his fingers effortlessly, and I wonder if it's a nerves thing, if it helps keep him calm while talking about something that clearly bothers him. "More specifically, bad hockey happened. The first time, I went down weird and basically jammed my leg up. Labral tear. Had to get surgery and missed almost an entire season."

"That sounds awful."

"It was absolutely brutal, but it was nothing compared to coming back the next season, having the best one of my career—like we're talking top of the league—then going down again in a conference final game and costing my team a shot at the Cup."

He barely looks at me when he says it, but the shame in his eyes is still impossible to miss.

He blames himself for it all.

"Ezra, I—"

He shakes his head. "Don't. Don't tell me how sorry you are. I hate that."

"I wasn't going to say that. I was going to say, I hope you know it's not your fault. Because it's not. It was an accident. It just happened. It's not like you did it on purpose, right?"

"Fuck no." He scoffs. "I loved that game more than anything in my life. I would have done whatever it took to keep it, and I did. I had surgeries and did physical therapy and trials for new drugs and everything else, but . . ." He sinks back in his chair. "Nothing. None of it helped like I needed it to, so I could keep playing. I still had—*have* the pain. It won't go away, no matter how hard I try."

The last words are so soft, so sad.

That same urge I had before to hug him hits me, but this time I resist. The last thing I want to do is touch him after what happened in here the other day.

My eyes fall to the spot where it happened, where I was practically mauling him on the corner of his desk. Where I had my hands on him, and my lips were pressed to his.

I peel my gaze away and am surprised to find Ezra watching me intently.

"Look, Summer, about the other day. I—"

"No, please. Let's not talk about it, okay? Let's pretend it didn't happen. I think that's best, don't you?"

He stares at me, his mouth open, and I get the strangest feeling he wants to argue. He doesn't. He snaps his lips shut, then nods.

And that's it.

We go back to work. I make the executive decision to add brussels sprouts to the menu and tack on more items—three different kinds of fries, a variety of grilled sandwiches, and a few appetizers. It's too crowded for such a small venue, especially since I'm nowhere near done with it, but we'll pare it down later.

It's four o'clock before I know it, and my shift has come to an end.

Part of me wants to stay, just to be near him, but I don't. I think I *need* this break.

"I'm heading out," I announce, gathering my things.

He doesn't say anything, and for the first time, I'm grateful for it.

I'm just stepping over the threshold when he speaks.

"Hey, Summer?"

I turn to him. His head is still bent, his pen moving across the page. "Yeah?"

"I don't want to pretend it didn't happen. Just so we're clear."

I don't say anything because what can I say? That I don't want to forget it either? I don't. Not really. How could I want to forget it when I liked it so much?

So I take a page from his book, and I say nothing.

I just walk away, and I'm left with more questions than ever before.

"Summer! Over here!"

Odette waves at me from across Dickie's Gourmet Burgers, a cute little place that has the best burgers around, and I grin in her direction.

I was surprised when she called me yesterday, asking if I wanted to get lunch, but grateful, because I could really use someone to talk to who doesn't work at the cidery and isn't my father.

I don't want to pretend it didn't happen. Just so we're clear.

Ezra's words from two days ago haven't left my mind, no matter how many times I've pushed them away, and trust me, I've tried. Over and over, but they won't budge.

What did he even mean? He was clearly horrified by what happened, so it couldn't possibly mean he wanted that kiss.

His "just so we're clear" was anything but clear.

I've tried asking about it so many times, but I keep chickening out. Plus, he's been gone these last two days. I've returned to working mostly with Warner while still trying to put together a decent menu that I plan to present to Ezra on Monday. He didn't give me a deadline or anything, but it seems like a good time to get started on it, considering that everything we've ordered should arrive within the next two weeks.

"You look great," Odette says as I approach. She wraps me in a quick hug before letting me go.

"Thanks, so do you."

"It's the fiancée effect." She winks. "Come on. Let's order. I'm starving."

We walk to the front of the small restaurant and place our orders—a bacon cheeseburger for her and a pastrami and Swiss burger for me, and two baskets of fries, because why not?

"I'm glad I could peel you away from the cidery," Odette says, a bottle of soda sitting in front of her. I always loved the little old-timey coolers they have here, stocked with drinks you probably forgot even existed. "Noah said you're working almost full-time. Is that because of the kitchen renovation? You're helping with the menu, right? Which, by the way, Noah and I are so thankful for you saying yes. We know it's a lot and you're on a tight timeline with the wedding coming up in just eight weeks, but it's going to be so big for Stick Taps."

"Of course. I'm happy to help," I say, twisting off the top of my orange cream soda.

"So, with all that work, does that mean you're staying in Port Harbor?" she asks.

I can't deny that the more time I spend here, the more my answer leans toward yes. I've missed it. Plus, it's been nice being around my dad again. Moving close to him wouldn't be the worst thing. He became my best friend after my mother passed, and being away from him for so long was harder than I let myself believe. And it's obvious he needs me around. If not, he'd probably be eating all the bacon the grocery store has to offer.

"I haven't made any final decisions yet, but I do know I'm going to be staying for a while still. My dad likes having me around, so we'll see."

Odette frowns. "I had heard about his heart incident. He's doing okay, right?"

I nod. "He is, especially now that I have him on a special diet. But still, you know what it's like watching your parents get older. It's hard. You want to be there for them."

"I completely understand. I mean, my mother isn't slowing down at all and has been having far too much fun with Ken lately, but I get it."

"As in the *very* good-looking man who owns Sunnie's? God, I love their fritters there."

"They are to die for, aren't they? But yes, the same Ken. They've been together for a while now. It's cute, especially since you know what my family has been through as far as the curse goes."

She rolls her eyes, but I recall how Odette used to fret over the alleged curse that had been burdening the women in her family. They all swore they'd never know true love, but look at them now. They seem to be doing quite well to me.

"That's amazing. I'm happy for her. And you, too, by the way. Can't believe your teenage crush on Noah came to fruition."

She giggles, her entire face lighting up just thinking about her fiancé. "I know. It's wild, isn't it? I'm just . . ." She sighs dreamily. "I'm in love. Like out of my mind in love. Is that silly?"

"Not at all. It's sweet. Can't say I've ever felt that. The only person who makes me feel out of my mind is . . ." But I don't finish that sentence. Instead, I take a swig of my soda.

"Ah, ah, ah. You're finishing that sentence, Summer Turner," she says, pointing her own drink at me. "Who is it? Do I know him?"

"Uh, you could say that." I take another quick drink before answering. "It's Ezra." Her eyes widen. "No, no. Not in the way you're thinking. I don't *like* him or anything. He's just infuriating, is all. Like so completely obnoxious. And a total grump to boot. Have you seen the way he walks around the cidery? He's constantly scowling—it's so frustrating working with him. His employees call him Grump Ass, and I can see why. That's exactly what he is. A grump *and* an ass."

She's grinning by the time I'm done talking, and I fidget in my seat because I don't like it one bit.

"What?" I ask when she doesn't say anything.

"Nothing. You just remind me of me."

"What do you mean?"

She lifts a shoulder, taking a swig of her soda before saying, "I was the same way when I was falling for Noah. I thought everything he did was annoying, but it turns out I was just completely in love with him."

I can't help it—I laugh. "You think I'm in love with Ezra Rawlings?"

"Maybe not in love with him, but it certainly sounds like you could have a little crush." She pinches her fingers together to emphasize it.

I laugh harder. "No, no. That is *not* what's happening."

"Why not? He's hot."

I raise my brows. "Does Noah know how you feel about his business partner?"

"Please." She waves her hand. "Noah is the only man for me. Everyone knows that. It doesn't mean that I can't acknowledge how good looking Ezra is, and he *truly* is. All the brooding he does. That perpetual frown. His green eyes."

"Are you *sure* it's Noah you want?" I tease.

"Yes, very much so. That man makes me so happy, I swear I see stars every time I kiss him."

Her words make me smile, but I can't deny they also make me feel a bit . . . well, jealous. The last time I saw stars was when I kissed Ezra.

I don't want to pretend it didn't happen. Just so we're clear.

I wish I could talk to Odette about this, ask her what he could mean, but now that she suspects I might have a crush on him—which I *so* don't—I'd rather not give her more ammo.

"Look," she continues, "all I'm saying is, it might not be a bad idea. Ezra doesn't do relationships anyway, so it could totally be fun to have a little fling, you know? I'm sure taking care of your father is stressful. Why not relieve the stress with him?"

It doesn't sound like a bad idea on paper. But it's a lot more complicated than that.

"He can barely tolerate being in the same room as me. Besides, did you forget that he's my boss?"

"Okay, first of all, Ezra can barely tolerate being in the same room as anyone. Secondly, he might be your boss technically, but is he really? Your dad forced him to hire you. I'm pretty sure that already blurs a whole lot of lines. And third, he's *handpicked* you to be his right-hand person for this kitchen remodel. That's kind of a big deal, no?"

"Well, I am a chef, so it makes sense."

She flattens her lips. "Hmm."

"Hmm? What does that mean?"

She sighs. "It's just . . . Ezra is . . . well, he's Ezra. He's very introverted. He never wants to hang out with me and Noah or do anything fun ever. I guess I'm just surprised he's so keen on spending that much time with you if he doesn't like you—he's very much a 'do it himself' kind of guy. He barely lets Noah help him with anything, and they're partners."

I shift in my chair. "It's only because I know a lot about the subject. That's all."

"I'm sure it is. But—"

"Order for Odette!" someone calls from the front counter.

"Hold that thought," Odette says as she rises from her chair to grab our burgers.

She comes back right away, setting my lunch in front of me, and we immediately dive into our food, she with more fervor than I.

I can't eat. I'm too focused on what she could possibly mean.

Why *is* Ezra spending so much time with me? Why was he so insistent that it was me who helped him with the remodel? There are plenty of other people he could have called on for that. Plenty of other chefs in Port Harbor too.

So why me? Why not someone else?

And why . . . why do I *want* to help him so much?

Odette never finishes her thought, and I never bring it back up either. All I want is to forget about Ezra Rawlings for one day.

Easier said than done.

CHAPTER ELEVEN

Ezra

"I don't give a shit what your boss said to you about the delivery. He promised *me* it would be here today, and I'm standing here looking at an empty hole where my *Jurassic Park* pinball machine is supposed to be."

"I—I—I . . . Sorry, I . . ."

"Is that it? Do you have anything else to say?"

The guy on the other end of the phone sputters a few more unintelligible words, and all it does is piss me off more.

I'm in a sour mood today, and it's not just because the machine I was promised has been delayed yet again.

It's been three days since I last saw Summer, and I'm beginning to wonder if I completely fucked things up with her. Not that there's anything *to* fuck up since she's just my employee and nothing can happen between us, but I was actually starting to enjoy working with her on the kitchen renovation. I have no idea what I'm doing in that regard, and her expertise is greatly appreciated.

Right, Ezra. Because that's all it is. Just her kitchen experience. Definitely not that you like spending time with her.

"Look, Kyle. It was Kyle, right?"

"Uh, Drake."

"Fine, Drake. Whatever. Just get me my pinball machine by the end of the day tomorrow. I don't give a shit who you have to piss off to make it happen, but make it fucking happen. Understood?"

"Yes, sir. I understand, sir."

"Good. Call me when the truck is on the road."

Then I hang up.

It's not usually how I conduct business, but I can't find it in me to give a fuck right now. I've been sleeping like shit, I'm up to my eyeballs in things to do, and I'm in desperate need of a vacation. The only thing I have going for me right now is that my hip has decided to play nice and is only a dull throb today.

I'll take the wins where I can get them.

"You good?"

I turn to find Noah staring at me with cautious eyes.

"Fine," I bite out, but he doesn't buy it. He can tell I'm on the brink of losing it.

"Drink?" he offers, already moving behind the bar.

I nod, then slide onto a stool.

I don't typically drink during working hours, even when the social setting calls for it. I like to keep a clear head, but I could really use a good pour right now.

He fills a pint with Empty Net, one of our newer flavors that perfectly balances pear and peach. It's sweet, damn good, and my current favorite. Then again, I've always had a bit of a sweet tooth.

"Thanks," I mutter as he slides it my way. I take a healthy sip, then set it back down before he can even grab himself something.

He settles across from me with what I assume is Glove Save, which is his favorite. "Want to talk about it?"

"Nothing to talk about."

"So you're yelling at people on the phone for no reason?"

"I didn't yell. I didn't raise my voice a single time."

Noah's lips set in a firm line. I'm being technical, and he knows it. I might not have yelled, but I was certainly a dick.

I sigh, then scrub my hands over my face. "Fuck, man. I don't know. I'm just . . . on edge, I guess. Getting stressed about shit."

"Like what? Talk to me, Ez. We're business partners, remember? You don't have to carry this workload alone."

I know that. I really do. However, I also know that Noah is extremely busy with our community iceplex and all the goings-on there, not to mention the numerous events we have scheduled here, managing the animals, *and* his upcoming wedding. I mean, sure, Odette's probably doing most of the work for it, being a wedding planner and all, but my point remains the same—he has enough going on too. I can't pitch in as physically as he can, so there's no reason I shouldn't be able to handle things like paperwork and money.

"And don't feed me some shit about how you don't want to bother me or how you got it handled," he says, essentially reading my mind. "Clearly you don't, and that's okay. Just say the word, and we'll figure everything out together."

Noah has always been this way. It's why he captained his former NHL team for as long as he did. The guy is good at figuring shit out, and he always wants to do it together. I respect that. It's why, when he came to me with the idea for the cidery, I wasn't even remotely scared to pack up my life and move to Washington and bet on him and the business.

He continues to stare at me, and fuck if it's working. My walls start to crumble.

"We're behind schedule," I say.

"Schedule for what?"

"The arcade. We're supposed to have the big opening next weekend, and we're still missing three machines, plus we're slacking on getting the press info out."

"Okay." He nods. "So then let's talk to Sophie about it. She's the one who posts on our socials, right? Have her double her posting. Get some boots on the ground and hang flyers around town. Hit the places that already stock our cider."

"And the missing machines?"

"Who cares? I mean, would it be ideal to have everything? Sure, but it's not the end of the world if we don't. We'll just tell people when they come in that we'll be adding more games and shit later. Give them an incentive to come back."

He has a point there. Hell, it might actually be smart.

"That could work," I say.

"It will work. What next?"

"What do you mean?"

"That can't be all that's stressing you out. What else is going on? You been sleeping okay?"

I shake my head. "Do I ever?"

"When your hip isn't being a bitch, yes. Is that the issue?"

I want to tell him it's always the issue, but it's hard to explain chronic pain to someone who doesn't live with it. They don't under-stand that you don't get breaks. You just get days that are easier than others. Right now it's easier, but it doesn't mean I'm not still dealing with the pain.

"My hip is my hip."

He nods with a frown, and I hate the fucking sympathetic look he gets in his eyes. It's the same one I always receive when I talk about my injury.

I think one of the only people not to look at me like that was Summer, and that's frustrating on a whole different level.

"I had the contractors in here yesterday about the kitchen. It looks like it's going to be a four-week renovation at a minimum, and they can't start for another week. So we add in roughly another buffer week just in case, and we'll be pushing it really fucking close to your wedding."

"Shit." It's all he says, but that's because he doesn't have to say anything else.

I'm the one who promised him that if we did this, we'd have it done before his wedding so that we could use the kitchen for it. Now I'm not so sure I can deliver, and it's killing me. I don't want to let him down. I don't give a shit about marriage myself, but I know it means something to Noah. I want this day to be perfect for him and Odette.

"Well, there's not much we can do about that now," Noah says. "We already knew we'd be pushing it with the deadline, so this just gives us even more motivation to get it done. I can pitch in with the contractors. Get things moving faster."

"Dude, Noah, no. I didn't mean that you'd have to do that on top of everything else you're dealing with. I just—"

"Let me handle it, okay? That's my area, Mr. Numbers."

He means it lightheartedly, I know he does. But it still sucks because he's right. That is his area, and it's only because I can't help him. I'm sure I could swing a hammer for a bit or tear some tile out, but I can't be down on my knees for long or stand on ladders or do just about anything else that wouldn't have me in excruciating pain for days or weeks afterward.

I'm fucking useless.

"Fine," I agree, pushing down the anger that always comes when I remember I'm never going to be able to move like I used to. "But I'm helping as much as I can, and you're not going to argue with me about it."

He wants to, but he doesn't. "Speaking of the kitchen, Odette had lunch with Summer yesterday, and she's really excited about the new menu."

Everything in me perks up at the mention of Summer, and I tell myself it's because I want this to work out for her too. I want to see her happy like that night she cooked for me. She can act as nonchalant as she wants about the whole thing, but I can tell she's excited about the idea of overseeing another kitchen. The way her face lit up when we were picking out equipment was like a little kid finding buried treasure. It was fascinating to watch.

I want to see that look again. I want this to work for her. I want Stick Taps to be a place people come to not just for cider, but for her menu too.

But I can't tell Noah all that. He'll think it means something else, and it doesn't.

"Cool."

"Cool?" Noah repeats. "That's all you have to say?"

I lift a shoulder, taking another drink of my cider. "What do you want me to say?"

"I don't know. Aren't you working closely with her on this? No comments or thoughts on the menu?"

"Not really. I trust her." I mean that. I trust Summer to make the best menu she can for the cidery, just like I trust her to make this kitchen run smoothly.

"Hmm."

"Stop fucking saying that," I practically growl at him as he takes a sip of his cider.

"What?"

I narrow my eyes. "You know what. Every time Summer gets brought up, you do this *Hmm* shit, and you make faces, and it's fucking annoying. There is nothing at all going on between us."

Noah tucks his lips together, fighting a smile. "I never said there was, but it's interesting that's where your mind went."

I flip him my middle finger.

"Shut up," I say into my glass as I chug the rest of my drink. I set the empty cup down, wiping my mouth with the back of my hand. "I'm going back to work. You should too."

"Yes, sir."

He salutes me mockingly, and I'd be annoyed if I wasn't so damn worried that he thinks something is happening with me and Summer.

There isn't. There can't be.

So why does it feel like there is?

◆ ◆ ◆

My body is aching. I've been sitting at my desk for the last several hours trying to get caught up on everything I've been avoiding. Order forms are scattered across my desk, pens and pencils with too many bite marks are haphazardly placed, and I have three different coffee mugs surrounding me.

I'm fucking beat.

I check the time. Realizing I haven't moved in at least two hours, I finally rise from my chair. My back pops as I stretch, my hip screaming only a little as I do. I try to shake out the stiffness of it as I make my way into the taproom.

The cidery is buzzing with people. Not nearly as many as there were earlier, but there are still plenty of customers spread around. A few are playing games, some are just shooting the shit, while others are attempting to wrangle their children. I wave to a few familiar patrons.

"Hey, Ezra," says Micah, the guy who owns one of the gas stations in town. "How goes it?"

"Good. Great. Busy as usual. You?"

We make light polite conversation, and while I genuinely do like Micah, I'm distracted the whole time because of *her*.

I clocked where Summer was the second I walked into the taproom.

She's behind the bar with Warner. Her head is tossed back in a laugh, and her brown hair, which is up in a ponytail tonight, swishes back and forth. Warner stares down at her like she's the only girl in the room. Part of me gets it, because clearly my eyes are drawn to her, too, but the other part of me is just plain pissed off that they're openly flirting.

What the hell is she doing? She kisses me, then flirts with *him*?

I mean, our kiss didn't mean anything, so she's free to do as she will, but . . . fuck. I'm still seeing green, and it has nothing to do with those pretty chocolate-colored eyes of hers.

I say goodbye to Micah, then make my way over there.

"Warner!" I snap once he's in earshot.

His back goes straight, and he turns to me. "Ezra, hey, I was—"

"This isn't *Love Island*. You're not here to flirt. You're here to work."

His eyes widen, and I don't blame him. Even I can hear the venom in my words.

"Oh, uh . . ." His eyes flash to Summer, who is staring daggers at me. "Sorry. I—I d-didn't mean to—"

"Don't apologize to me. Apologize to Summer for being inappropriate in the workplace."

His cheeks redden. "S-Sorry, Summer. I—I—"

"Don't worry about it, Warner. I didn't mind at all."

She might have addressed him, but she was talking to me.

She's mad. Good. I'm glad because I'm mad too. And more than that, I want Warner gone. I can't be near him right now, or I might fire him just because, and he doesn't deserve that. Not really.

"Someone made a mess in the bathroom. It needs to be cleaned up." I don't know if this is true, but it'll get him gone, and that's exactly where I want him right now.

Nobody moves. Warner watches Summer, and Summer watches me.

"Well?" I say, finally dragging my stare away. "Aren't you going to take care of it?"

"Oh. Shit. Right. Yes. I'm on it, boss," Warner says. He gives Summer one last longing look before hurrying away toward the bathrooms.

Summer doesn't budge. No, she just keeps glowering at me. I can feel her eyes boring into the side of my head.

I want to look at her. I really fucking do. But I fear that if I take one glance at her, I'm going to do something really stupid, like jump over the counter and show her the real definition of being inappropriate in the workplace.

So instead I turn, ready to head back to my office.

Then I hear it. It's whispered, but it feels like it's shouted through a bullhorn.

"You really are an ass, Ezra."

She's right. I am. And I want her to keep thinking that. Keep saying it. I want her to hate me because it makes it easier to do what I should have been doing all along when it comes to her.

I walk away.

CHAPTER TWELVE

Summer

"Come on, come on, come on."

I turn the key in the ignition again, but nothing happens.

"Shit!" I slam my hands against the steering wheel repeatedly. "Fuck!"

This isn't the first time that my father's old cruiser has decided to die on me. This was his squad car back in the day, and when the department decided to retire this model, he bought it for dirt cheap because he just couldn't let it go.

I guess the good part is that I've always had something to drive when I visit Port Harbor, but it would be nice to have something far more reliable. If I did, maybe I wouldn't be stuck in the parking lot of Stick Taps at nearly eleven o'clock on a Tuesday night with nobody around.

My first instinct is to call my father, but I know he's been pulling a lot of late shifts over the last week or so to give his deputies a bit of summer with their families. I hate that he's working so much, because there's no way the stress is good for his heart, but that's just the kind of stand-up guy my father has always been. He's always sacrificed for the happiness of others.

I know that Noah and Odette live a mile or so up the road, but I really don't want to bother them this late. I'd rather call a tow truck than bug the almost newlyweds. I'm sure they have better things to be doing tonight than helping me. And I don't have Warner's number saved.

You could call Ezra.

The thought flits through my mind, but I push it away instantly.

My boss is the last person I want to see right now, especially after that stunt he pulled on Sunday with Warner, sending him to clean the bathrooms because he thought we were flirting. It was embarrassing, but more than that, it was infuriating. What right did he have to act jealous? He's the one who pulled away from our kiss and has been cold toward me since. Hell, he hasn't even spoken to me since he walked away two nights ago.

I push thoughts of Ezra from my head as I sling open the door and pop the hood of the car.

I'm under the hood when a loud noise rings out through the otherwise quiet night. At first I think it's one of the animals. There are so many of them hanging around here that it could easily explain it.

But then I see them off in the distance—headlights.

So no animal, then. It's a car. And it's going *fast*.

The driver whips into the lot of Stick Taps before I know it, and my entire body begins to buzz.

Somehow I know exactly who it is speeding into the parking lot, as if they're in a car chase or something.

The car skids to a stop when they see me, their headlights shining directly into my eyes. I hold my hand up to block them, even though it barely does anything.

The door opens, and out steps a six-foot-three frame I am all too familiar with.

"What's wrong?" Ezra's deep voice floats through the air, and I hate how the little hairs on my arms stick up.

Despite my traitorous body, I don't have the patience to deal with him tonight, not when the car won't start and all I want to do is go home, eat something, and crawl into bed. I'm tired. It's been a long day.

"Hello to you too," I say as he stomps toward me, his limp a bit more noticeable today.

That's not the only thing noticeable. His hair is wet, making his already dark locks even darker, and he's not wearing his typical slacks and button-up shirt. He's traded them for black joggers and a simple gray T-shirt, and even though I didn't think it was possible, it's even hotter than his math teacher wannabe look.

He looks good. *Too* good.

I stare anywhere but at him.

"Hi," he says curtly. "What's wrong? Car trouble?"

"No, I just thought I'd change my oil before I went home." I roll my eyes. "Yes, car trouble. It won't start."

"Hmm. Have you tried—"

"I swear, if you say jiggling the key, I might scream. I've tried everything and nada."

He nods. "All right. Mind if I look?"

I wave my hand, moving out of the way. "I didn't realize you were a mechanic, but sure, be my guest."

"I know enough to get me in trouble."

Oh, I don't doubt that at all.

He slips past me, and I'm hit with the scent of his soap again. It's earthy and clean and smells entirely too damn good, and that's the problem. No matter how annoyed I am with him, I still find him attractive. Which is why it's impossible to peel my eyes off him as he leans over the car, and even harder when I notice how his T-shirt stretches over the muscles in his back.

"Well, I've got nothing," Ezra says after a few minutes, and I snap my gaze back to him.

"I figured. It's fine. I'll call a tow truck."

"A tow truck?" He looks offended that I even suggested it. "What for? So they can charge you an arm and a leg to get picked up in the middle of the night? Not a chance. I'll drive you home. I just have to grab something from inside real quick."

"What? No."

"Yes."

"No," I say, more firmly this time. I am *not* going anywhere with him. He can bat those long lashes at me all he wants. It's not happening.

He sighs like *he's* tired of me. "Summer, I swear—"

"What? What do you swear, *Ezra?*"

He pinches the bridge of his nose, his lips set in a hard line, and I don't care. I don't give a shit that he's mad. I don't care if I'm being stubborn. And I really don't care if I have to walk back into town. It's infinitely better than being stuck in the car with him.

"Look, it's been a long fucking day, okay? So, can you not be stubborn just this once? Please?"

Please.

It's such a simple word, and I hate how it undoes all the false bravado I've been holding on to. That, coupled with how tired he truly does look . . .

Ugh, I hate myself for it, but I snap my mouth closed and nod. "Fine. But I'm giving you gas money."

He huffs. "Whatever you say, Sunny."

Then he leaves me standing there as he heads into the cidery.

I watch him leave, already regretting my decision, then make my way over to his sporty-looking sedan. I don't know much about car culture, but it's evident that whatever this is, it's expensive. And likely very fast.

Something about that sends a rush through me as I open the passenger door. There's a pizza box from I Heart Pizza Pie sitting in it, and the smell of oregano and tomato sauce has my stomach instantly rumbling.

I grab the box containing the best sourdough pizza I've ever had and slip into the seat, holding it on my lap, reveling in how warm it feels on the cool summer night.

Ezra comes out a few moments later, then slides into the driver's seat and hands me a folder.

"What's this?"

"Plans for the kitchen," he explains as he buckles his seat belt. I do the same. "I was going to go over them before bed."

"But it's late," I say absently as I flip open the folder and begin looking everything over. I immediately see issues with it. The placements are off, and it doesn't flow well. He should move the stove, the prep tables, and the storage.

"I don't, uh, I don't sleep very much." He turns his car around, the engine rumbling loudly, even though we aren't moving fast. "Might as well be productive."

"Makes sense," I say, but I can't help but feel a bit sad thinking of Ezra sitting up at night alone in his place, just working. Does he do anything else? Does he not have people to hang out with?

Then I remember what an ass he is, and all my sympathy goes out the window.

"We can get your car looked at tomorrow. Do you work?"

"You're the one with my schedule memorized. You tell me," I say sarcastically.

He casts me a side-eye glance as he pulls out of the parking lot, and all it does is make me want to antagonize him more. I don't know what that says about me, but right now I don't care. I want to rile him up like he's riled me up.

"What? You're not going to speed out of here like a bat out of hell?"

"Is that a challenge? Because that sure sounds like a challenge."

I snort. "Please. I doubt you could win a race against a sloth."

His eyes narrow momentarily before he says, "Hang on to that pizza, will you?"

And it's the last thing I hear before I'm thrown back in the seat. My heart settles into my throat as I hug the box tightly. My initial reaction is to scream at him to stop, but I don't. I trust him, and that thought scares me a little.

He presses on the pedal more, and I glance over at him, and I'm surprised to find the pure elation on his face. I don't think I've ever seen him look so happy before. It's like everything that sits so heavily on his shoulders is lifted, and he's free.

It's a really good look for him.

"You good?" he shouts over the whine of the engine, and I don't dare look at the speedometer.

"Yes!" I yell back.

He goes a little harder, then downshifts and eases onto the brake, the car slowing down but not in a way that jerks you forward. We roll to a stop at the end of the road leading up to the cidery, and I'm instantly annoyed by the grin stretched across my face.

"Fun?" Ezra asks with a smile of his own.

I shrug. "It was fine."

"Fine, my ass. That was a fucking blast, and you know it."

My lips twitch involuntarily, and I force a stoic face. "Whatever."

But Ezra doesn't stop grinning, and dammit if it doesn't make me want to grin again too.

"God, I could do that every day if it weren't for your father always busting me. It reminds me of being on the ice. It feels like flying." His words are laced with longing, and I'm suddenly hit with the desire to be able to rewind the clock for him so he could do things differently and get hockey back. "But that's why we have the iceplex. It's my way of connecting with the game again."

He doesn't say anything else, and I don't offer anything either. I don't know what to say. Losing my kitchen is nothing like what happened to him. I can still cook. He only has his dream from the sidelines.

"You're really clinging to that pizza," he says as we drive through town. He's not going a single mile over the speed limit, and I wonder if that's because of Noah getting onto him about his speeding, or if he's actually heeding my father's warning.

"What kind is it?"

"Pesto chicken with balsamic glaze."

My stomach rumbles loudly. Ezra doesn't miss it.

"Hungry?"

"Yeah. And their pesto chicken happens to be my favorite pizza ever. I missed it in Chicago."

"Not a fan of deep dish?"

"Blech. Not even a little. Give me a good sourdough any day of the week."

"Agreed." He flicks his eyes down to the pizza, then up to me. "You want some?"

His words are so casual that they take me off guard. There's no way I heard him right. There's no way he wants to share his pizza with me.

"What?"

He chuckles lightly, like he knows I'm stumbling over his words. "I have no business eating a whole pie by myself. We could split it."

It's a bad idea. I know it is. But I am hungry. We didn't get a lot of downtime tonight with our bingo night, so I haven't eaten since lunch. A pizza sounds a lot better than going back to an empty house and warming up the leftover chicken and broccoli pasta I made for my dad and me last night. Plus, he does need help with those kitchen plans. Whatever he has going on isn't going to work. It's better to fix that now than try to change it later.

But I shouldn't. I really, really shouldn't. I . . .

"I don't want to intrude."

"Wouldn't have invited you if you were. Besides, I could use your help with the kitchen plans. The contractors want me to review them by Friday so we can finalize everything and get started next week."

Well, when he puts it that way . . . "Yeah, sure."

"Don't sound so excited." He flips his turn signal on and drives in the opposite direction from my father's house. "Are you still thinking about opening your own restaurant?"

His words surprise me. He remembers me saying that?

"Uh, I guess I always am. Why?"

"I don't know. Just curious. I could look out for some places for you, if you want."

It's actually . . . nice of him.

And confusing. I swear, he's giving me whiplash. He was a jerk before, but now he's offering me pizza and helping find a space for a restaurant? I don't understand him.

"I'm not really looking."

"Why not?"

Because I'm scared, I think to myself. "Because it's not the right time."

"That's what everyone with a dream says. They always push it off until it's too late. You shouldn't do that. You should go after what you want. Don't wait. You never know when you won't have the chance again."

I know deep down he's right, but it doesn't change the fact that I'm still not ready.

So I don't say anything. I just watch the streets go by before he eventually pulls into a modest neighborhood. It's not one I'm too familiar with, as it's something that went up shortly before I moved away.

"I'm just up here," he says.

He pulls into the driveway of a newer ranch-style house, and I can safely say it's not at all what I was expecting. I figured he'd be in one of the townhomes or an apartment. Definitely not a white-picket-fence-worthy house with an oversize two-car garage.

"This is nice," I say as he puts the car in park.

He shrugs. "It's home. Needs a bigger garage, but it's not bad."

"Bigger? How many cars do you have?"

"Five."

"Five? I don't even have *one* that runs!"

"A problem for another day. Now come on. Let's get inside before the pizza gets cold."

His hand brushes against mine as he grabs the box and pushes open his car door. If he feels the electric jolts, too, he doesn't show it. He just gets out of the car and leaves me sitting there, the folder clutched tightly in my hands.

I take a deep breath, trying to ignore what a bad idea this was, then grab the handle.

Only it's not there—the door's been wrenched open, and Ezra is standing there.

I peer up at him in shock because, well, I *am* shocked. I didn't think Ezra had a single gentlemanly bone in his body.

Enigma. That's what he is. There's no other way to describe him.

"Did you change your mind?"

"Hmm?" I realize I'm still sitting in the car, staring at him. "Oh, right."

I climb out, Ezra stepping back to give me space, and I almost wish he hadn't.

No, no. Not that. I'm annoyed by him, remember? Be annoyed by him, Summer!

But I'm not, even though I wish I were. He's so hot and cold, but so are my feelings toward him, and I just wish we could each pick a lane and stay there.

Maybe tonight will be the night we get back on track and strike a balance.

I follow him into his house, and as soon as we step inside, I'm hit with the same scent I always am when I'm too close to him, but this time it's everywhere.

He flips on a light, then takes off his shoes. I do the same and trail behind him deeper into the house, taking it in as we go.

The first thing I notice is how clean it is. And I don't just mean he's good at picking up behind himself. I mean *clean*. There's nothing out of place anywhere, which is so funny, because I've been in his office before, and his desk is usually a complete wreck.

No photos line the walls, very few knickknacks sit on the bookshelves that take up one side of the living room, and his couch looks like nobody has ever sat on it.

We step into this kitchen—which is equally untouched—and I want to cry at the beautiful stove he has.

"Do you approve?" he asks, setting the pizza on the counter.

"Approve? Are you kidding me? I could *kill* for a stove like this. It's gorgeous."

He laughs lightly. "I don't think I've ever heard someone call a stove *gorgeous* before."

"Then you're not hanging out with the right people."

"Clearly," he deadpans. He flicks his chin toward the fridge—again, gorgeous—and says, "Grab us some drinks? I'll get plates."

I pull open the stainless-steel door and laugh.

"What?"

"Um, you realize your fridge is empty, right?"

"No, it's not. There's ranch dressing in there. Cider too."

"And not much else. Do you not cook at all?" I ask, looking over my shoulder.

He shrugs as he reaches into the cabinet. "Sometimes, but it's nothing like what you do."

I'm not proud of it, but I stick my head farther into the fridge at his compliment. I have to or else he'll see just how red my cheeks are.

When I feel like I don't look strawberry red, I grab us two ciders and take them to the counter.

Ezra plates the pizza, and we settle onto the stools tucked beneath the island.

I can't help but groan at the first bite of pizza. "Holy shit. This is so good."

"Right?" He eats half the slice in one bite, chews, then swallows. "It's easily my favorite part of living here."

"Where did you move here from?"

"Technically, Minnesota," he says, popping open his cider. It's Empty Net, my favorite. "I went back home after . . ."

His words trail off, and I instantly know what he means—the hockey accident that took him out of the game for good.

He clears his throat. "Before that, I was in Tennessee for three years."

"Did you like it?"

"It wasn't bad, but it was not a place I could see myself settling down. Too crowded for me. I'm sure this might come as a shock, but I'm not much of a people person, so I didn't love the going-out culture they had, you know? It felt like every night the guys wanted to hit up a bar or something, and I wasn't down for that."

"Yet now you own a bar."

"It's not a *bar*. It's a cidery. There's a difference."

He has me there. Sure, Stick Taps serves alcohol like a bar does, but it's nowhere near the same vibe as Hank's here in town.

"Besides, I might own a bar, but it's not like I'm really that involved with the day-to-day of actual . . . barring."

"Barring?" I laugh. "I'm pretty sure that's not how you use that word."

He wrinkles his nose. "Whatever. I'm tired. Leave me alone."

"You should sleep more."

"Tell that to my hip."

I stop myself before I can frown, instead shoveling more pizza into my mouth.

Ezra polishes off two more slices, and I finish another myself before declaring that I'm done.

"Thank you. For sharing your pizza, I mean," I say as I hop off the stool, taking my plate to the sink.

"What are you doing?" Ezra asks, and I jump.

I had no idea he was so close. And by close I mean take-a-step-back-and-be-pressed-up-against-him kind of close.

"Uh, the dishes."

"No," he says, reaching over me and grabbing the plate from my hand.

"Ezra, stop. Just let me wash it."

"Not a chance, Sunny. You've been on your feet all day. Go sit down."

I want to argue, because that's my natural reaction when it comes to him, but suddenly my feet are aching, and I'm realizing just how long of a day it really has been.

"Fine," I mutter, then resume my spot at the counter, but not before snatching up the plans for the kitchen.

I sip on my cider as I look it over again. I was hoping it was just the bad lighting in the car, but my first impression was right—this isn't going to work.

"Well?" Ezra asks, and I look up to find him still standing at the sink, his back now to the faucet, a towel in his hands as he dries them off.

His hair is dry now, lying messily on his head like he's been running his hand through it, and there's a wet spot on his shirt, causing it to cling to him.

I hate how good he looks like this. So relaxed. So unbothered. He's not even scowling like he usually is. He looks . . . at ease, and it's doing wonders for him.

"See something you like, Sunny?"

I snap my gaze from that damn wet spot to his eyes.

"Excuse me?"

He nods toward the plans sitting in front of me. "The layout. Do you see something you like?"

"Oh." I give myself a mental shake, frustrated that I let him get inside my head again. "Uh, no. Actually. This sucks."

Just like that, his scowl is back. "Jeez, tell me how you really feel."

"I feel like you could do better."

"Ouch."

"Oh, I'm sorry. Is it just you who gets to be the asshole?"

His eyes narrow, but only for a moment before he exhales heavily and nods. "That's fair." He carefully slips the towel back around the handle on the stove, then pushes off the counter and stalks closer until he's standing right next to me. "Listen, Summer, I—"

I hold my hand up. "Stop. I don't want to hear your excuse."

His brows furrow. "Excuse? What excuse?"

"Whatever bullshit you're about to feed me about why you were a dick the other night with Warner. I don't want to hear it. Let's just go over these kitchen plans and keep it strictly business."

His nostrils flare, his eyes darkening, jaw setting tight as he takes another step closer. I should move. Hell, I should run away.

I don't.

Not even when Ezra leans in closer and says, "What if I don't want it to be strictly business?"

A steady *whoosh* fills my ears as my heart rate climbs.

I draw in a deep breath, and I know right away it was a mistake.

Rain showers. Fresh evergreens. Soap. Ezra.

I exhale shakily. "Well, that's too bad because that's what it is."

"Is it? Was it strictly business when you kissed me?"

Heat climbs up my cheeks at the memory of him pulling away from me. I've tried so hard to forget it, but it's impossible, especially when I swear I keep seeing him looking at me like he did just before our lips touched.

Like he is now.

I drop my gaze back to the plans, but they just look like a jumbled mess. I can't focus, and it's all Ezra's fault. He's standing too close.

"I thought we decided we were going to forget that ever happened," I say to the paper.

"No, that's what *you* decided. I remember distinctly saying that I didn't want to forget."

I don't want to pretend it didn't happen. Just so we're clear.

"Was it distinct? Because ever since then, you've been avoiding me."

"I've been working."

"Avoiding." I dare a peek at him. "And torturing your employees."

"Working," he insists. "And disciplining them when they need it. When they're being . . . insubordinate."

"We were just talking."

His jaw tics. "You were flirting. On the clock, mind you."

I tip my chin higher, meeting his heated stare head-on. "So what if we were? What's the big deal, huh? Warner's a nice guy. He's funny and he's sweet and *cute.*"

He is objectively good looking, but he does nothing for me. Ezra doesn't need to know that, of course, especially not when it's so obvious it riles him up. His eyes are practically black, his breaths coming in sharply, so I keep going.

"So who cares if I flirt with him? Or if I date him? Who cares if—"

"I do!" He takes another step closer, so damn close that he's mere inches away, and I can see the freckles that line up just over the bridge of his nose. "I fucking care, Summer."

"Why?" The words aren't nearly as sharp as I intend them to be, and it has everything to do with our proximity. "Why do you care so much, Ezra?"

One.

Two.

Three.

That's how many seconds it takes for him to answer me.

"Because he's not me."

And then Ezra Rawlings is kissing me.

CHAPTER THIRTEEN

Ezra

She tastes like pears and peaches, and all it does is make me like my favorite cider even more than I already do.

She's just as soft as she was before, maybe even a little softer, as I slide my hands through her hair, cupping the back of her neck and pulling her closer because I have to. I want to feel her against me. No, I *need* to feel her against me.

Summer must feel the same way, because her fists grip my shirt, holding me to her as our lips move together like they've done this dance a hundred times before when they haven't. It's only been once, and my hip ruined it. It already takes so much from me. I refuse to let it spoil this too.

I swipe my tongue against her lips, and she moans, opening for me, and I don't dare waste the opportunity. I lick inside her mouth, tasting every inch of her as our tongues slide together in a frenzy.

Fuck, this is good. Almost *too* good.

No, that's not possible.

I slip my hands through her hair, which I've been wanting to touch since the moment I saw her sitting in the sheriff's station. I wanted to know if it's as soft as it looks, and it is. The slightly wavy brown locks feel like fucking silk beneath my fingertips.

It's incredible. *She's* incredible.

Suddenly she pulls away, and I want to curse at the loss of her.

"Ezra . . ." she says through strangled breaths. Her chest is moving up and down so fast that if I didn't know any better, I'd say she just skated all two hundred feet of a rink and back again. "What are we doing?"

"We're kissing." I press my lips to hers again.

She laughs, pulling away once more. She rests her forehead against my chin, still gulping in air. "I . . . I know that. I mean . . . we can't, right?"

"No," I agree. "We can't. You're my employee. This is definitely against the rules."

"It is. We should stop."

"We should."

But I don't take my hands off her. If anything, I hold her tighter. I drag her closer.

"Ezra . . ." I think it's supposed to sound like a refusal, but it comes out as a plea, and I'm not about to deny her anything.

I couldn't if I tried.

I just kiss her again, and she sinks into me.

I slide my hands under her ass and lift her into my arms. My hip pinches, but I ignore it as I spin us around, setting her on the counter and stepping between her thighs.

She lets out a soft gasp, and I swallow the sound with my mouth.

I kiss her softly, then hard and soft once more, just because I can. I can't get enough. It's like I'm addicted to her, and I've only just begun.

Her hands slide into my hair, and I groan at the touch. I can't remember the last time someone had their hands on me like this. Maybe two years ago? More? I don't know, but fuck, it feels fantastic.

I pull my lips from hers and kiss across her jaw right up to her ear, then back again just because I can. I do it on the other side, wanting to taste every inch of her, then trail my way down her neck. She moans when I press my lips against her throat, her nails scratching against my scalp in the most delicious fashion.

"Fuck, that feels good," she says through labored breaths.

"Tastes good too." I run my tongue against her. "You taste like vanilla cupcakes, Sunny."

She laughs. "It's my bodywash."

"I love it. Never stop using it."

"Stop telling me what to do."

"Always a brat." I lick at her again, and she moans. I smile against her. "But I bet I know the way to make you finally shut up."

"Oh? And how are you going to do that?"

I trace a path back to her lips, kissing her until we're both breathless and desperate. When I finally pull away, I say, "By fucking you."

She lets out a loud gasp as I drag her off the counter. She wraps her legs around me on instinct as I carry her through the kitchen and living room and down the hall to my room.

My hip screams at me the entire trek, but I push the ache away. Having her in my arms is worth all the pain.

Her mouth hasn't left me the entire trip. She's been peppering kisses all over my face, and I fucking love it.

I stumble into the bedroom, thankful I left the bedside lamp on to guide me as I take us to my king-size bed.

I've never had anyone else in here before.

The thought hits me out of nowhere, and I realize that I'm glad it's Summer. There's something about her that's gotten under my skin from the moment I met her. She drives me wild, but it's in a good way. Like right now, as she sinks her teeth into my neck with the gentlest of nibbles.

I stop at the foot of the bed and lower her to the floor. She slides down my body, pressing up against all the right spots.

She catches my gaze, her chocolate eyes cloudy with lust, but I still see the silent question in them.

Are you okay?

I know she's asking about my hip. I wait for that near-constant frustration I have when someone asks about it, but it never comes. I'm too fucking happy to have her in my arms to give a shit.

I answer her by capturing her mouth in a searing kiss, my fingers finding their way beneath the short, cropped sunshine-colored shirt that's captured my attention the second I saw her standing in the Stick Taps parking lot.

She shivers under my touch, and I take it as permission to continue, slipping my hand higher until I'm grazing the underside of her tit. She groans at the slight contact, and I know it's not enough for her. She wants more, and I do too.

I break away from her and tug her shirt over her head. She reaches for her bra, but I stop her.

"Let me."

She nods, dropping her hands, and I step back to admire her. I rake my eyes over her, taking in the vision before me. Her tits, full and perfectly pert, are barely contained by her simple white bra. It's nothing special at all, but on her it looks like a million bucks.

Her brown locks are tousled from me running my fingers through them, her chest flushed from all the kissing we've been doing, and her eyes are so dark they look nearly black in this lighting.

She looks fucking gorgeous, and I want to commit this moment to memory because she was right. This is wrong, and we shouldn't be doing this for so many reasons. She works for me, for fuck's sake. I'm doing her dad a favor.

He can't know about this, just like this can never, ever happen again.

But until then . . .

I reach for her, and my fingers find the clasp of her bra. I undo it, letting the material fall away between us.

There's no way she doesn't hear the stutter in my breath as I get my first look at her.

She grins, but it's not a cocky kind of grin. It's sassy and sweet, and all it does is make me want her more.

I curl my hand around her waist, tugging her closer, and she comes to me easily. Her nipples brush against me, and I'm suddenly very aware of how much clothing is between us.

As if she's just realized it, too, Summer's hands push my shirt up, and I let her drag it over my head, tossing it aside for us to clean up later.

Her eyes roam over me, and I love the appreciation I see in her gaze. I might not be a hockey player anymore, but I take care of my body as if I were, hitting the gym several times a week. I have to. Not just for my own mental health, but for my hip too. It's the only way to keep my mobility where it's at.

"I knew you had a six-pack. And not just of cider."

She winks, and I laugh at the awful joke.

"Shut up and come here," I say, and we reach for each other at the same time, both sighing as our skin touches and our mouths crash together.

I can't tell which one of us is more desperate, but I don't care. All I care about is mapping every inch of her body until the wee hours of the morning.

If I have only one night with her, then I'm going to make it count.

I kiss from her lips down her chin and over her throat, which works against the soft touch. I capture a nipple for only a moment before continuing south as I drop to my knees before her.

When my fingers find the button of her jeans that look ridiculously good on her, she says, "Ezra, you don't have to. I know you—"

"Want to." I meet her worried gaze. "I want to, Summer. Let me taste you. *Please.*"

Her eyes spark, and she nods, her teeth sinking into her bottom lip. "All right. But only because you asked so nicely."

One corner of my mouth lifts as I flick open her jeans. The zipper is loud as I drag it down the track, and I watch Summer every step of the way.

She doesn't try to stop me. Not when I hook my fingers into the waistband and tug the denim down. Nor when I take her panties along too. Not when she steps out of the material and stands before me completely bare.

And when I grab her leg, setting it over my shoulder, nuzzling my nose against the soft curls that sit between her thighs, she doesn't say a peep.

It's only when I finally drag my tongue against her that she says anything, and it's just one word—my name.

"Ezra."

It's like fucking gospel to my ears, and I live up to it by worshipping her.

Her hands slip through my hair as I slide my tongue through her center, paying extra attention to her clit. She groans loudly, tossing her head back with a heavy eye roll.

My hip may be throbbing, but it's nothing in comparison to my cock doing the same thing. I don't think I've ever tasted anything so sweet in my life.

I could stay here all night, my tongue in her cunt, listening as she comes undone. But I have other ideas, too, like burying my cock inside her until she's nothing but a mess beneath me.

I suck her clit into my mouth, flicking my tongue against it quickly, and when her legs start to shake, I know it has nothing to do with the position we're in. She's close.

And, honestly, so am I. Embarrassingly so, and if I don't get inside her soon, I'm going to make a mess inside my joggers in a way I haven't since I was seventeen.

"Oh god. Right there," she mutters through heavy breaths. "Don't stop."

I indulge her request, not breaking my rhythm as she begins rocking her hips ever so slightly, taking whatever it is she's seeking. I let her practically fuck my face as I continue the torture with my tongue until I feel her whole body go taut.

Then she's melting right into me, her grip tightening on my hair so hard it nearly hurts, but I don't care. I'd take any kind of hurt right now if it meant her getting her release.

I taste her through her shakes, and the aftershocks, too, until she's literally wrenching herself away from my assault. Only then do I pull away to catch my breath.

I place her back on her feet and settle on my haunches as she falls down to the bed behind her.

"Holy shit," she says, her legs still shaking as they hang off the edge of the bed. "That was . . ."

"Incredible, huh?"

She pushes back up to her elbows, looking down at me with a lopsided grin. "Very much so. I don't think I've come that hard in . . . well, maybe ever."

"Good." I rise to my feet, ignoring the cry from my hip at all the up and down.

She reaches for my joggers, tugging at the waistband, and I snatch her wrists in my hands.

"But . . ."

I shake my head. "Another time. If I feel your mouth on me right now, I'm going to explode, and while the idea of filling that bratty mouth with my cum is enticing, I want to fill your sweet pussy first, Sunny. Understood?"

She swallows roughly, then nods. "Yes."

"Good. Now, crawl up the bed, will you?"

I swear she's moving before I even get the words out, and I chuckle as she goes, enjoying the scramble far too much.

I pad to the en suite bathroom in search of the box of condoms I'm fairly certain I have stashed in there. When I find them behind the mirror, I check the date just to be sure and am relieved when I see they're still good.

Protection in hand, I step back into the bedroom and pause.

Summer's lying in the middle of the bed. She's up on her elbows, one leg kicked out straight, and the other bent at the knee. The lamp casts a yellowish hue over her, to where she's almost glowing, and I suppose that's fitting for the nickname I've given her.

She's stunning. There's no way around it. Made even more beautiful by the fact that she's not trying to cover herself up and that she doesn't look ashamed to be lying naked in the middle of my bed. Her confidence just makes her all the sexier.

When I finally meet her eyes again, she has one brow lifted in a silent *Well? Aren't you going to fulfill your promise?*

And yes. Yes, I am.

I stop at the foot of the bed, tossing the box of condoms onto it before hooking my thumbs in my pants. Summer doesn't take her eyes off me as I push them down my legs and kick them aside.

Which is how I know she likes what she sees. *A lot.*

Feeling's mutual, I say to myself as I take my cock in my hand, giving it a few pumps. Not because I need to, but because if I don't, I might die.

It sounds dramatic, but I've never been such a fucking wreck before. I've never been so goddamn eager for *more* in my life.

I place one knee on the bed, and Summer's tongue slides against her lips in anticipation.

I drag the other up, then crawl to her, my heavy cock swaying between my legs the entire journey. She spreads her thighs for me, and when I finally settle between them, we both sigh as I slip against her warm, wet center.

I rock into her just because I can, and she moans, tossing her head back.

"Yes." She drags the word out through a hiss. "That feels . . ."

"I know," I say when she doesn't finish her sentence. "I know, Sunny."

Then I press my lips against hers because I can't stand not kissing her any longer, and she twines her arms around my neck, pulling me down closer until I'm resting against her. It's not my full weight—I don't think she could handle it—but it still feels damn good to be so close to her.

I'm not usually one for physical contact, but I find that with her, I crave it.

That seems to be the case in more ways than one.

I try not to read too much into that as my cock brushes against her clit again, and she groans into my mouth.

"Ezra," she says, pulling away. "I don't think I can wait much longer."

"Me either."

"Then do it. Fuck me already."

How could I possibly say no to that?

I push onto my knees and reach for the condoms. I rip into the box, then open a foil packet with my teeth in an act of impatience, and just as I'm about to roll it over my shaft, Summer speaks up.

"Let me."

It's the same thing I said to her earlier, and I nod, handing the rubber to her.

She places it over my tip, using both of her hands to roll it on, and *fuck, fuck, fuck.* I could come right now. I could explode in her hand before I ever get the chance to be inside her.

She drags her palm over me once, then twice. When she goes for a third time, I grab her wrist to stop her.

"Problem, Mr. Rawlings?" she teases.

I narrow my eyes at her. "Brat."

She shrugs, unbothered by the name as she falls back to the bed. She's looking up at me with hooded eyes, and I fall on top of her, lining myself up with the part of her that I can still taste on my lips.

This time when I kiss her, it's soft and sweet. Such a contrast to what I want to do when I finally get inside her.

Her hips search for my touch, and when they find it, she sighs as I slip inside her easily, like I was made to fit her. Or she was made to fit me. Either way, it's unlike anything I've ever felt before.

"Oh god," she cries out as I press into her more. "Fuck, Ezra. I . . ."

But her words die on her lips as I drag my cock out of her, then slam back in.

And I get it, because I feel the same way. I don't think I could speak right now if I tried, and honestly, I don't want to. I just want to be in this moment. I want to feel every inch of her. Want to learn by rote every sigh and plea and buck of her hips as I fuck into her.

Her nails drag from my scalp over my neck and down my back. They're sure to leave a mark or two, but I couldn't care less. It's worth it for this.

"You feel so good," I tell her, my lips at her ear. "Like a fucking dream come true."

"I could say the same about you," she says, her breath heavy as I thrust into her again. "I didn't think it would be this good."

"You've thought about it?"

"And you haven't?"

"Of fucking course I have. How could I not? You're . . . you."

I feel her smile against me, and all it does is spur me on.

I push back up onto my knees, eager to wring another orgasm from her and barely holding on to my own as I pound into her again. She traces her palms over my chest and down across my abs, never once taking her eyes off me, and I fucking love it because I want to watch her as she comes apart.

And come apart she does just a few moments later.

I can tell it slams into her out of nowhere, because it does the same to me, and I'm a roaring mess as I fill the condom with more cum than I ever have before. Summer's cunt squeezes me tightly, making sure there's not a drop left behind as I fuck her through each wave, giving her everything I can until there's nothing else to offer.

I collapse on top of her, and her lips instantly find the side of my neck.

I'm not sure how long we stay that way—me trying to remember how to breathe and her peppering kiss after kiss against me, but it's long enough that I'm very close to making a real mess between us if I don't move soon.

With reluctance, I peel myself away and climb off the bed to dispose of the condom.

I make my way into the bathroom, resting against the sink as I wash my hands. My hip is practically burning at this point, but I don't care. That was worth it and more.

Summer takes my place when I get back, and when she's finished, she climbs under the sheets beside me.

She snuggles up against me, and my arm goes around her automatically as if this were something we do every night.

Panic races through me in a flash at the normalcy of this all.

What the fuck am I doing? What the fuck are *we* doing? This is such a bad idea. I need to find a way to make her leave. Say something assholeish to make her run away. We should put as much distance as possible between us.

Yet . . . I can't find it in me to do any of that.

All I want to do is pull her closer and sleep.

So that's what I do.

"You know," she says after several quiet moments. "We never did look over those kitchen plans together."

I chuckle, dragging my fingers through her hair that's sufficiently tangled at this point. "No, I guess we didn't. We'll deal with it later. Right now I need sleep. Apparently I have a long day of reconfiguring a kitchen tomorrow."

"Deal." She kisses my chest, then curls into me, and I tighten my grip on her, almost like I'm afraid she's going to disappear in the middle of the night.

She might. She should. Because this really is a bad idea. Possibly the worst one I've ever had.

But I can't deny that I want to do it again.

I am so fucked.

CHAPTER FOURTEEN

Summer

Sweat trickles down my neck, waking me from my slumber.

I'm hot. Sure, it's summertime, but this is the Pacific Northwest. Even when it's hot, it's never *this* hot.

No, this is something else. Like an inferno, flames lick up the side of my body. This is—

The memories of last night slam into me, and I spring up in bed, looking to my right.

Ezra.

He's on his stomach, his arms stretched out under his pillow, one leg kicked up. The sheet barely covers his naked ass as he takes deep, steady breaths. He's even frowning in his sleep, and it's almost unfair how absurdly hot that is.

I have the urge to lift the sheet and get a look at him in the morning light, but I refrain.

Holy shit! I slept with Ezra!

Not even just once either. The second time came a few hours ago when I woke up to his hand between my legs, fingers pumping into me. I was shocked by how wet I was when he pulled me onto his lap, where I rode him until we were both completely spent.

I don't even remember falling back asleep, but clearly we did.

I glance at the clock on the bedside table, and I can hardly believe it when I see it's nearly eleven. I can't remember the last time I slept so late or so damn peacefully. It must be his big, comfy bed. Or maybe it was the orgasms. Or perhaps it was just sleeping next to someone for the first time in . . . shit, I can't actually remember the last time I did.

I roam my gaze over my bedmate once more, and I wonder what he's dreaming about that has him so grumpy even in his sleep. He carries too much on his shoulders.

I slip from the bed as quietly as I can, grabbing the first piece of clothing I can find and throwing it on before stopping in the bathroom. I do my business, then find some toothpaste and give my teeth a quick brush with my finger.

Ezra's still in the same position when I'm finished, so I sneak out in search of my phone. I'm a grown adult and don't need to check in with my father about anything, but I also know he's a bit of a worrywart. He can claim it's the law enforcement man in him, but I think that's just part of being a parent. Besides, I want to make sure he's okay. Aside from me working, it'll be the first time we've spent an evening apart since I came back to Washington, and I admit that I worry about him more now than I did before his heart incident.

I find the device on the kitchen counter, unsurprised that it's completely dead.

"Shit," I mutter, looking around for a charger.

I locate one stashed away in what looks to be Ezra's "junk drawer," a term I use very loosely for him, considering there's an organizer in it and everything seems to have a place.

While waiting for my phone to boot back up, I make my way to the fridge. I think I saw some orange juice in there last night, and it sounds too good to pass up at the moment.

"Oh, great. You're one of those people."

I whirl around, orange juice sloshing from the container and down my chin at the intrusion.

Ezra is leaning against the wall, one leg crossed over the other, in nothing but his joggers from last night, and they are slung low. And I mean *low*. So damn low that I can very clearly make out the V that points straight down.

It's hot. *He's* hot.

"Pardon?"

He nods toward the juice in my hand. "You drink straight from the carton."

"Oh shit. I did, didn't I?" I replace the cap, then slide it back into the fridge. "My bad."

He grins, and it looks so . . . easy. It's almost disarming. I'm not used to him smiling. I'm used to the frowny Grump Ass version of him.

But this . . . this I could get used to. I could like this *too* much.

"It's fine," he says, pushing off the wall and padding into the kitchen until he's standing next to me. He opens the fridge and retrieves the carton I just put away. He twists off the cap and takes a large swig before saying, "I do it too."

Something tugs low in my belly, and even though I've had three incredible orgasms in the last twelve hours, every part of me could go for another, and I still don't think it would be enough.

The thought is terrifying because it *has* to be enough. This can't happen again. I am technically his employee for the time being. It goes against so many rules, and the last thing I want is to lose this kitchen because I can't seem to keep my pants on around him.

This was a onetime thing only.

"Sleep okay?" he asks, still grinning. Still disarming me, and it makes me wonder . . . *Does this really have to be the last time?*

My cheeks heat because I can just *hear* the insinuation in his voice. *Sleep okay?* sounds more like *Get fucked okay?* The answer to both is the same.

"Uh, yeah. Has anyone ever told you that your bed is absurdly comfy?"

"Considering I've never had anyone else in my bed before, no."

He puts the carton away and closes the fridge, then turns to me like he didn't just announce that so casually. As if it's not completely loaded with so many things that my brain can hardly process right now.

Ezra brought me to his house. Ezra took me into his bed. Ezra fucked me until I could barely keep my eyes open.

I want to ask him why me, but that's likely the beginning of a whole different conversation, one I'm not quite sure we're ready for.

"So," he starts, taking a step toward me, and I find myself holding my breath. Why? I don't know. But I seem to do a lot of things that I don't understand when it comes to Ezra, like sleeping with my employer, for starters. "Breakfast?"

"You have nothing here, remember?"

"I have cereal and milk."

I lift a brow. "Really?"

"Yeah? Why do you sound surprised by that?"

"I don't know. I guess I just didn't really peg you as a cereal kind of guy. I can't imagine you sitting on the couch with a bowl of Cheerios, watching TV or anything."

"That's because it's not Cheerios, it's Froot Loops, and I would never eat it on the couch. I'd eat in bed with the TV on."

It's safe to say I was a bit preoccupied when Ezra carried me into his bedroom last night, so I didn't notice the television he has in there until this morning.

It surprised me, mostly because I just can't picture Ezra sitting down to scroll Netflix or something. He seems like he's always too busy for that.

"I don't sleep much, remember? I need something other than work to keep me occupied in the middle of the night," he explains as if he can tell I'm trying to sort that out in my mind.

I nod. "That makes sense. Though I'm still shocked you keep sugary cereal here. You strike me as a guy who opts for the healthier stuff."

"Cereal is where I draw the line, and I might have a bit of a sweet tooth."

You taste like vanilla cupcakes, Sunny.

Uh, yeah. I remember.

I clear my throat, shoving away the memories of him tasting me last night. "Cereal in bed it is, though you really should hit up a grocery store every now and then. Learn to cook, even if it's just the basics."

"Are you going to teach me?"

He's not even trying to be flirty. It's a genuine question, and my instant reaction is to say yes, because what kind of chef wouldn't want someone else to fall in love with cooking?

But then I remember how we're not supposed to be doing this—whatever this is—which means we definitely aren't supposed to be making plans together.

"We'll circle back to that," he says at my pause, moving toward the pantry. He opens the door and looks back at me over his shoulder. "Now, do you want Froot Loops, Lucky Charms, or Cinnamon Toast Crunch?"

Five minutes later, we're back in his bedroom, under the same sheets we were tangled in last night, each of us holding a bowl of too-sugary cereal, the TV playing quiet reruns of *The Office* in the background.

I know I should probably check my phone and get hold of my dad, but I'm too content right now. I'll do it later. He's a big boy and can take care of himself for one night.

"God, I forgot how good this was," I say as I shovel a bite of Cinnamon Toast Crunch into my mouth. "I don't remember the last time I had it."

"It's my second favorite. I'm still a Froot Loops kid through and through. My uncle was about as skilled in the kitchen as I am, so I ate a lot of it growing up."

"Is he how you got into hockey?"

"Sort of?" Ezra shrugs. "I mostly got into it because it was something to do. My uncle worked hard to keep a roof over our heads, so I was often alone. There was an after-school program at my local rink, so I'd go there and watch the kids skate. I was mesmerized by it. I'd never watched hockey or anything until then, but it looked fun as hell. One day a coach saw me and asked if I wanted to give it a go. I didn't have equipment, but they found me some, pushed me out onto the ice. I didn't love the skates at first—way too unreliable—but once I actually gave it a real shot, I was hooked." He grins. "They would have to practically drag me from the rink every night because I never wanted to leave. It was like being in a different world. I was no longer just the kid who lost his parents. I was someone else. I was . . ."

"Free?" I finish for him, unable to contain my own smile. He looks so happy talking about the game, and though I know he doesn't want my sympathy, it still makes me feel so bad that he lost it.

"Yeah, that. How'd you know?"

"Because you get this look on your face when you talk about hockey, and it's the same look you have when you're speeding down the road. It's . . . peaceful. And kind of beautiful. Terrifying when you're doing a hundred, but still beautiful."

He laughs. "I wasn't doing a hundred."

I raise a brow at him.

"It was 105, thank you very much."

"Yes, because that's *so* much better." I roll my eyes.

"Hey, it's the closest thing I can get to an adrenaline rush these days, thanks to my hip. I'll take the win where I can get it."

"Is that why you drive a manual? I can't imagine that's easy, given your restricted range."

"Yes, that's why. And it can be uncomfortable, but it makes me feel useful again."

I want to say so many things about that—like how he's still useful even if he isn't who he used to be—but I don't. That's too heavy a topic for us. Instead, I take another bite of my cereal that's starting to get soggy. I chew, then swallow.

"I forgot how quickly this gets mushy," I say, pushing the pieces around in the milk.

"Yeah, that's the only downside of cereal. You have to eat it fast."

We finish off our bowls, and Ezra takes them, setting them on the bedside table.

It makes me smile.

"What?" he asks when he notices.

"I was just thinking about how shocked I was by the state of your house. It's like a museum in here or something with how clean it is, especially compared to your office."

He scratches at the stubble that felt so good between my legs last night. "You noticed that, huh?"

"It's kind of hard not to."

"Yeah, it is a bit weird. I don't know." He shrugs. "I feel more at home at work, if that makes any sense. I spend so much time there that I feel more comfortable. This place feels like a museum because it practically is one. If I'm home, I'm usually in here in bed, and that's it."

"Then why'd you get such a big house? Why not just an apartment or something smaller?"

"I told you already—garage space."

"Ah, yes, for the ten billion cars you have."

"It's only five. For now." His hand sneaks over, pinching at the edge of the shirt I threw on earlier. "Nice shirt, by the way. It looks like mine."

"Sorry. I just grabbed something to throw on real quick."

"It's fine. I like you in my clothes." His voice drops an octave, his eyes darkening as they settle on my lips. "They look good on you."

He's inching closer, and even though my head is screaming *Stop! We can't do this again!* my body is saying *Kiss him! Kiss him! Kiss him!*

I never was the best at listening to my head.

Our lips connect in a frenzy, like we're both starved for each other's touch, which can't be true, though it certainly feels like it.

Ezra tastes like Froot Loops and mint, and it's a horrible combination, but I can't get enough of it. I can't get enough of him.

I'm not sure who reaches for the other first, but I'm suddenly slinging my leg over him and climbing into his lap.

His hands cover my waist, holding me tight as his mouth devours mine. Our tongues slip and slide together, and I'm all too aware of his hard cock resting against me. I remember how good it felt last night inside me, the way he hits all the right spots like he knows my body innately. I want to feel it again.

I rock myself against him, and his grip on my hips tightens, and he drives up to meet me move for move.

He hisses, and I pull away instantly.

"Shit. Are you okay?"

"Yeah, yeah. Fine. Just my hip," he says, reaching for me again.

A thought slams into me, and I lean away.

"Wait . . . Is that why you pulled back when we kissed in your office?"

He swallows thickly, darting his eyes away, almost like he's embarrassed by it. "Yes."

I frown. "Why didn't you say something?"

"What could I have said? *Hey, sorry my weak-ass hip ruined the moment? Let's try again?*" His words are bitter, and he looks disgusted with himself. "No, I couldn't. So I let you go. It was probably for the best anyway. We shouldn't . . . we shouldn't even be doing this, Summer."

He's not wrong. I've had the same thought over and over again this morning and last night, for that matter. But . . .

"I'm not even really your employee."

His dark brows lift. "Oh, you aren't?"

"No. I mean, it's not like you handpicked me or anything, right? We just got thrust into a shitty situation, that's all. A favor for my father."

He nods, understanding that I'm grasping at straws here, trying to find *any* reason not to stop this, even though we both know that we should.

This is an absolutely terrible idea. Likely one of the worst ones I've ever had.

Still, I find myself saying, "Besides, it's not like we're worried about real feelings getting involved, right? You don't do girlfriends and love, and I'm not sure I'm staying in Port Harbor. What's the harm?"

His olive eyes narrow only slightly, and for a split second I think he might actually refute that, but then he nods once more. "Right. No harm at all."

"Okay, then . . ."

"Then . . ."

And we're kissing once again, and it's even more desperate than before, like all the walls we had standing between us are now gone, and we're free to just *be*.

I grip his dark hair, and his hand drops between us. It's then that he discovers the secret I've been holding on to all morning.

He pulls away, his gaze capturing mine. "You're not wearing any panties."

I grin, shaking my head. "I'm not."

"Jesus, Summer."

Then he kisses me fast and hard, plunging two fingers into me roughly, and I gasp into his mouth.

"Do you have any fucking idea how hot that is?" he says, his lips ghosting over my jaw, his teeth scraping against me as his fingers work me over. "Knowing you've been walking around in my shirt all morning with no underwear on? With this pretty cunt of yours ready for me to take at any moment?"

"Then do it, Ezra," I say desperately, because that's exactly what I am right now—desperate for more. For him. "Take it. Take me."

"Oh, I plan to."

He reaches for the box of condoms sitting on the bedside table with his free hand, then gives it to me.

Worry falls over me. "Are you sure? I don't want to hurt your hip."

"I'm fine," he says as he presses against my clit with his thumb, and I have to bite my lip to keep from crying out. "All I care about right now is how good your pussy is going to feel squeezing my cock."

I waste no time ripping it open as he pushes his pants down just enough to free himself. He hisses as I slide the rubber over him, stroking him a few times just because I can. Just because I want to.

"Fuck, that feels good," he mutters, kissing my neck now.

"Bet the real thing would feel better."

"Let's test that, shall we?"

I have no idea how he does it, but suddenly his fingers are gone, and I'm impaled by his cock.

I was right—the real thing does feel better.

"Fuck," he says through gritted teeth as all of him fills me. "I don't think I could ever get tired of this."

Same.

But I don't say it out loud. I'm too scared of just how true it might be.

I *don't* think I could get tired of this, because nothing has ever felt this good before. Not even when I was told I'd be getting my own kitchen. Nothing compares to how it feels to have him inside me. To have him looking at me like he is right now—like I'm his whole world.

"I need you to move, Sunny. Ride me."

I nod and lift up, then grind back down, loving the sounds that leave him as I do.

"God, you feel so good."

"You too," I tell him, moving against him again.

His hands never leave me as I ride him as instructed. They play with my hair, they trace patterns over my back, they hold on to my waist, and then my ass, as he ruts up into me.

I feel like I'm being worshipped, and it's intoxicating in a way I've never experienced before, which is why I'm not surprised when I feel myself already teetering on the edge of orgasm.

"Touch me, Ezra. Please," I beg him. "I'm so close."

He slips his hand back between us, his thumb pressing against my clit as I continue my stride.

He surges up into me every so often, always hitting that spot that makes me see stars, and combined with his touch between my legs, I'm coming before I even realize it's happening.

"Oh shit, shit, shit," he mutters, his head falling into the crook of my neck. "That feels . . . You're . . . *fuck.*"

None of it is coherent, but that doesn't matter. I understand everything as his body shakes and his cock pulses as he fills the condom with a force.

I slow my movements until I'm just sitting on him, slumped against Ezra as the last twelve or so hours catch up with me.

I'm exhausted. Completely spent. And even though I slept so well last night, I could fall right back to sleep if given the chance.

Ezra must have the same idea, because he lifts me off him and lays me against the pillow. I watch as he climbs out of bed with a stilted gait, and it tugs at my heart. How could something so incredible cause him so much pain? And why does he keep trying to put on a brave face when it's obvious he's hurting?

I want to ask him that and so much more, but I don't. Those are the kinds of things you talk about with your boyfriend, and Ezra isn't mine.

This is nothing. Harmless fun. That's all.

It has to be, because if it's not, then what the hell am I doing here?

CHAPTER FIFTEEN

Ezra

"Did you find a date for our wedding yet?"

I barely spare Odette a glance, then go right back to my work in front of me.

I'm stationed at the bar today, and I tell myself it's because I needed a change of scenery, and that it has nothing at all to do with the brown-haired beauty behind the counter.

Nothing she said about us sleeping together made sense, because no matter how we spin it, even if it is a favor for her father, I am still her boss. But I couldn't find a single fuck to give about that, especially not when she was sitting on my lap, looking every bit like a goddess. And especially not after I knew how good being inside her felt.

I would have agreed to almost anything she said just to have her again.

And I did. Have her again, that is. And again and again and again.

Summer's been spending a lot of time in my bed since I drove her home from Stick Taps last week. We claim it's because we're working on the remodel, and it just makes sense for her to come to my place, but that doesn't explain why our planning sessions always end with us naked.

With the kitchen plans finalized and approved by Summer, construction officially kicked off a few days ago, and the crew is already making significant progress. I'm hopeful that the project might even be completed sooner than they quoted, but I'm trying not to cling to that idea too tightly, just in case.

I'm trying not to hold on to anything *too tightly.*

My eyes slide to Summer, and I look away almost instantly.

"Uh, hello? Earth to Ezra?" Odette waves her hand in front of my face, as if I don't know that she's there or talking to me.

"Noah, please tell your girlfriend to stop being obnoxious or I'm going to ban her from the cidery."

"Fiancée," Odette corrects. "And you won't ban me. You like me."

I grunt, only because I can't tell her that she's right. It'll go to her head.

"Not to mention Ezra here forgets he's not the sole owner of this joint. I get a say in who's allowed in, too, and Odette always is."

"See? Noah agrees with me." She elbows me, and my pen scratches against the page in the wrong direction. "Oops. Sorry."

But she doesn't sound sorry at all. She just wants my attention.

I sigh, setting my pen down and turning toward her. "What do you want?"

She smiles sweetly. "I want to know if you found a date for the wedding."

"No, and if you keep asking me about it, I'll rescind the *yes* on my RSVP."

"Uh, you're the best man. Don't think you can."

Noah laughs. "Don't put it past him, Odie."

I point at my partner. "What he said."

Odette rolls her eyes. "Whatever. Just find a date, okay? We need even numbers for the tables."

"I highly doubt anyone is going to be counting the number of people seated at each table."

"Ezra . . ."

The single word is threatening, and I raise my hands. "Fine. I'll find someone. You happy?"

"Yes. Now we just need to find a date for you, Summer."

"Um, what?" the woman in question says from down the bar, where she's been working on the menu. Or at least that's what she claims she's doing. She hasn't actually moved her pencil in over thirty minutes, and I would know, since I've been sneaking glances at her all day.

I wish I could keep my eyes off her, especially here at work, but it's hard to when I know just how beautiful she looks when she comes or just how absolutely fucking stunning she is with my cum dripping down her chin as she stares up at me from her knees.

We did that this morning. She wasn't supposed to stay over, but I certainly wasn't mad that she did. And getting my cock sucked in the kitchen this morning didn't warrant any complaints either.

"Our wedding. You're still coming, right?"

"Of course I am. I wouldn't miss it."

Summer's gaze catches mine just for a moment, but it's long enough for me to see the apprehension in it.

The wedding is still six weeks away. Is Summer planning to stay in Port Harbor that long? I know we didn't talk about a timeline on this . . . *thing* we're doing, but I can't deny that I'm happy about her sticking around, even though I shouldn't be.

"Great. You need a date." Odette gasps. "Oh, you can go with Ezra!"

"What?" Summer and I both say it at the same time.

Odette laughs. "See? You're already in sync. It's so cute."

If only she knew just how in sync we were when I had Summer bent over the back of my couch.

"Stop teasing them, Odie," Noah says.

"Yeah, *Odie*, knock it off," I tell her.

"Okay, first of all, you don't get to call me that." She points at me. "And secondly, why not? You're both single. I'm not asking *you* two to get married. Just go together."

I flick my gaze to Summer for only a moment, and I can tell just from her posture that she doesn't know how to respond to her friend.

So I step in and do it for her.

"No. Now drop it."

My word is firm. Final. Odette doesn't bring it up again.

And Summer doesn't look my way the rest of the day.

For the first time in I don't even know how long, I'm sitting in my office, staring at the clock, counting down the minutes until the cidery is closed.

Until I can talk to Summer without the extra eyes and ears.

Until I can figure out why she's been avoiding me all day.

I told myself it's because she was uncomfortable with Odette teasing her about us going to the wedding together, but I'm beginning to wonder if I said something wrong. Even after they left, she didn't want to be around me. Every time I tried to catch her eye, she would turn away. And when I did try to talk to her, she'd hurry out of the room and put Warner between us.

He hasn't been flirting with her lately, and I'm grateful for it. It's not that I think Summer would flirt back at this point—though we haven't talked about us being exclusive—but because I'm not quite sure I would trust myself not to pummel the guy if I had to witness it.

Twenty minutes until we're closed, and I'm not even close to getting what I need done tonight.

I try to force myself to focus, but just five minutes later, I'm back to glancing at the clock. I toss my pen down and go in search of Summer.

There are still a few people straggling behind. A family of four is in the arcade, which has been bringing in a lot of new customers, and Micah is closing out his tab now.

"Hey, Ezra," he says when he spots me. "Been hiding in your office all night again?"

"Someone has to do all the hard work around here," I tease, shaking his hand. "How are you doing?"

"Good. Can't complain. Hey, Summer here was just telling me about the kitchen remodel and the new menu."

I glance at her, and though it looks like she's not paying us any attention, I can tell by how her body is canted toward us just slightly that she's hanging on to every word.

"Yep. We figured it was time to expand a bit."

"Well, I have to say, I'm mighty glad about that. No offense, but your current offerings leave a lot to be desired. Can't tell you the number of times I've stopped by Hank's for grub, then come out here for a drink."

I hold back my wince. "I appreciate the honest feedback, Micah."

"Of course. I always shoot straight with you, which is why I can't wait to try the brussels sprouts. Summer was telling me about those too."

I dart my eyes to Summer again. She's still pretending not to be listening in. "She's doing the whole menu for us. Used to be a chef in Chicago."

"Oh, kid." He laughs heartily. "She was a chef long before that. She used to make food with her momma, and let me tell you, every potluck this town had? Their dish was the first one gone. You'd have to get there at least a half hour early if you wanted even just a nibble."

She used to cook with her mom? Is that why she loves it so much?

"Man, I miss Rebecca."

Since I'm still looking at her, I don't miss how Summer's shoulders sink at the mention of her mother. It's the same thing they did when Odette brought her up.

She misses her, and I'm sure being back in her old hometown is bringing up all sorts of memories of her. No wonder she escaped to Chicago. I would have done the same thing.

"I'm sure she was a lovely woman, and that she'd be proud as hell of what her daughter is doing for Stick Taps."

For the first time since this morning, Summer looks at me.

And fuck me, she's gorgeous. She's always pretty, but there's something about the way she's staring at me right now that makes me wish we were alone.

"Excuse me, did you pay already?"

We turn to find the family ready and waiting for their turn at the register.

"He did. I can help you over here," Summer says, turning up her smile and waving them down the counter.

Micah and I say goodbye, and the family isn't far behind him. I follow them to the door, bid them good night, and flip the sign from *Open* to *Closed*.

Finally, we're alone.

But when I turn back around, Summer's disappearing out of the taproom again. Instead of racing after her like I want to, I give her space. I think she could use it right now.

I go back to my office and shut everything down for the evening, put my laptop and files into my bag, and then make my way out to my car.

Then I wait.

Ten minutes go by, then twenty, but I don't dare think of leaving.

I have to see her first.

When she finally comes out thirty minutes after closing, I release the breath I've been holding.

She stops when she sees me leaning against my car.

"Another one?"

I glance back at my matte white Audi RS 7. "Another one."

She sighs, then joins me, resting against the hood. "What are you doing, Ezra?"

"Waiting for you."

"Why?"

"Because I upset you earlier, and I want to know what I said and how I can fix it."

The words tumble free, and it surprises me just how much I mean them. I usually don't care if I piss someone off. That's their problem, not mine. But when it comes to Summer, I *do* care. I care a lot.

"You didn't upset me. *I* upset me."

"What? Why's that?"

She's quiet for several moments, and I begin to worry she's not going to say anything.

"Because I cared that you didn't want to go to the wedding with me, even though I know *why* you said what you did. You were trying to keep suspicions off us, which I appreciate. And . . . and . . . ugh. I don't know. I just had a moment. A total girl moment. It was dumb."

I push off the car until I'm standing in front of her. I reach out for her, tipping her head up so she's looking at me, because I need to see her when I say this.

"I want to go to the wedding with you."

She laughs, her coffee-colored eyes rolling back in her head. "You're just saying that to make me feel better."

"No, I'm not. I know we haven't known each other that long, but I'd hope that you know I don't use my words lightly. I don't say things I don't mean. I want to take you to the wedding, Summer."

Her lashes cast shadows on her cheeks, gaze softening. "Ezra . . . you can't."

"I can too. We're friends, right?"

"Sort of."

I smirk because I know what she means. We aren't exactly friends, but we're not *not* friends either. "Well, *sort of* friends can go to weddings together. Besides, if I don't find a date soon, I think Odette might set me up with one of her aunts, and I don't think you hate me enough to let me endure that torture."

"I've known them my whole life practically. They aren't that bad."

"Have you seen them take over the diner on Sundays? They're menaces."

She laughs lightly. "All right. That's fair. I just . . ." She sinks her teeth into her bottom lip for a moment before saying, "Are you sure?"

"Yes, I'm sure."

"You know people will talk."

"Let them."

For the first time in maybe ever, I mean that. I don't care if people are talking. I just want to see Summer smile. And that probably means a whole lot more than I'd like it to, but I ignore it.

"But I'm not dancing. Just so we're clear," I say.

"Not even the Cha Cha Slide?"

"Not a fucking chance."

She giggles, then pushes up on her tiptoes and presses her lips against mine.

It's a sweet kiss. Gentle. But it quickly becomes so much more. Our tongues slide together. Her hands tug at the shirt tucked into my slacks, and mine trail down to her ass, hiking up the little black skirt she's wearing until I can feel her bare skin against me.

I pull away. "A thong? Really?"

She shrugs. "It's hot out."

"I really don't like the idea of you prancing around in this tiny-as-hell skirt with *fucking Warner* wandering around."

She laughs. "Your jealousy is kind of cute."

"I'm not jealous."

"You are, too, Ezra. But you know you have nothing to worry about, right?"

I tip my head to the side. "I don't?"

She shakes her head, nuzzling her nose against mine. "No. It's just you."

Even though I knew that deep down, a weight lifts off my shoulders hearing the confirmation.

"Just you," I echo, and then I take her mouth again.

It's such a different kiss than our last one. There's nothing sweet about it. It's hard, it's fast, and it gets out of hand way too quickly.

I slip my thigh between her legs, and almost instantly she begins rubbing herself on me. She pulls my shirt up, her hands diving underneath, fingernails dragging against my skin. I'm going to have marks tomorrow, and I don't care. I'll wear them like a badge of honor because this is fucking heavenly.

"Oh god." She moans as she ruts against me. "I think I could come like this."

"Then do it, Sunny." I drag her against me again, her ass warm and soft in my grasp. "Come on my leg. Make a mess on me."

"But you . . ."

"I don't care about me. I just want to watch you come undone."

She yanks my lips back to hers as she humps my leg, and I can tell when she's close. Her movements are becoming jerkier and her breaths growing more inconsistent.

I sneak a finger between her cheeks, pulling at the thin string tucked in there. She groans, pushing herself faster, harder. It spurs me on, and I dive deeper until my finger is pressed against her hole.

It's all it takes, and Summer's coming in my arms.

Her shudders and sighs fill the summer night air, and it's the sweetest sound I've ever heard. It doesn't matter that my cock is straining against my pants, harder than it's ever been. Hearing her get off was the most satisfying thing in the world.

When her shakes subside, I drag her mouth back to mine, kissing her tenderly until my lips begin to go numb.

I pull away, and she's grinning up at me. "Well, that was unexpected."

I chuckle. "I'm not sorry."

"Don't be. I think I've had more orgasms in the last week than I've had in my entire life."

"Come home with me. I'll give you another. Maybe two if you ask nicely."

She hums happily. "While that sounds amazing, I can't tonight."

I'm surprised at the disappointment that courses through me, and I tell myself it's just because I won't be getting off tonight. It has nothing to do with missing her. It can't.

"My dad is expecting me. I haven't been home much, and if I'm not there to check on him, he might eat a whole pound of bacon just out of spite."

"If it weren't for his heart, that'd be impressive to see."

"That's what I said." She shakes her head with a grin. "We're doing a movie night."

"This late?"

"Hey, take it up with my boss. He's the one who keeps scheduling me for closing shifts, though I'm starting to think it's because he has ulterior motives."

Boss.

It's a reminder that what we're doing is technically wrong, and that if Noah found out, he might actually kill me.

Still, it doesn't deter me from kissing her again.

When we break apart this time, I step back. Then again. I'm afraid that if I keep standing so close to her, I might keep kissing her.

God, what is wrong with me? Have I really been so deprived of human touch that I can't even keep my hands to myself for five minutes?

Yes, that's what it is.

I lead her to her car, opening her door for her. She grins up at me as she slips behind the wheel of the old cruiser.

"Thank you."

"For the orgasm?"

She rolls her eyes. "And for staying."

"Of course. We're good, right?"

"We're good," she confirms. "Good night, Ezra."

"Night, Summer. Text me when you get home."

She promises she will, and I watch her pull out of the lot before getting in my car and following behind her.

We go opposite ways when we reach town, she toward her father's and me toward my house. While I usually like being there, tonight I'm not feeling it like I normally would. Not even the idea of eating cereal in bed sounds appealing.

When I pull into my driveway, I sit there, watching my phone, waiting for her text.

It comes five minutes later.

Summer: Made it home.

Summer: Thanks again for tonight.

Me: Anytime, Sunny.

And the scariest part of it all is that I mean it.

CHAPTER SIXTEEN

Summer

"How's it going with Ezra?"

I pause mid–pancake flip at my dad's question. "What?"

We've come to an unspoken agreement about my late nights and sleepovers, and as far as I know, he doesn't have a clue Ezra is responsible for keeping me out way past appropriate, but does he know what I've been up to anyway? I've gotten good at making sure I don't look a complete wreck when I sneak inside in the mornings, but has he picked up on it anyway?

"At the cidery, kiddo. Keep up."

Oh. I breathe a sigh of relief as he pours himself his second and final cup of coffee for the day.

"How's it going out there?" he continues. "Is he treating you okay?"

I pray my father can't see the blush that steals up my cheeks at the question.

Is Ezra treating me okay? Considering he's given me an orgasm every day for nearly two weeks now, I'd say he's treating me far more than just okay.

But I can't tell my father any of that.

Instead, I say, "Uh, yeah. It's going well. And Ezra is . . . nice."

"Really?" he says incredulously. "I mean, he's a good kid and all, but he's kind of a dick."

"Dad!" I admonish, finally letting the pancake drop into the skillet. It's a rare day when Dad's going into work late, thanks to some election stuff, so I was able to make him breakfast this morning.

"What?" He shrugs. "It's true. He wasn't like that back when he was playing hockey. I don't think he ever stopped smiling then, and I'd know, because we all followed his whole career. He was going places. We're talking on-the-path-to-winning-multiple-Cups kind of places. That damn hip injury really screwed it all up. Think it changed him in other ways too." He takes a sip from the Garfield mug in his hand. "Don't get me wrong—I think he's a good man, but he sure isn't trying to win any kind of Mr. Congeniality award, that's for sure."

He's not entirely wrong. Ezra can undoubtedly be an ass, but there are also so many other sides to him that he doesn't let people see. Like how he eats sugary cereal in bed or how he texts his uncle damn near every day, just to check in on him. Or how he's always working so hard on the cidery, not just to make a bigger profit, but to make it better for the customers. That's why he's remodeling the kitchen. It's a big headache for him, but he knows it'll make his patrons happy.

Ezra is an ass, but he's selfless too.

"He's not always a dick," I defend him, even though I don't have to. "And he hasn't been one to me for weeks."

My dad straightens up at that, his eyes darkening. "He was mean to you? What'd he do? Do I need to kick his ass? Arrest him?"

I point the spatula at him. "Simmer down, Sheriff. He was just . . . I don't know. There's another guy who works there—"

"Warner?" Dad asks. "That kid hits on everyone, I swear. Heard he's dating the Hendersons' son now."

"He is, but this was before that. He was hitting on me, and Ezra saw it. He didn't care for it, so he stepped in. He was such a jerk in the moment, but in retrospect, it was actually kind of nice." I smile, thinking of how Ezra called him *fucking Warner* the other night and how jealous he sounded. I've never found that an attractive trait, but there was something so hot about the fire in his eyes that I couldn't deny being into it.

"Hmm," my father says in response, and I dare a glance over at him.

I don't at all like the way he's looking at me. It's like I'm a case and he's trying to work out all the missing puzzle pieces to it.

Shit, did I slip up and say something I shouldn't have? Did I defend my boss too much?

"What?" I ask, knowing I should turn back to the pancake that's on the verge of being overdone, but I can't. "Why are you looking at me like that?"

"Like what?" He takes another sip of his coffee, hiding behind his mug. "I'm not looking at you like anything."

"Sure you aren't," I say, narrowing my eyes, but I don't push the subject.

My dad is a damn good cop, and the last thing I need to do is incriminate myself in front of him. He'll put two and two together far faster than I'd like. I can't help but think he'd be disappointed if he knew what I was doing with Ezra. Not that I think my father would really care as long as I'm happy, but there is a whole power dynamic at play, even if we don't want to acknowledge it.

I finally flip the pancake onto the plate, and just as I suspected, it's overcooked.

"Shit," I mutter. "I'll make you a new one."

"Nah. Don't worry about it. I actually need to run anyway. Got a few things I need to take care of before heading into the station."

"Oh." I deflate. Other than our movie night several days ago, I feel like I haven't seen my dad in weeks. I was looking forward to breakfast together. Plus, I was enjoying cooking, even if it was just pancakes and turkey sausage. "Are you sure?"

"Yeah. Rain check for Saturday?"

I nod. "Sure. That sounds good."

He leans forward and presses a kiss to the top of my head. "Thanks, kiddo. I'll see you later."

"Yeah, later, Dad. Be careful."

"Always am."

He grabs his holster off the table, then his hat.

Just before he steps out of the kitchen, he pauses, then looks back over his shoulder. "Maybe take that into the cidery. See if Ezra wants breakfast."

Then he disappears, leaving me staring after him.

It confirms everything I need to know.

◆ ◆ ◆

"Come on. We're closing early."

I snap my head up from the menu I'm *still* working on. I should have been done a week ago. I could blame it all on Ezra—he's the one who keeps distracting me, after all—but it's not entirely his fault.

It's me who keeps changing my mind. I know how important this is for him and the cidery, how much they're talking about the kitchen remodel on social media and promising this new, explosive menu, and I just want to live up to that. I'm terrified I won't.

Truthfully, I feel out of practice with cooking. Sure, I've been making things here and there for my father and myself, but nothing compared to the scale of what I'm used to doing. I haven't gotten the chance to really be in a kitchen since I made the mac and cheese for Ezra, and considering the state of it back then, I'm not sure that even counts.

"What? Why?" I ask.

Ezra gestures toward the completely empty cidery. "Because everyone in this town, including my business partner, is at the charity event in Pine Square. There's no reason for us to be burning up the electricity by keeping this place open."

He has a point. I think we've had two customers all day, when typically, on a Saturday, we'd be packed. Even my dad had to bail on our breakfast this morning to get to the event early—one he seemed relieved I wouldn't be attending, mostly because nobody wants a repeat of me in handcuffs. He was even pulling deputies from the next town over to help with crowd control.

"Don't you technically have to keep it on anyway to continue making the cider?"

"Shh. No logic. Not today. Just come on."

He holds his hand out to me, and I can't help myself—I drop my pencil and take it.

He leads me out from behind the bar, and then with his hand on the small of my back, we go toward the door.

"Aren't we going to close everything?"

"We can come back here later. We'll just lock up for now."

I don't even argue with him. His excitement is far too palpable for me to do so. It's not a side I see from him often, and I like it far too much.

We climb into his car, and I love how it rumbles to life under us. We're in his BMW—the same one we sped toward town in when he drove me home the night the cruiser broke down—and I giggle as he peels out of the parking lot, his tires chirping against the asphalt.

"Where are we going?" I ask.

"The iceplex."

I've heard a lot about the community center he and Noah have put together, but I haven't yet made it out there. I was never into hockey like my father was back in the day, so I'm eager to see Ezra in his natural environment.

"I need to grab a few things from my office there. Figured we could take a break and maybe go for a skate. If you're up for it, of course."

"I've never ice-skated before." The stunned look on his face makes me laugh. "You look like I just told you I like pineapple on pizza."

"Another fucking travesty," he comments, flipping his turn signal on and speeding past a car that's already doing at least five over the speed limit.

I'd chide him for it, but honestly, I kind of love watching him drive. There's something so hot about the way he shifts gears. His long, strong legs pushing the clutch in makes me feel things I really shouldn't be feeling.

Thanks to his inability to obey the law, we're pulling into the Stick Taps Community Iceplex in no time.

He surprises me by reversing into a spot in the very back of the lot.

"What?" he asks when he catches me looking at him funny. "I don't want anyone to scratch my baby."

I roll my eyes and stay seated as he climbs out of the car and crosses my way.

I let him help me out, trying my best to ignore the tingles I feel when he places his hand on the small of my back as we make our way through the lot.

I try not to be disappointed when he drops his hand as we walk inside. Then he surprises me by taking my hand.

I glance down at where our fingers are linked together and back up at him, but he's not looking at me. He's too busy leading us through the building like he owns the place, and I guess he does.

Several people say hi to him, but not a single one seems bothered by us being together, and it's only when we reach the rink that I realize it's because nobody here knows who I am. They don't know that I'm his employee too.

All my worries slip away when I take in the ice.

"Wow," I say, looking around, feeling so small as I look up at the seats that feel like they go on forever from this angle. "This is incredible, Ezra."

"It's nothing compared to the real thing, but it's not bad. The kids love it, that's for sure."

There are a few of them out on the ice on the other end. They're gathered around on one knee, listening to who I assume is a coach. It's kind of cute, seeing all the little kids with their gear on. They look like they're playing dress-up.

"This is the five- and six-year-old group," Ezra says, watching as they all lean in, putting their hands in the middle. "Not a single one of them knows what they're doing, and it's kind of adorable."

"They're just trying to be like their idols." I bump my shoulder against him. "Like you."

"I don't think I was ever anyone's idol."

"You were," I tell him, absolutely sure of it. I might not have watched him play before, but I remember how much my dad talked about him. There's no way kids weren't clamoring to be just like him.

He smiles softly and squeezes my hand. "So, want to skate?"

"You were serious about that?"

"Yes, but only if you want to. I know you said you don't know how, but I'd love to teach you. We could call it an exchange. You give me cooking lessons, I give you skating lessons."

"But we haven't started your cooking lessons yet."

"That's because you can't keep your hands off me, Sunny."

I shove him, and he doesn't budge an inch. "That's *your* fault, too, Mr. Rawlings."

"I don't hear you complaining," he says with a knowing smirk.

My cheeks flush. "Quit bragging and find us some skates."

Ezra leads us around the rink, waving to the coach on the ice, who looks like he's wrapping up the practice with the kids, then down a tunnel. We stop in the equipment room, where we find a pair of skates to fit me, then head to his office, where he says he keeps his own bag of gear.

When we make it back out to the rink, the kids are gone and the ice is completely clear. I'm glad because I would have been really embarrassed if the five- and six-year-olds showed me up with their skating skills.

I watch as Ezra expertly puts on his skates, and I try to mimic him but give up.

He laughs. "I got you, Sunny."

I don't miss his wince as he drops down in front of me, and I know it's because of his hip. He tries to act like it doesn't hurt him, but I see how he favors his left side and the faces he makes when he stands and sits. He's in pain, and I wish he'd talk about it more than he does. I wish he knew it was okay to not be okay. I'm not going to judge him if he isn't 100 percent all the time.

"How do those feel?" he asks.

"Uh, weird? You said they felt unreliable before, right? That seems like an understatement now."

He smiles. "You'll get used to it. Let's get on the ice and see how they feel then."

I let him help me up, my knees shaking as I try to figure out how to stand on the impossibly thin piece of metal. How this is even considered safe, I don't know, but I'm willing to give it a shot.

"Want to watch me do a few laps first while you get comfortable with the skates?" he asks when we reach the edge of the ice.

"Please."

"Just hold on to the boards."

I nod, gripping them tightly as he lets me go.

He steps—no, more like jumps—on the ice, and then he's gone. He's *fast*. Much faster than I anticipated, given his injury. There's no way I'll be able to keep up with him.

I watch as he takes a few laps around the rink, his thick thighs pumping. He should look silly out there in his dress shirt and slacks, but he doesn't. He looks completely natural and at ease.

If I thought he looked free when speeding down the two-lane roads, I was wrong. It's nothing compared to how he looks right now.

Sadness tugs me. I hate that he lost this. I hate that he had to give up something that meant so much to him.

"You okay?" He comes to a stop in front of me, snapping me out of my haze.

"Huh? Oh, yeah. Just worried about keeping up with you." It's not a complete lie, but I also don't want him to know that I was feeling sorry for him. He'd hate it, and I know that because I'd hate it too. We're a lot alike in that regard.

"I promise I'll go slow. I won't let go until you're ready."

He holds his hand out to me just like he did at the cidery, and just like then, I relinquish all my trust to him and slip my palm against his.

Slowly, he pulls me onto the ice. It's immediately slippery, and my first instinct is to flail my arms out to try to steady myself.

"Engage your core," he says, gripping my hand tighter.

"Core? I don't even have a core!"

He laughs. "You do too. You've got it."

"I'm going to fall!" I yell, feeling my legs slip out from underneath me.

"Engage! Engage!" he instructs, grabbing my other hand. "Come on, Sunny. You've got this."

And maybe it's his encouragement, or maybe I just get tired of failing, but he's right—I do have this.

I follow his instructions as he tugs me farther away from the wall, feeling more stable as we move. My knees are still knocking together, but I trust myself just a little more.

"There you go," Ezra says, grinning proudly. "You're doing it."

"I'm pretty sure those five-year-olds were better than me."

"They were, but that's okay. They've had practice. You haven't."

"Were you ever this bad?"

"I fell right on my face the first day. In front of everyone, including all the older kids. It was mortifying."

"You're just making that up to make me feel better."

"I am not. It really happened. They called me Bambi for three years after that."

"They did not."

"Did too," he argues from a few feet away.

Wait—he's a few feet away!

"Hey! You let go!" I feel myself slipping right away. "You said you wouldn't!"

"I said I wouldn't let go until you're ready, and look at you. You're doing good. Just keep your core engaged. Keep your legs in it. You've got this."

His words urge me on, and before I know it, we make an entire lap around the two-hundred-foot rink.

Sure, we go infinitely slower than Ezra did on his three laps, but I do it.

I'm out of breath by the time we make it back to where we started, and I cling to the boards like a lifeline.

He chuckles, then hands me a water bottle he stashed on the benches before we started.

"You okay?"

I nod, taking a long drink. I wipe my hand over my mouth when I'm done. "It's fun. Not nearly as cold as I thought it would be. I'm actually sweating a little."

"I know." He reaches out, swiping a bit off my forehead, then wiping it on his fancy shirt. "It's a workout, huh?"

"Big-time. No wonder hockey players are always out of breath on TV."

"Want to sit and take a break?"

"Yes, please."

We make our way over to the bench, and I sigh as I sit down. My legs are killing me, so I don't know how Ezra is doing this when he's already in pain.

"So, what'd you think?" he asks after a few quiet moments. "Are you going to be the next PWHL star?"

"Uh, no. I'll stick to staying in the kitchen, thank you very much."

"Good. I like you there." He wrinkles his nose. "That would have sounded really bad if you weren't a chef, huh?"

I laugh. "Just a little."

"How's, uh, how's the menu coming? I mean, not that I'm rushing you or anything. I know that kind of thing takes time."

"But we're getting down to the wire. I know." I exhale heavily, doubt creeping its way in. I had felt so confident about the menu when I first agreed to make it, but now I'm fretting over every item because I don't want to fail Ezra or myself. "I don't know. Is it silly that I'm sweating it a bit? This is the first time I've made a menu all on my own. Before, I just made whatever people told me to. I've never had the chance to make it my own. I thought it was what I always wanted, but now that I'm getting the opportunity, I'm feeling the pressure."

"Well, don't. It's nothing serious. It's just a cidery."

I level him with a look. "It's not *just* a cidery, Ezra. It's your business. It's your baby. I don't want to mess that up for you."

"And the kitchen is *your* baby. It's okay if you mess it up. That's part of being a business owner. Sometimes we get it right and sometimes we don't."

"I don't own the kitchen, though."

He rolls his lips together. "No, I guess you don't, but you understand the point I'm trying to make."

I nod because I do. He's telling me this is my project and that I should make it my own. I love how much he trusts me, but it doesn't make me any less nervous that I'm going to screw this up completely.

"Hey," he says, his hand cupping the back of my neck and rubbing at the tension I hadn't even realized I was holding there. "You're going to do great. I know you will."

"Thanks." I lean into his touch. "That feels good. I like having your hands on me."

"Yeah? I like having my hands on you."

I'm not quite sure who makes the first move, but we're no longer sitting side by side. I'm between his legs, my arms around his neck, and my lips on his. His big hands hold me steady on my skates, and I relish the way they feel wrapped around me, making me feel safe and cared for. Ezra seems to have a way of doing that, and though I'm trying my best not to get used to it, I am anyway.

When I finally pull away, we're both out of breath, and his pupils are dilated so much that the green is almost nonexistent.

"We should probably go," he says. "Before I do something reckless and fuck you on this bench."

"That doesn't sound reckless to me."

"There's another class in ten minutes."

I wince. "Okay, so maybe a little reckless."

"Just a bit." He kisses me again, this time just a quick peck, then pats my ass. "All right. Let's go. We still need to close the cidery, and apparently I have a cooking lesson to get to."

CHAPTER SEVENTEEN

Ezra

The skating might have been a bad idea.

I admit that I pushed myself out there to impress Summer, and I'm paying for it now.

I pull a bottle of Advil from my pocket and pop two more for the third time today. It's more than I'm supposed to be taking, but I need it. I've been more active in the last three weeks than I've been in a long time. Between the skating last week, my regular lessons with the kids, and all the incredible sex, I'm pushing my limits.

Not that I'm complaining about the sex. How could I? It's never felt like this before. And even when I am in pain, Summer realizes it, and she takes over. I've never had someone understand what I've needed so well before. It's kind of scary, but not so frightening that I want to stop what we're doing.

I should, though. *We* should. My feelings about relationships haven't changed, and even if they did, it wouldn't matter. Summer is going back to Chicago at some point. This could never work long term. I guess it doesn't matter if I stop it, then. I should just enjoy the fun while it lasts, right?

And fun is exactly what it's been. In more ways than one too. Even when my first official cooking lesson went so badly off the rails that we had to air out the kitchen from all the smoke, it was still a good time.

Can I really be at fault, though? If Summer hadn't worn that apron that had no business being so fucking hot, I wouldn't have burned dinner. I don't even know where she got it from, but it gave me all sorts of ideas and images that I couldn't help but kiss her.

Though she distracted me, it was nice to see her in her element. It makes me feel even more confident in her ability to run the Stick Taps kitchen. She's so savvy and innovative that there's no way she's not going to make something amazing that our customers will love. Just sitting here today, I've already had three people stop by and tell me they can't wait to try whatever we're cooking up.

Luckily for us, the remodel is still on schedule, so they may get their wish before too long.

"Hey, boss." I look up from my laptop, which is sitting on one of the many pub-style tables in the taproom, to find Warner staring at me.

"Yes?" I've been slightly less cold to him since Summer reassured me there's nothing going on between them, but it still annoys me that he flirted with her so openly.

"Uh, wanted to let you know that Summer's going home early."

My blood rushes to my head, and I'm flying out of my chair in record time. "What? Why?"

"She threw up. She thinks it's something she ate."

Summer is sick? I start shoving papers into folders, not knowing if that's even where they go or not, and close my laptop.

"She's grabbing her stuff now and getting out of here," Warner continues. "Just wanted to let you know, since it's trivia night. We might need extra hands."

"Call Sophie. Get her in here. Promise her Saturday off in exchange for the hours."

"You got it." He nods, but he doesn't move.

"What?" I bark at him. "Something about that confusing?"

"Uh, no. No. I just . . . Where are you going?"

"I'm going to check on Summer."

"Ah." He pushes his hands into his pockets. "I'm sorry. I didn't realize."

"Realize what?" I ask, tossing my laptop into my bag.

"That you two were a thing."

I pause, casting a glance up at him.

He puts his hands in the air. "Hey, it's fine. My lips are sealed. I just wouldn't have been hitting on her had I known she was off the market."

"Well, she is." *Fuck. Why did I say that?* "I mean, it's not . . . we're not . . ."

He chuckles. "It's fine. Your secret's safe with me, boss."

He gives me a knowing smile, then raps his knuckles against the table before turning to leave. I stand there staring after him, wondering where the hell he got the idea that Summer and I are together.

I mean, we are. Sort of. But how the fuck would Warner know? We've been careful at work. We hardly even interact. Checking on my employee shouldn't be a red flag either. I'd do that for anyone.

"Warner!" I call out to him.

He about-faces. "Yes?"

"How?"

"What?"

"How do you know?"

He lifts a shoulder. "Just a hunch. I don't think I've ever seen you so happy before. Couldn't help but notice it started when she showed up."

He dips his head toward me before carrying on.

If he's noticed, does that mean others have? Does Noah know? Does Summer's dad? She's barely spending time at home. He has to be aware that *something* is going on. Not necessarily with me, but still.

Are we making this more obvious than we think?

I don't know. All I know is that I need to find Summer and make sure she's okay.

Five minutes later I'm walking out of the cidery just as she's pulling open the door of the old cruiser that's still somehow running. It spent three days in the shop getting the starter replaced, and apparently that's not the first time in the last year. It was on the tip of my tongue to offer her one of my cars to drive, but I never did.

"Sunny!"

She looks up at me, and I can tell instantly that she doesn't feel good. She's pale, her eyes rimmed red like she's been crying, and her lips are chapped, likely from lack of fluids.

She was fine this morning when I arrived at the cidery. I wonder what happened between now and then.

I jog the rest of the way over to her, my hip hating me for doing so, but I ignore it.

She holds her hand out when I get close. "Stay away. I've been puking, and I'm sure I smell awful."

I ignore that, too, pressing closer. I tug her close, and she melts against me instantly, her arms going around me limply.

"No offense, but you look like shit."

She laughs lightly. "You keep being so sweet to me, and I might think you like me."

I do like you.

The words rocket into me, and I'm stunned by how true they are. Not just for obvious reasons, like the sex, either. No, it's just her, and that fucking terrifies me.

"What's going on?"

"I don't know. I was tired after my shift yesterday and didn't feel like cooking just for myself, since my dad was busy at a function for the election. So I grabbed a salad from the grocery store. It looked fine, but apparently it wasn't. My stomach has been off all day, and I finally threw up a little bit ago." She huffs out a breath, like she's tired just from talking. "I thought it was just going to be a one-and-done deal, but once I started, it wouldn't stop." Another deep breath, almost like she's trying not to puke right now. "I am never eating salad again."

I repress my urge to laugh, because even though this isn't funny, there is something so cute about seeing her so sullen over lettuce.

"Come on," I tell her, dragging her away from her car.

"What? Where are we going?"

"I'm taking you home."

"What?" She tries to dig her heels in, but it's pointless. "No, Ezra. You couldn't. It's broad daylight. People will see us."

"I don't care. You're sick, Summer. You look like you're about to pass out at any moment. You're in no condition to drive. I'm taking you."

"But . . ." Except that's all she says, allowing me to continue steering her toward my car.

I unlock the BMW M6 Competition and help her into the passenger seat. She winces the whole way, and I hate that she's feeling like this. I'd give anything to trade places.

For a split second, I worry about her getting sick on the ride, but then I realize I don't care. It's a car. I can clean it up.

I reach over her, pulling the seat belt across her chest. She must really not be feeling good, considering she doesn't protest.

Once she's strapped in, I hurry my way to the driver's side and slide behind the wheel.

"Do we need to stop for anything on the way?" I ask her as she curls into herself, facing the door.

"Maybe some soup? Gatorade?"

"I can handle that." I start the car, and she grimaces at the rumble from the engine. Even though it's summer, I turned the heat up because she's shivering. "I promise to drive the speed limit."

"Thank you, Ezra," she says softly.

"Anytime, Sunny."

And I mean it more than she knows.

Traffic is surprisingly rough. With Port Harbor being such a small town, it's not usually something we have to worry about, but some days I swear everybody is out on the road.

Today is one of those days.

When I finally manage to pull into Summer's father's driveway, she's passed out in the passenger seat.

I shut off the car and round the front to her side. She barely wakes up as I lift her into my arms and carry her toward the house. My hip protests the whole time, but I don't care. I'm not about to make her walk.

"Sunny," I say softly into her ear. "I need to get you inside. Do you have a key?"

"Hmm?" She blinks once, twice. Then she looks around, realizing what's going on. "Wait, what are you doing? Ezra, your hip."

"Shh. I'm fine," I tell her, readjusting her, and she's already turning into me and snuggling closer. "I just need your key."

"Code. No key."

"What is it?"

"Zero-three-one-five. Mom's birthday. Dad never wants to admit it out loud, but he misses her. I do too."

I smile at her sleepy confession, then punch the numbers into the keypad. The door makes a whirring noise, and I try the handle. It opens.

I'm surprised that, despite the house's exterior looking a bit older, the inside has been updated. It's not as modern as my place, but it's not as dated as I had pictured it would be either.

I save my exploring for later and carry an already-sleeping Summer through the house to where I assume the bedrooms are. I try two before I find what I think is hers.

A pale-pink floral wallpaper covers most of the room, and the rest is painted a soft color to match it. The furniture appears to have once belonged to a teenager, but it's still nice and clearly well maintained.

I couldn't imagine going back to my childhood home like this. I feel so far removed from that life. Summer's braver than I am, that's for sure.

I settle her onto her small twin-size bed, and she stirs.

Her eyes flutter open. "Ezra . . ."

"It's me." I sit down next to her, practically hanging off the tiny mattress. "Just rest, okay? I'll warm up your soup and get you something to drink. Are you feeling all right?"

She extends her hand, wiggling it back and forth.

I laugh lightly. "Just call out if you need me."

She nods, and I wait for her to close her eyes again before I move.

I hurry out to the car for the supplies I grabbed from the grocery store, then head for the kitchen. It takes me a while to locate a pot so I can warm up the chicken-and-stars soup I found in the refrigerated section. Once it's going, I take the three different flavors of Gatorade I got into the bedroom for her, along with some aspirin, just in case she wants it. I don't know about her, but whenever I'm sick, I always get a splitting headache.

She lies curled on her side, her mouth slightly ajar, her hair moving up and down as she snores softly.

For someone who is so clearly miserable, she still manages to look beautiful. I have the urge to bend down and kiss her forehead, but I don't want to bother her. So I force myself to leave and check on the soup instead of standing here staring at her like some weirdo.

On the way to the kitchen, the photographs lining the wall catch my eye, and I slow down to take them in.

The first is of Summer as a baby, and she somehow looks so much like she does now, and completely different all at once. The second is of her and—if I had to guess—her mother. Their smiles are identical, almost eerily so. And the third is of her parents at what appears to be their wedding. They look happy, like they'll never get tired of each other. You can *feel* the love pouring out of each photo, and I wish that Summer never lost this. I wish I had never lost it too. I don't often think of my parents, but I suddenly find myself missing them in a way I haven't in a long, long time.

I peel my gaze away and check on the soup. Once it's ready, I scrounge around for a bowl and a spoon and take it to her.

To my surprise, she's awake.

"Hey," I say softly. "How you doing?"

"Tired. Hot. Cold. So many different things."

I hold out the bowl of soup. "Want something to eat?"

She grimaces. "Yes, but also no. But yes."

I chuckle. "Maybe try a few bites, then reevaluate?"

She nods, pushing up to a sitting position, then scooting over.

I toe off my shoes, then climb in beside her, careful not to jostle her too much. The bed is comically small for me, and even Summer notices.

"You look absurd in my bed."

"I'm sure you tell all the boys that."

She rolls her eyes, still somehow sassy even when she's sick. "There have been no other boys in here, Ezra."

"Not even when you were a teenager?"

"Are you kidding me? I wasn't cool enough for a boyfriend back then."

"And are you now?"

She raises a brow. "Careful. That almost sounds like you're asking to be mine."

I wait for that familiar panic to settle in whenever something is mentioned to me about relationships, but it doesn't. In fact, it never comes. Not when I practically hand-feed Summer soup just like a boyfriend would do, or when I open her Gatorade. And it doesn't even come when she gets sick again, and I end up holding her hair back for her.

That's scary in and of itself, but I try my best not to read too much into it as I get her back in bed.

"I'm sorry," she says as she curls against me, shaking from the chills.

"For what?"

"Getting sick. I know it's trivia night, and I'm sure you have a lot better things to do than sit around taking care of me."

"I'm exactly where I want to be."

It's the truth. I would much rather be here than at the cidery listening to the remodel construction or poring over the invoices I was working on before Warner came and told me about Summer.

I feel her smile against my side. "Thank you. It's nice of you to risk getting sick for me."

I think I'd risk a lot more than just that, but I don't say anything.

Instead, I wrap my arm around her tighter and hold her close as she falls back asleep. After a while, I feel a wet spot form on my shirt, but I don't dare move. I couldn't if I wanted to. I'm too determined to see this through, and honestly, even though she's sick, I don't want to leave her. I want to be the one there to take care of her for whatever she needs, and I'm not sure what that means, but it's something for me to sort out later.

Right now I just want to be here with her, so that's exactly what I do.

I jolt awake, and the first thing I think of is Summer.

I reach beside me and am surprised to find that the bed's empty and cold.

What the hell?

I groan as I lift off the tiny mattress, my hip stiff and aching as I set my feet on the floor.

My eyes go to the old-school alarm clock on the bedside table. *Holy shit.* It's after eight, which means I've been out for a solid three hours at this point.

I scrub a hand over my face, then go in search of Summer. I find her quickly, the light shining from beneath the bathroom door a dead giveaway.

"Summer?" I call out to her. "Are you okay?"

There's no answer, and I lean closer, straining for any signs she's getting sick again, but there's nothing.

It's quiet.

Unease settles into my gut, and I push the door open slowly.

My stomach drops at the sight before me. She's curled up on the floor, her arm clutching her stomach, her hair a matted, sweaty mess.

"Fuck, Summer," I say, shouldering my way into the small room.

She stirs, trying to blink open her eyes. "I got sick again."

"I can see that." I drop to my haunches in front of her, my hip pinching at the movement. "Can you get up?"

"Maybe with some help?"

I get her to a standing position, then tug on the shirt she's wearing. She never changed after she got home from work, and I imagine she's in desperate need of some new clothes.

She lets me lift the material over her head. She holds on to me as I undo the button on her jeans, then shimmy them down her legs until she steps out of them. I unclasp her bra, and she takes her panties off on her own as I reach around her and turn on the shower.

When the water is warm enough, I help her in, frowning at the way she leans against the wall for support.

"Do you want me to stay?"

She shakes her head. "You don't have to."

"That's not what I asked. I asked if you wanted me to."

She hesitates a moment, then nods. "Please."

I strip out of my clothes as fast as possible and step into the tiny tub-and-shower combo, getting behind her. I squirt some shampoo on my hands and massage it into her scalp. She moans as my fingers dance through her hair.

"That feels so good," she murmurs.

It's all we say through the entire routine. I clean her hair, then condition it. After that I squirt bodywash onto the loofah she points to and scrub it over her body. Not once does my cock twitch or do I get the urge to press against her to do anything other than hold her steady, and it's not because I don't find her attractive even now. I'm too focused on getting her better.

When she's nice and warm and clean, I wrap the towels I find in the small closet around us and help her out. We make our way to her bedroom, and I slip back into my dress shirt, leaving it unbuttoned, and pull just my slacks on. When she falls asleep, I'll go out to the car and grab my gym bag for a change of clothes.

I strip her bed bare, figuring she might want clean sheets to sleep on.

"They're in the hall closet," she says without me having to ask where new ones might be.

She helps me make the bed, and I can't stop thinking about how domestic this all feels. Sure. I'm here taking care of her because she's sick, but is this what it would be like if we were really together? If she wasn't going back to Chicago? If I weren't so dead set against relationships?

And is it really so bad?

Once the bed is made, we crawl back into it, and Summer snuggles against my side like she's done so many nights before.

"Feeling any better?" I ask, my lips against her forehead.

"Marginally. I think I might be done puking for the night."

"That's always good. Do you want more soup?"

She shakes her head. "No. I just want to sleep. Is that okay?"

"Whatever you want, Sunny. I'll be here."

"My dad gets home at eleven."

It sounds so silly. She's a grown woman. She can have anyone she wants in her bed. But I get the feeling she's not telling me because of that.

She's just sticking to the rules we made when we started this thing, the ones that are becoming less and less clear.

"I'll be gone before then."

She kisses my chest. "You're a good guy, Ezra."

"You say that like you're surprised by it."

"I'm not. I always knew your grumpy side was just a front." She yawns. "You hide behind your pain, use it as a wall. I like it when you let it down for me."

It's the last thing she says before she falls asleep.

Instead of following her into slumber, I watch her until it's time for me to go. I kiss her forehead and text her instructions to eat and take some more medicine, then slip into my car and head home.

The whole drive there, all I can think is, *I like letting it down for you, too, Summer.*

CHAPTER EIGHTEEN

Summer

It took three days, but I'm finally feeling human again, *and* I'm still swearing off grocery store salads for the foreseeable future.

As embarrassing as it was to throw up and be a general mess in front of him, I'm glad Ezra was there to help take care of me the first night. I haven't seen him since, and I'm eager to tonight.

"Are you sure you're ready to go back to work?" my dad asks from across the kitchen table, worry lacing every single word.

My appetite still hasn't returned to normal, but I was determined to get out of bed today and make something for us, even if it is just oatmeal and toast.

"Dad," I say in warning. This is the fourth time he's asked me since I came out of my room. "I'm sure. Please stop asking."

He sighs. "I'm sorry. You might be a grown adult, but you're still my kid, and I worry about you."

"I know, and I love you for that, but I'll be fine. Promise."

He gives me a small smile, but I don't miss how he keeps sending glances my way. He could tell right away that something was wrong with me when he came home. He always was able to do so when I was younger, too, so I guess I shouldn't be surprised that it hasn't changed over the years.

He kept me supplied with soup and electrolytes ever since, even calling off work one day to watch old movies with me from his recliner. It was like being a kid all over again, and it made me wonder yet again what it would be like if I stayed here. It's not like I'd live here with my dad forever, but I'd be able to spend actual quality time with him, and I don't hate the idea of that in the least.

"All right. I'll back off. I just don't want Ezra overworking you, that's all."

Just hearing his name sends a jolt of excitement through me. He's texted me every day, and not once has it been to ask when I'll be back to work. I think he'd give me the rest of the week off if I really wanted it. No, he's texting to check on *me*, and that makes me happier than I care to admit.

I still can't believe he stayed like he did. Or that he climbed into the shower with me and bathed me. It was intimate in a way I'd never experienced before, and not because we were naked. It had nothing to do with that. It was how gentle he was. How caring his touch felt as he cleaned me up with absolutely zero judgment or lust in his gaze.

I've never felt so exposed to someone before. Nor have I ever felt so safe.

If I'm not careful, I could get used to it, and that's the last thing I need to do, all things considered. It's just a fling. Just a bit of fun. Even if—and that's a big *if*—I do stay in Port Harbor, Ezra has made his feelings about relationships clear. This is nothing serious. It can't be.

"Did you hear that Ken's selling Sunnie's?"

I pause mid-bite. "What?"

"Yep. I saw the for sale sign in the window yesterday. I don't know when he made that decision, but can you believe it? Sunnie's has been a staple in this town for . . . shit, for as long as I can remember. I can't imagine not having those fritters around. Your mom loved them." He smiles. "Ken has been keeping that place open since Sunnie passed, but we all know it was never his baby like it was hers. I guess it's time, you know?"

My heart thuds at the idea of that building being up for sale. Sure, Sunnie's has been around since I was a little girl, and I—along with the rest of Port Harbor—hold a lot of love for the place, but I can't deny that my thoughts are running rampant with ideas. That space would be ideal for a restaurant. It's a prime spot for foot traffic, and the view of Mount Rainier is stunning. It would be perfect.

You failed before, a little voice whispers in my head.

It's not wrong. I've failed before, and I'll probably fail again.

"You know," my dad says carefully, "I saw that sign and got to thinking about that dream of yours. You could—"

"How's the campaign going?" I cut him off, my heart stampeding in my chest. Every word he spoke got me more and more excited, and I don't need that.

My father frowns, and I know it's because he wants to talk about this more. He knows better than anyone how much I've always wanted my own restaurant. While he knows the gist of what happened, he doesn't know just how deep I got cut in Chicago. I'm already working in a kitchen at Stick Taps. Can't that be enough?

"This new guy is good, no doubt about that," my father says, letting me change the subject. "I'm still ahead in the polls, though, so that's always a plus."

"Good or not, your opponent doesn't stand a chance against you. The county loves you. You know that."

"Yeah, but I doubt they'd feel that way if they knew about my heart thing."

I realize I've been so caught up in Ezra and the remodel that I haven't even asked about it in a while. He hasn't complained, so I've figured he's okay. He would say otherwise. We've always been honest with each other.

Like you're being honest by sneaking around with Ezra.

I push that thought away. "Speaking of that, how have you been feeling this week?"

"Not bad. Just a little heartburn, but nothing my pills can't fix."

Now it's my turn to frown. "Are you sure it's just heartburn? Do you need to see your doctor?"

"If I'm not allowed to worry about you, then you're not allowed to worry about me."

"You can worry about me, Dad, but being sick for a few days is different than me getting a call in the middle of the night because of your heart." I shoot him a glare. "If this campaign is causing you stress, then you need to drop it. You don't have to be the sheriff."

He looks offended I've even suggested that, but I bet the thought has crossed his mind a time or two. My dad isn't exactly old, but he's not as young as he once was either. He has more than enough time under his belt to retire. It might even be good for him.

"Being sheriff is all I've known for the last fifteen years. I'm not looking to hang up my badge just yet."

"Dad, I—"

He holds his hand up. "I'm okay, Summer. I promise if I feel like I can't do this job, I'll consider retirement."

I don't miss his wording. He'll *consider* retirement. That's not good enough, but I know it's all I'm going to get.

"Fine. I just love you, okay? I want you happy and healthy."

"How many times do I have to tell you that I'm happy as long as you're happy?" He winks at me, then points to my half-eaten food. "Now finish your meal. You need the calories after being sick."

"Yes, Sheriff," I smart off, earning me a glare.

We finish breakfast, and I promise to text him and let him know how I'm feeling in a little while before he leaves.

I take my time getting ready, then climb into the cruiser ten minutes before I actually need to leave for my shift at Stick Taps. I tell myself it's because I want extra time to get there in case of traffic, but this is Port Harbor, for crying out loud.

I'm going early because I want to stop at Sunnie's. I can't stop thinking about it, even though I shouldn't. Even though that little voice is still whispering in the back of my mind.

You failed before, Summer. How will this time be any different? Face it—you couldn't hack it. You're a has-been.

I pull up to the bakery and park along the curb in front, and my heart begins to hammer when I see that it's true.

Right there in the corner of the window is the sign.

FOR SALE BY OWNER

I can't seem to stop myself from opening my door, dying to know more. I say it's just because I'm curious why he's selling it, but I know that's not true. I want to see if he has a buyer.

"Summer!" Ken, the owner, grins at me from behind the counter when I walk into the cute little shop. "How are you, kid?"

I laugh. I think everyone in this town will always call me that, thanks to my father. "Good, Ken. How are you?"

"Not too bad. I was just getting ready to hang my apron up for the afternoon and hand it off to the crew."

"Hot date with Elaine?" I wiggle my brows at him.

He blushes at the mention of Odette's mother. "Now, now. You didn't come all this way to tease an old man. What can I get for you?"

"Four fritters, please. Whatever flavors you have left are fine."

"Sure. Are you on your way to Stick Taps?"

"I am."

"Then I know just what you're looking for."

Tongs in hand, he grabs one apple, one chocolate banana, one mixed berry, and one that I'm unfamiliar with.

"What was that last one you put in the box?" I ask as he tapes it shut.

"Froot Loops. It's Ezra's favorite."

I grin, because of course it is.

I hand over a twenty and tell him to keep the change, which earns me a grin from the older gentleman.

It should be my cue to leave. To take my fritters and walk right out of here. Yet, I linger.

Ken notices.

"Something on your mind, kid?" he asks, crossing his arms over his chest.

"I, uh, I noticed you're selling the place."

He smiles sadly, nodding. "Yep. It's time. This place always belonged to my late wife. This was never my passion. It was hers. Now that I have Elaine and things are going so well there . . . I don't know. It's time to do something different, you know? I want to travel. I want to see the world. Is that hokey?"

I understand that more than he realizes. It's what I felt when I was looking at culinary schools. I wanted to be far away and experience something new. Now, though, all I feel is a longing for home.

"Not at all, Ken. You deserve that. It's just a bummer because Sunnie's has been such a core part of this community for so long. The people will be sad to lose it." I roll my tongue over my lips, swallowing down the lump that's formed in my throat. "Have you had any offers yet?"

My heart pounds in my ears as I wait for his answer.

"A few, but most of them are for chain places, and that's not my style. I think if I'm going to sell Sunnie's, it should be to someone who has the same love of cooking as she did. Not someone looking to make a quick buck and bring something nonlocal here."

So many ideas run through my head all at once.

Dark lighting, a modern refresh on the exterior, new tables and chairs, and a fresh coat of paint inside. It would be moody yet inviting. It would be a must-eat destination.

It would be mine. I could move back here, find an apartment in town or rent Mr. Looper's place. I could be close to my father. I could do whatever I wanted.

My mind spins, and I'm feeling more alive than I have in days at the idea of finally having my own restaurant.

I want to scream out loud that I'll buy it. That he should sell it to me because I would keep it local, and I would honor his wife's memory.

But the words never come. Not just because I have zero financial backing, but because all those fears that I've been holding on to since walking out of Lore come crashing onto my shoulders. I feel dreadful all over again.

You can't run a business, Summer. You could barely hold a kitchen together, let alone deal with all the other things that come with owning a restaurant. Hell, you're still working on a menu for the cidery. How could you possibly do that for a full-scale restaurant?

I can't. I'm not ready. I might never be.

I force a smile. "Well, I hope you find the right person."

"Me too, kid. Me too."

I wave goodbye to Ken, and the sign catches my eye on the way out. That pull to ask him about it more tugs at me, but I pay no heed to it. I can't. I have other things I need to focus on right now.

Maybe I'll get my own restaurant one day, but it won't be today.

◆ ◆ ◆

"You're doing it wrong."

Ezra glares at me over his shoulder, then goes back to stretching out the dough far too thin.

Much to my chagrin, he wasn't at the cidery today. Apparently he had to borrow Noah's truck and go pick up a new pinball machine that they were having trouble getting the company to deliver.

Instead, it was just me and Warner, who was on his absolute best behavior all day.

Ezra texted me around the time I got off with one single word.

Tonight?

I couldn't deny him, which is why I'm standing in his kitchen, watching him butcher the crescent rolls we're having with the chicken pesto pasta we're making.

"You're pulling them too thin. They're going to do—that." I sigh as it rips in half. "Break."

I want to shove him out of the way and take over because it's just in my nature, but I refrain. I pick up another chunk of dough and hand it to him.

"Try again," I instruct. "And stop overworking the dough."

"Yes, Chef," he teases, and I swear the words have never been hotter.

Our second cooking lesson is going much better than our first. In hindsight, I probably should have started with something a little easier, like I did tonight.

This time, when he spreads out the dough, it's perfect, and I coach him on how to fold it so it looks pretty. While it doesn't, it's still edible, and that's all that counts, right?

"Better?"

"I mean, it's in one piece, so that's always a plus." I point to the noodles on the stovetop that should be just about done. "Check on those and drain them while I finish the rolls?"

He nods, then wipes his hands on his apron, and I have to bite my lip to keep from smiling. If he keeps doing that, we might have a repeat of last time when we smoked the kitchen out because we couldn't keep our hands off each other.

I quickly finish the rolls, then move on to the chicken with Ezra.

We get everything plated, take off our aprons, and then sit down at the table that we set earlier. There's something about eating across from each other, a bottle of wine sitting between us, that feels so . . . well, kind of romantic. Definitely different from eating cereal in his bed, that's for sure.

"Oh shit. That's actually good," Ezra says through a mouth-ful of food.

I'd tell him he's being gross, but he's right—it is good. It's almost like he knows what he's doing.

"Any improvements you'd make?" I ask, twirling the pasta onto my fork, then stabbing a piece of chicken.

"The chicken is just a bit overcooked, but that's my bad. I should have taken it off the burner when you told me to." He points his utensil at me. "But that's your fault."

"How?"

"The apron, Sunny. You know what it does to me." He winks at me over the top of his wineglass.

"Eat your food, Ezra."

"Yes, Chef."

I narrow my eyes at him, shifting in my seat, hoping he doesn't notice it. If he does, he doesn't say anything.

"Sorry that I wasn't at the cidery for your first day back," he says a few moments later. "Those damn delivery guys kept giving me the runaround with the machines. I won't be ordering from them again."

"That sucks. But you got it sorted, right?"

"Yep, she's plugged in and looking good. Plays nicely too." He takes another sip of his wine, then sets the glass down. "Saw something interesting on the way home tonight."

"Oh?" I ask, shoveling another bite of food into my mouth. He's right that the chicken is just a bit overdone, and I'm impressed he realizes that.

"Sunnie's is for sale."

I've been doing so well all day not thinking about it. Or at least trying really, really hard not to. But the second he says it, my heart does that same hammering thing it did earlier.

"I heard something about that." My words are cool and calm.

"Could be a good place for a new restaurant. Great location, that's for sure."

"Mm-hmm," I say noncommittally, taking a bite of the crescent roll, even though I'm suddenly feeling full. I just need something to do to distract me from the hopeful way Ezra is staring at me. It reminds me too much of the look my father gave me earlier.

He sets his fork down. "I'm saying you should buy it, Summer."

I sigh, pushing my plate away. "No."

He works his jaw back and forth. "Why not?"

"Because not all of us are former hotshot hockey players with money burning holes in our pockets, Ezra. I can't afford it, for starters. And even if I could, I'm not doing it. I don't want to."

"Okay—I get the financial aspect of it, but I'm not buying that you don't want to. I've seen the way you're giving your all to the menu at the cidery, and I'm excited as hell to have you working there, but imagine doing that for a place that's all your own. You deserve that."

"You've never even seen me in a kitchen. Not really. How do you know I don't suck?"

"Because I know *you*, Summer, and I believe in you."

He believes in me? I hate that such a simple statement makes my stomach do flips, especially when this . . . whatever this is we're doing . . . it's not supposed to mean anything.

When it *doesn't* mean anything because it can't.

"Look," I say, rising from my chair, my plate in hand as I take it over to the sink. "I appreciate your vote of confidence—I truly do—but my answer is still no."

He sighs, following behind me. "Fine, but we aren't done talking about this."

"Are too."

"Are not."

I glare over at him and point to the mess we've made in the kitchen. "Stop being annoying and start cleaning."

"Yes, Chef," he says with a grin, grabbing a towel and slinging it over his shoulder.

We work together for the next twenty minutes to restore the kitchen to where it was before we started his lesson, and I spend the entire time thinking about Ezra's words.

Because I know you, Summer, and I believe in you.

I wish I had the same faith he does, but I don't. Once upon a time, maybe, but losing something you've worked so hard for, like I did—folding under the pressure—it does something to you. It shakes you up. I . . . I can't trust myself anymore. I've never admitted that before, but it's true. It's why it's taking me so long to refine this damn menu for the cidery. It's why I'm dragging my heels in deciding to stay in Port Harbor. Because what if the choice I make is the wrong one? What if I try something and I fail again? Can I bounce back from that?

I . . . I don't know, and I'm not willing to find out.

"Hey, Sunny?" Ezra says a while later. We're lying in his bed, his fingers playing with the ends of my brown locks as we watch something mindless on TV.

"Yeah?"

"I'm not trying to push you into something, you know that, right?"

I exhale slowly and nod. "I know that, Ezra."

"I just . . . I wish you could see yourself in the kitchen like I see you. When you're cooking, it's like you're in a different world, like nothing could touch you in there. Nothing could get under your skin. You just . . . fuck, you look happy, almost like you're in love, and I know what that's like. I had it with hockey, and I lost it. I fucking lost my one true love, and I don't want the same thing to happen to you just because you're scared. I get it—more than you know. So I'm not pushing you, I swear. I'm just letting you know that if you do decide to follow your heart and take a risk, I'm in your corner."

Tears sting my eyes, and I blink them away. I've had people in my corner before—my dad has always been my number one fan and my mother, too—but I've never had someone like Ezra there for me before. Someone who doesn't *have* to believe in me, but chooses to.

"Thank you," I whisper.

He kisses my forehead. "Anytime, Sunny."

I get the feeling that he means it.

We stay like that the rest of the night. His hands don't wander any lower than my back, and we don't spend the evening fooling around. We just watch TV until we fall asleep, and it might be the most restful night of sleep I've had.

And it has everything to do with Ezra.

CHAPTER NINETEEN

Ezra

"Nice job, Marshall!" I clap loudly, grinning as I watch him drop right back into position after stopping the other kid's attempt at going glove side on him.

He stops the next six shots, which come in quick succession, and pride swells in my chest. He's done so much better since that day he said he wanted to quit, and I'm beyond proud of him for pushing through and sticking with it.

I just wish Summer would do the same.

She hasn't been back to my house since we talked about her buying Sunnie's. We've been sneaking in kisses after work, but it's clear something is distracting her. Part of me hopes it's that she's rethinking the idea of potentially purchasing the space, but I can't be certain. I plan to talk to her tonight about it during our third cooking lesson, where we've graduated from pasta to chicken Parmesan.

The timer on the scrimmage runs out, and Marshall's team is the winner. The kid looks ecstatic about it too.

"Good work out there," I tell him as we skate toward the tunnel leading back to the locker rooms.

"Thanks, Coach. I was hoping for a shutout, but a win is a win."

"That's right. And a win means ice cream, right?"

"Heck yes it does!"

I laugh as he darts off the ice, joking around and carrying on with his teammates, as I help the other coach clean up.

We're just about done when the door to the rink opens and in walks the last person I was expecting to see today.

"Sheriff Turner." I skate over to him. "How are you?"

"Not bad, Mr. Rawlings." His eyes roam over the rink. "Nice place you got here."

"Thanks," I say, but I get the feeling that's not what this visit is about. In fact, I get the feeling he's here about something else entirely. *Someone* else. "Was there something I could help you with, Sheriff?"

He clears his throat, tucking his hands into his pockets. "I wanted to thank you, Mr. Rawlings."

"Pretty sure we know each other well enough at this point that you can call me Ezra. And thank me for what?"

"For taking care of my daughter. I got an alert on my doorbell when she was sick. I saw that it was you who brought her home, and I just wanted to say thank you for taking care of her. Summer's a stubborn girl, and I'm sure she said she could handle herself, but I appreciate you not leaving her alone."

If he received an alert on his camera, that must mean he knows how late I stayed, which was long past the appropriate time for a boss to be taking care of his employee.

He knows. About me and Summer, he knows.

And that's why he's really here. He doesn't want to thank me. He wants me to be aware that he's aware.

I keep my face and tone neutral as I say, "It was no problem, sir."

His eyes narrow for only a moment, but I know what it means all the same. He's sizing me up. He's trying to suss out if he should be worried or not.

He shouldn't. I have no intention of harming Summer.

You also had no intention of even starting anything with her, and look how that turned out.

I drive the thought away.

He nods, like he's satisfied with whatever goes unsaid between us, then says, "How's the remodel going?"

"Good. We're just about done. There are a few more days left on construction, then the grand opening is after Noah and Odette's wedding."

"Ah. Explains why my kitchen looks like a war zone."

I tip my head to the side, unsure what he means.

"Summer," he explains. "She's been cooking up a storm, working on the menu. She's testing recipes left and right. Pretty sure I'm going to burst if I have to eat another brussels sprout or mac and cheese ball."

Relief floods me. She's not avoiding me. She's cooking.

Now that I know, it makes me happy she hasn't been around. I'm glad she's feeling inspired enough to stay away. And I hope more than anything it was because of our conversation the other night.

"White cheddar and Gouda?" My stomach rumbles at the thought of the last time she made mac and cheese for me. I don't know how she turned something so simple into a culinary experience, but she did.

"Yep. She's adding Parmesan too. Really kicked it up a notch."

I grin at that. I wish I could be there to see it, but I understand that this is her process. She can have it for herself—for now.

Sheriff Turner relaxes for the first time since he came in here and leans against the boards. I do the same. "I haven't seen her this happy since she was leaving for culinary school. I guess I have you to thank for that too."

I tilt my head to the side. "Me? What'd I do?"

"You have given her the space to do her thing. Gave her a nudge." He sighs. "Honestly, I was scared she was going to give up after Chicago."

Summer's been fairly tight-lipped on what happened there. All I know is that she had a shot at her dream, and she lost it. She's never given specifics, but whatever they are, it's obvious they had an impact on her confidence.

"That old boss of hers was a real piece of work. Used to berate her for the smallest mistakes, even when they weren't her fault. Change the menu on her at the last minute *after* hours of prep, then blame it all on her for not being able to handle it. She wanted to be an executive chef so badly, she kept her mouth closed and took it."

I can't see Summer ever letting someone walk all over her like that. She's never let me do it, that's for damn sure. Never had an issue standing up for herself, and I've always admired that about her.

Is that what rattled her? Her old boss? Is she . . . Is she worried I'm going to do that same thing?

"I was proud as hell of her when she finally spoke up for herself," the sheriff continues. "Sure, she could have chosen a better time to do it—not in the middle of dinner rush and maybe not have yelled at the entire kitchen and stormed out—but still proud." He frowns. "They blacklisted her in Chicago."

I whip my head toward him. "What? Are you serious?"

"You didn't know?"

"No, I didn't. She never . . ." I clench my teeth, shaking my head. "She never told me."

"I'm not surprised. She's embarrassed as hell over it. She feels like she failed. Hell, I don't think I'd even know she was blacklisted if I weren't following food blogs, looking for any mention of how incredible a chef my daughter is. Didn't expect to see the whole debacle getting picked apart in the comments."

I want to tell him never to read the comments, but I'm still reeling from this new piece of information.

Fuck, it makes so much sense now. No wonder Summer doesn't want to pursue Sunnie's. They broke her. They took away her dream.

But doesn't she know that this town would rally around her until the end of the earth? That her father would do anything to see her succeed? Doesn't she realize I would do the same?

I'm not quite sure when that became the truth, but it did. And fuck if that doesn't scare me like it should.

"Why are you telling me this, Sheriff?"

"Because Sunnie's is for sale."

I swallow the knot in my throat. "I know."

"So you've already talked to her about it?"

I want to deny it, because that would imply that Summer's been spending time with me that she shouldn't be, but I don't think it matters at this point.

"I have."

"And?"

"And she said no. She's scared. She doesn't believe in herself."

"So believe enough for her."

I do.

The weight of those two words is heavy, and even more so because of how honest they are.

The sheriff grins, and it's one of those annoying kinds of grins. The *knowing* kind.

"What?" I snap at him.

He just laughs, and it pisses me off.

"Stop it."

He rolls his lips together in an attempt to stop, but it does nothing to quell the irritation clawing at me.

I don't know what he thinks he knows, but he's wrong, whatever it is.

I push off the boards, my hip throbbing. "Is there anything else you needed, Sheriff?"

"Nah, son. That's all. Just wanted to make sure we're on the same page when it comes to my daughter and her dreams."

I nod. "We are."

"Good. So don't let her blow this. Don't let it pass her by. Don't give up on her. She might try to push you away or run, but don't let her. She's done it once already, and it damn near broke me to see her so down about it. She's my little girl, and I want the world for her. Her happiness comes first for me. It has since the day her mother died. The only way that's going to happen is if someone is there for her. Someone she trusts. Someone she cares about. Someone like you, Ezra."

His words are heavy, made even heavier by the fact that I feel the same way. I trust Summer, and I care about her in ways I never expected to.

"Don't let her walk away from her dream," he says. "And don't let her walk away from you either."

◆　◆　◆

When I get back to the cidery, not even locking myself in my office and burying my head in work seem to help distract me from my conversation with Sheriff Turner.

Don't let her walk away from her dream. And don't let her walk away from you either.

We parted ways after that, and all it did was leave me in a sour mood.

What the hell was he getting at? Why did he keep giving me that look that said *I know something you don't?* Why did he have to tell *me* not to let her walk away from her dream?

I don't control Summer. Nobody does. She's made that clear since the day I met her.

But it doesn't escape my notice that she's been cooking up a storm since our conversation at my house when I told her I was in her corner.

Did that mean more to her than I thought? Did she really hear what I was saying beneath those words? Did she know how much I meant it?

"Hey."

I'm so lost in my head that I didn't even hear my door being pushed open.

Summer stands in the entryway with a soft, almost mischievous smile. She's not even on the schedule today.

"Hey, what are you doing here? I thought you were coming over later."

She lifts a shoulder. "I was bored."

But her eyes are sparkling far too brightly for that to be true.

"Want to play some pinball?"

I check the time and am surprised to see that the cidery is five minutes from closing.

Where the hell did the day go?

"Uh, yeah. Just let me wrap this up, and I'll be out there."

"Okay, but don't take too long. I still owe you a rematch from last time."

I smile. "I'll be quick."

I watch her go until she disappears around the corner at the end of the hall, and I breathe a sigh of relief.

I'm glad she's here. Of course I am. But after the conversation with her dad earlier, I'm honestly not sure I want to be near her right now. All it does is make my head foggy and make me feel things that I . . . fuck, things I really shouldn't be feeling.

Things I *can't* feel.

I wait until fifteen after to go out there and bid good night to our closing bartender. If they're wondering why Summer is here this late, they don't question it. I'm sure they figure it has something to do with the remodel.

I find Summer standing at the *Jurassic Park* machine, her bottom lip trapped between her teeth, brows furrowed in concentration as she mashes down on the buttons. Fuck, she looks good. She's wearing another tiny skirt, and I wonder if she's bothered with real underwear tonight or not.

The machine's lights go off, the music playing loudly, and Summer pumps her fist excitedly at whatever she just accomplished.

"Oh shit!" she exclaims, pushing the button on the side quickly.

She's not fast enough, and her shoulders sag at the loss of her ball.

I laugh, and she whirls around at the intrusion.

"I lost."

"It's because you got cocky."

"I did not," she argues, though we both know it's a lie. "You distracted me."

"You didn't even know I was here."

"Please." She rolls her eyes. "I always know where you are, Ezra."

I always know where she is too.

But I don't tell her that. Instead, I roll up the sleeves of my dress shirt and step up beside her. "Does the pro get a chance now?"

She waves her hand toward the machine. "Be my guest."

I pop a few quarters in, position myself against the machine, then pull the lever back. I hit my target immediately, then again. I do it over and over until my points far exceed whatever Summer had up on the board, and I delight in how salty she looks beside me as I keep going.

"You suck," she says when I finally lose, my score three times as high as hers.

I point out the numbers with multiple commas. "That says otherwise."

She huffs. "Whatever. It's not fair. You've had more time to practice over the last few days than I have."

It's the first time she's mentioned her absence, and now that I know what she's been up to, I feel like I have to tread carefully.

"Well, that wouldn't be the case if you were around."

She grins, and there's something flirty about it. "Why, Ezra, is that your way of saying you missed me?"

Yes.

"You wish," I say instead, grabbing her by the waist and tugging her close. She comes to me easily, her arms going around my neck, that smile stretched across her ruby-red lips.

"Hi," she says on a giggle, batting her lashes up at me.

"Hi yourself. How was your day?"

"Better now."

"Do anything fun?"

It's marginal, but I feel her stiffen in my arms, and I don't miss when she darts her eyes away as she answers me. "Not really. Just been working on the menu."

I wait for her to tell me about the recipes she's testing out, the ones that have worked and the ones that haven't, but she doesn't elaborate.

I should probably be mad that she's holding her cards so close to her chest, but I can't be. Not when I've missed her so much, and I'm just glad to have her in my arms.

"It's going to be amazing," I tell her, dragging her even closer. I run my nose against her cheek, loving the hitch in her breath. "And you want to know how I know that?"

"H-How?"

"Because . . ." I kiss her cheek, then again, this time closer to her lips. "You're amazing, Sunny."

Then my mouth is on hers because I can't wait another second. I have to touch her. Kiss her. *Devour* her.

I don't think I have an option anymore.

She kisses me back with equal ardor, and all it does is make me want her that much more.

Summer's hands drop to my belt, then my zipper, and I'm being pulled free from my boxer briefs in record time.

"Fuck," I hiss as she takes me in her hand. "That feels so good. It's been too long."

She laughs. "Three days is too long?"

"When it comes to you? Yes."

We pause because *holy heavy*, but I don't regret saying it. Not when I mean it as much as I do.

Then we're more frantic than ever before, our lips connecting as Summer continues to stroke me. I tug her T-shirt free because I *need* to feel her bare skin beneath my hands.

She sighs when my fingers brush against her stomach, a shudder racking through her.

"That feels good."

"*You* feel good," I counter.

She smiles against me. "I know something else that will feel good."

Then she's dropping to her knees, taking me into her wet, warm mouth before I can even register what's happening.

It's not the first time she's worshipped my cock with her tongue, but it still somehow feels like it is, and I think that's because I'll never quite get used to being with her like this and how absolutely fucking euphoric it is.

"Summer," I say, my hands sliding into her hair. I don't know if I'm pulling her closer or trying to push her away. "I'm gonna come like this."

She pulls off me long enough to say, "Pretty sure that's the point."

Then her mouth is back right where I want it, and I'm lost in the feeling again as she sucks me to the back of her throat.

It's too much, having her tongue swirl around me, one hand working over my cock, the other cupping my balls just the way I like it.

"I'm warning you, Sunny," I say, tugging her silky brown locks. "If you don't stop, I'm going to make a mess."

She flicks her gaze up to me but doesn't let go.

A minute later I'm delivering on my promise, and she sucks me down like she's never wanted anything more.

I don't think I have either.

I pull her up almost instantly, pressing my mouth to hers, not caring that I just came inside it. I just need to kiss her. Need to feel her against me.

I only break our kiss long enough to tug her shirt over her head. I toss it aside—a problem for later—and find her lips again. After devouring her mouth, I kiss my way down her chin and over her throat, nipping at her just because I can.

When I see the little marks I'm leaving behind, only one word goes through my mind—*mine.*

It's absurd. Absolutely fucking preposterous considering we're not really anything, but I can't stop thinking it.

Mine, I chant as I push her skirt up.

Mine, I say again as I slide her panties to the side.

Mine, I think as I press two fingers into her needy cunt.

"You're so goddamn wet for me, Sunny."

She nods, her head thrown back. "All for you."

"Want to fuck you." I pump into her, hooking my fingers and pressing on that spot I know drives her wild. "Can I do that? Can I bury my cock inside you until you're whimpering in my arms?"

"Please. Please, Ezra," she begs, and the sound is like the perfect song.

I pull my fingers from her and grab her by the waist, sitting her up on the pinball machine she's been pressed against. Thank god for tempered glass, or else I'd be scared of breaking the top.

"Get your tits out. I want to see them bounce as I fuck this beautiful pussy," I tell her.

She scrambles to do just that, and I have to stop and admire her once the material is tossed to the side.

Her skirt is up around her waist, her panties pushed to the side, showing off her glistening center. Her hair is wrecked from my hands, her lips swollen from my kisses, and her neck peppered with bite marks. She's a fucking vision. A true work of art.

"What?" she whispers into the quiet cidery.

"You're perfect."

She laughs lightly, darting her gaze away. "I'm not."

"No, Sunny," I say, grabbing her chin and forcing her to look at me. "You are. Believe that. Believe me. Believe in yourself."

Her eyes flash, and she knows exactly what it is I'm referring to, and it has nothing to do with this moment.

Believe in your dreams. Believe in your passion. You're not a failure.

Then she grabs and pulls me to her. She kisses me hard as she scoots to the edge of the machine. My cock brushes against her, and I could cry at how good she feels as I press into her.

Too good, actually.

Shit.

I wrench my mouth away. "Wait, wait. I need—"

"No," she says, reading my mind. "No, I want to feel you. *All* of you. If that's okay."

"Okay? Jesus, Sunny, it's more than okay. I don't think I've ever wanted anything more. But are you sure?"

"Yes. I'm good if you're good."

"I'm good."

"Then do it, Ezra. Fuck me bare. Leave your mark on me."

I slide inside her slowly, with more patience than I've exhibited before.

Mine, the word echoes in my head as I bury myself to the hilt.

I pause, letting her get used to the feeling of me. Hell, letting myself get used to the feeling of her.

I've never been with anyone like this before, with nothing between us. And now that I've had it . . . I'm not sure I could ever go back. I wouldn't want to, not with her.

"Ezra, I need you to move."

"I can't."

She laughs. "Why not?"

"Because if I do, I might come, and I really want this to last. Give me a second?"

She nods and lets me have it, my head resting in the crook of her neck while I talk myself down from the edge. I have no business being ready again so soon, but this is Summer we're talking about. I'm always ready.

When I get my heart rate as under control as it's going to get, I move.

She groans when I do, and I want to say *The feeling's mutual,* but I keep it to myself as I pull out until just the tip is sitting inside her.

Slowly, I push back in.

"Fuck. You feel like heaven, you know that?" I say as I look down, watching myself slip inside her again. "Unlike anything I've ever felt. And I can't . . . I can't hold back, Sunny. I just fucking can't."

"Then don't." Her leg wraps around me, drawing me into her more. "Give me everything you have."

I pound into her, the machine thumping against the wall. For a moment I worry about it breaking, but I realize I don't care. Let it break. I'll buy a new one and grin as the money leaves the bank account.

My hip throbs as I thrust into her over and over and over again, but I push the pain down. Besides, it's nothing compared to how good it is to be inside her like this.

And it is good. So good that if I don't get her off soon, I'm going to completely fucking embarrass myself. I sneak my hand between us, pressing my thumb against her clit and drawing short circles.

"Yes." She moans into my ear. "Yes, that. More."

I press harder, and I'm rewarded with another pleasure-filled sob.

"Ezra . . ." she says, digging her nails into my back. "I'm going to . . ."

"Do it, Sunny. Come on my cock. Let me feel you milk me dry."

I barely get the words out before her pussy spasms around me, and it's all it takes to send me right over the edge behind her.

I come and I come and I come some more. It's more than I ever have before.

When we're both spent and out of breath, only then do I pull out. I look down and grin at the mess that's leaking out of her and all over the machine.

Unable to help myself, I gather the mix of us on my finger and push it back into her.

She groans, tossing her head back as I slide my digit in and out of her slowly. I'm not doing it to get her off. I'm doing it because I want every drop of me in her.

After a while I pull away, helping her down off the machine onto shaky legs, and she smiles up at me.

"That was . . ."

"Definitely going to require me to scrub the security tapes?"

She laughs. "Yeah. That."

She presses to her tiptoes, laying her lips against mine softly, and I sigh.

"Thank you, Summer," I say.

She pulls back, tipping her head to the side. "For what?"

"For giving me all of you. For giving me you. For being . . ."

Mine. The word comes back in full force, and I choke it down.

"For being you," I finish.

"You're welcome." She winks with a smirk. "I'm going to go get cleaned up."

I nod, letting her walk away.

I watch her go, my mind racing with so many things I want to say to her. So many things I shouldn't be thinking.

I had no idea that whatever it is between us would lead us here. That I'd be deep in thoughts I never thought I'd have. That I'd be feeling a way I swore I would forever avoid because I'm not whole, and someone like her deserves someone who is.

But I am, and I have no idea how I'm going to stop.

Or that I want to.

CHAPTER TWENTY

Summer

The new menu is officially set.

Ezra had said he trusted me to create something he knew the customers would love, so that's what I did. I spent the last week perfecting it, and there's not a single change I would make.

To say I'm excited to show him, Noah, and Odette the final menu is an understatement. I just have to get through today and tomorrow, and then I'll have my opportunity.

It's not a group date—not technically—but I'd be lying if I said it didn't feel like it a little bit, especially after our time in the arcade the other night.

I'd never been with anyone like that before. I was always too scared. But with Ezra? It just made sense. *He* made sense, as scary as that is.

Terrifying or not, it was incredible. I'd never felt so close to someone before while being so exposed, and I'd do it all over again in a heartbeat.

"Who are we daydreaming about, and why is it our hot boss?"

Fuck.

I glance over at Warner. "I have no idea what you're talking about."

He laughs dryly, then hops up on the counter, even though said boss would rip him a new one if he saw it. "Come on. I have eyes, Summer. I know what being in love with someone looks like."

Now it's my turn to laugh. "I am *not* in love with Ezra."

He holds his hands up. "Okay, maybe not in love with him, but you're certainly in lust. You've been staring at him for the last ten minutes. And I don't just mean like a faraway kind of stare either. You're tracking him like he's your lifeline."

"I am not," I say automatically, pushing off the counter. Needing something to do with my hands, I start rearranging a set of glasses.

But he's right. I have been.

Ezra's been chasing Tootsie around at least five of those minutes, and I really have been following his every move through the big glass windows that take up the back side of the cidery. Not just because it's comical to watch, but because I can't help it. I like looking at him. I like being around him. And I really, *really* like kissing him.

"It's just funny watching him try to corral the chicken, that's all."

"While that is absolutely hilarious, that's not why you're staring at him. You like him," he teases, stretching out the word *like* obnoxiously.

I cut him a glare. "Stop it."

"Stop being so obvious. If anyone else were here, they'd also know something was going on with you two."

I pause. "What are you talking about?"

"I'm talking about you sneaking around. I'm talking about you sleeping with our smokin'-hot boss."

"Shh!" I admonish, glancing around the cidery. There are far too many people in here for him to be saying stuff like that. Luckily for us, though, nobody is up at the bar. Everyone is spread out among the tables, the outdoor seating, and the arcade. And thank god for the music that's pumping through the speakers, which hopefully masks this conversation.

"Sorry," he says, leaning closer. "But I'm right, aren't I? You two are together?"

I should probably deny it. Should tell Warner to fuck off and get out of my business. But I've been bursting to tell *someone* about this since it began.

"Yes," I answer quietly. "We're together. Well, kind of."

"Kind of?" he asks, his eyes sparking with interest. "Do tell."

"We're not labeling it. We're just . . ."

"Fucking?"

"Warner!" I hiss at him and tug him off the counter. I pull him away from the crowd as much as I can while still being behind the bar.

"Well, that is what you're doing, isn't it?"

I could dignify that question with a response, but I don't have to. The answer is apparently written all over my face, based on the way Warner grins.

He holds his hand up for a high-five. "Good for you, Summer."

I yank his hand down, glowering at him. "Okay, you're done."

He laughs. "Look, I'm just proud of you. Ezra's been on everyone's *to-do* list for years."

"I thought everyone called him Grump Ass?"

"They do, but it doesn't mean we're not all aware of how good looking that man is. I mean, those dress shirts? Those slacks? I want to ask him to be my tutor, and I'm not even a student."

I can't help but smile because I've thought the same thing myself.

"See? You get what I'm saying. So," he says, leaning into me, "not dating but still fooling around, huh?"

"Yeah, basically."

"And that's because he's all anti-love and -relationships, right?"

"How do you know about that?"

"I've been around for a while. You learn shit. Plus, he gets all queasy looking whenever Noah and Odette get lovey-dovey in front of him. It's not hard to figure out."

That's true. He does do that. Not as much as he used to, but it's still clear he's uncomfortable with all their PDA.

Me? Well, uncomfortable is the last thing I am. I'm actually kind of jealous. I wish I could touch Ezra freely like that, even if we aren't labeling this thing we're doing. But I have to respect his feelings on the situation, so I don't push it.

Plus, there's that pesky little fact that I'm still his employee too.

We might have made some really bad, really loose excuses when we first started this, but we can't really use those now. I *am* his employee. Hell, I'm his head chef. What we're doing is wrong. Completely unethical. There's no way to spin it otherwise.

I trust Warner not to say anything, but if my other coworkers got wind of this, I don't think they'd be as understanding, and they shouldn't be. I wouldn't be if the roles were reversed. I'd constantly wonder if favorites were played or if opportunities that weren't earned were given simply because of the circumstances.

It's just another reminder that I'm fucking this up all over again. I'm getting in the way of my own dreams again and again. I'm failing.

"Hey, whoa. Are you okay?"

"Huh?"

Warner points between my eyebrows. "You're angry. What's wrong?"

"Nothing," I say, the word harsher than intended. "Sorry. It's just . . . Can we stop talking about this? I really don't want anyone to overhear."

"Sure, yeah. Of course. I just . . ." He leans down again. "For what it's worth, I think it's a good thing. Maybe against the rules, sure, but still a good thing. You've certainly made Ezra a more tolerable boss, so whatever this thing is, keep it up."

He shoots me a wink and a thumbs-up, and I laugh just to get him to leave me alone.

But on the inside, I'm freaking out. Am I self-destructing because of what happened in Chicago?

No, no. I can't be. That can't be what this is. How could it be when it feels so right?

My eyes find Ezra again—who is still chasing the chicken around—and I'm making my way over to him before I even realize it.

"I'll be back," I call out to Warner.

He laughs, and I try not to let the sound bother me as I push open the doors to the back of Stick Taps, where the animals are housed.

Like he can sense me, Ezra pauses, then looks over his shoulder. Our eyes connect, and he grins. My stomach does a flip.

"Hey, Sunny."

"Hey," I say back. "You good out here?"

"I would be if *someone* would cooperate with me." He glares at the chicken, who couldn't care less.

"Want some help with her?"

Ezra was right—Tootsie is harmless. The chicken and I have become friendly since our first encounter, and I've spent more time than I'd like to admit chasing her back to her pen. We have a rapport of sorts by this point.

He huffs, putting his hand on his hip and squeezing it, almost like he's trying to stave something off.

"Are you in pain?"

"What?" He shakes his head. "I'm fine."

But I don't think he is fine. Now that I'm standing so close, I can see the hidden discomfort in his green eyes. Can see how hard he's clenching his jaw, his molars undoubtedly rubbing together.

"Help me get her back in her coop?"

He's deflecting, but I let him have it.

I step around him, creeping my way toward the chicken. "Hey, Toots." I keep my voice soft. "Let's get you back in your coop, okay?"

Cluck.

"I know you don't want to go, but you have to."

Cluck.

"Stop being sassy, or you're not getting any treats."

Cluck cluck.

Ezra snickers. "I'm pretty sure she just told you to fuck off."

"I think so too."

I go to reach for her, but she's too fast, moving out of the way before I even bend over fully. That's how the next five minutes go—I chase her, she runs away. Ezra tries, too, and it's the same result.

Eventually we get her in her coop, and she doesn't like it one bit, clucking at us from the corner.

"She's cussing like a sailor," Ezra says with a grin that wobbles around the edges, his hand still on his right hip. "We really should fix this hole."

"Is that how she keeps getting out?" I ask, looking up to where he's staring so intently.

"Afraid so. This is more Noah's department, but with the wedding just three weeks away, I don't think it's a high priority right now."

"So let's fix it, then."

I don't bother waiting for Ezra's answer. I go to the storage shed and pull it open, figuring there has to be a ladder stashed in here somewhere.

I'm right. I reach for it, but Ezra's there, elbowing me out of the way.

"Hey, stop. I got it. Let me—"

But the protest dies on my lips when I see the look in his eyes.

Back off, it says.

So I do.

It's clear he's determined to do this himself. Usually I trust him to know his limits, but I get the feeling he's pushing himself too hard.

It's confirmed as I trail behind him back to the coop, and his limp is far more pronounced than I've seen it in a while.

How long has he been hurting like this? How long has he been hiding the pain?

"So, how is this going to work exactly?" Ezra asks when we get back to the coop. He sets down the ladder and presses on his hip again. To anyone else, it might look like nothing, but I know him. I know his body. I know he's uncomfortable.

"Um . . ." I say, pulling my gaze from where he's gripping his hip to the spot where Tootsie keeps escaping from. "I don't know exactly. Patch it?"

He waves toward the ladder that's propped up against the coop. "Have at it then."

I don't know why, but his words make me angry. Usually I'd be all about a guy not trying to step in and take control because I'm a woman, but I know Ezra is saying it because he's hurting. He just won't admit it.

"I don't do heights." I have no problem with them, but he doesn't know that. "After you."

He works his jaw back and forth, and all it does is piss me off more.

"What's wrong, Ezra? Are you scared of heights too?"

He gnashes his teeth together even more tightly, and I can't help it—I keep pushing.

"Or is it that you're hurting and you don't want to admit it?"

"Yes!" he explodes. "Yes. My fucking hip is killing me. Is that what you want to hear?"

"Yes," I say, crossing my arms over my chest. "Why can't you just admit it?"

He laughs scathingly. "You can't be serious."

"Oh, I'm very serious. So you have hip pain? Who cares. It doesn't define you."

He scoffs as he begins to pace back and forth, his steps uneven the whole time. "It does, though, Sunny. It fucking defines me more than you know."

"I know it makes things hard, but, Ezra, it's okay that you can't do everything you used to be able to do."

"It's not okay!" he yells, his eyes more like a forest green than their usual Granny Smith apple. "I'm fucking weak, Summer. *Weak.* Don't you get that?"

In that moment I see it. Ezra isn't mad that he's in pain. He's mad because he thinks that somehow his injury makes him less of a person.

He's mad because it's entirely out of his control. Angry because he doesn't feel whole.

"Ezra . . ." I grab him on yet another endless lap. He stills, and I have to physically turn him so he's facing me.

When he is, I can't believe I didn't see it before. It's all right there in his gaze, in his trembling bottom lip.

He believes he's broken.

I slide my hand over his cheek, and he presses into the touch, exhaling heavily. It kills me to see him like this, to think he's not good enough because of an injury that he had no real involvement in. I knew he blamed himself for what happened, but I didn't realize his hate for himself was so deep.

"You are not your injury. You are not your sore hip. You are not your pain. You're enough, Ezra. For me, you're enough. Just the way you are. You don't have to hide your hurt, especially not from me. I'm not going to judge you. I want to know you. *All* of you."

There's no way he doesn't remember when he said those three words to me. It was just two nights ago when I let him fuck me bare.

He thanked me for giving all of myself to him, and now I want the same in return.

I want all of him, even his perceived flaws.

His shoulders sag, and I catch him as he falls forward, his face buried in my neck. I circle my arms around him, holding on to him.

I could love you.

The words slam into me, and their weight barrels right behind them. They're so heavy that I stagger.

Ezra doesn't do relationships. He doesn't do love. He's made that clear from the start, and I was fine with that. I was on board with just having fun and this being nothing serious.

But now . . . now, I think I could want both with him.

After a few moments Ezra pulls away, blinking quickly, but I see the moisture in his gaze anyway.

"Sorry," he says. "I just . . ."

But he doesn't finish his sentence, and he doesn't need to. I understand it all the same.

"Don't apologize. You're not weak, you know. In fact, that thought has never crossed my mind in the almost two months that I've known you. The opposite, usually. Do you not know how many times you've carried me? Or how many times you've tossed me around your bed like it was nothing? And don't even get me started on your stamina."

He grins wolfishly. "It is pretty impressive, huh?"

"Careful, Ezra. Cocky looks good on you."

"You look good on me too."

I laugh, but it's cut off with his kiss. His lips move against mine in a slow, sweet dance. There's nothing rushed about it. Nothing urgent. We're just kissing because we can't *not* kiss.

I'm acutely aware that we're out in the open and anyone could see us, but I can't find it in me to care.

I'm too swept up in the moment. Too swept up in him.

I fear it might always be that way.

CHAPTER TWENTY-ONE

Ezra

You're enough, Ezra. For me, you're enough.

I didn't know I needed to hear those words as badly as I did until Summer said them.

I've spent so long feeling weak after my labral tears, but maybe she's right. I am not my injury. It's just something that happened to me. It doesn't have to define me. I don't have to let it win.

"More cider?"

I shake my head at Odette. "No. I'm driving, so I'm a one-and-done kind of guy."

"Suit yourself," she says with a shrug. She pours another pint of Neutral Zone, then one of Glove Save for Noah, before settling back down at the counter.

"Thanks, Odie." Noah presses a kiss to the side of her head, and while usually I'd be annoyed by all public displays, I don't mind it as much as I typically do.

I know it's because if Summer were here, I'd be doing the same thing.

"I'm starving," Odette complains. "When is dinner being served?"

We're gathered in Stick Taps waiting for Summer to put the finishing touches on her menu debut.

She showed it to me this morning after I woke her up with my tongue between her legs, because she was worried about what ordering would look like. She had nothing to panic over, though, because it looked perfect. It's balanced with a mix of Pacific Northwest–themed dishes and more universal options, and I can't fucking wait to try it all.

"She said ten more minutes."

"That *was* ten minutes ago." Odette groans. "I've been fasting for this all day."

"That's incredibly unhealthy," I say, and she flips me off.

I chuckle, and her jaw drops.

"Ezra Rawlings, are you . . . *laughing?*"

I stop, my smile flipping into a frown, my eyes thinning. "No."

"Shut up! Yes, you were!"

"I was not. Noah, tell your girlfriend she's being annoying."

"Fiancée," he corrects. "And she's right. You were laughing. It was weird."

"I laugh."

"Yeah, but not often." Noah takes a sip of his cider. "Though now that Odette mentions it, you've been laughing a lot more lately. Smiling too."

"I have not."

Except I have. I know it, and he knows it.

I can trace right back to where it started, too—*Summer.*

She's been so giddy all day, running around the cidery, buzzing with excitement as she works in our new state-of-the-art kitchen. The crew officially wrapped up yesterday, which was perfect timing for a "friends and family night" tonight. We can try out the menu and give the kitchen a mini–test run before Summer begins training the new staff we've hired for our grand reopening.

"You're doing it again," Odette points out, poking at my face.

I pretend to try to bite her, and she swats at me.

I've never had a little sister, but I imagine if I did, we'd be a lot like this, always picking at each other.

"Would you two grow up?"

"Oh, sorry, *old man*. Are we bothering you?" Odette sasses her fiancé.

He might scowl at her, but it's clear she amuses him.

Is that . . . Is that what I could have if I let myself? With Summer? Is it even something I want?

I don't have time to analyze that more, as Summer chooses that moment to stop hiding out in the kitchen.

"Oh my gosh, food!" Odette cheers as our chef rounds the corner with two trays stacked tall with grub.

I rush off my stool to help her—and this time, when my hip aches, I don't let the anger set in like it usually would. That moment in the chicken coop yesterday changed something in me.

You're enough, Ezra. For me, you're enough.

"Here, let me take that," I say, grabbing one of the plates.

"Aw, look. Ezra *can* be nice," Odette comments.

Summer giggles. "Ezra's always nice."

Odette scoffs, and while Noah says nothing, I can still feel his eyes on me.

I pretend I don't and help set the spread of various foods on the counter.

"This looks amazing," I say, taking everything in. "Are those pork belly bites?"

"Yes." Summer smacks my hand away as I go to grab one. "And you need to wait. I have another tray in the kitchen. Can you grab it?"

On instinct, I move in to kiss her. Her eyes widen, and she steps back, playing it off like nothing happened.

But something *did* happen, and a frozen Odette and Noah tell me they saw it too.

Fuck, fuck, fuck.

I clear my throat and mutter out a quick "I'll be back" before hightailing it to the kitchen.

I don't exhale until I'm out of sight.

What the fuck was that, Ezra? You almost gave everything away! What were you thinking?

I wasn't, and that's the problem. It was pure instinct to kiss her in that moment. At least for me it was. Not for Summer, though. She knew we couldn't.

Maybe she's not as wrapped up in this as I am.

An ache forms, and this time it's not in my hip. It's in my chest. I rub at it, trying to scrub it away as I push all thoughts of Summer and how natural it feels to want to kiss her out of my head.

We're not here for that tonight. We're here for the new menu. I can sort the rest out later or bury it deep inside where I never have to think about it again.

Yeah, that part sounds good.

I grab the last tray and take it out to the taproom.

Odette, Noah, and Summer are all laughing.

"What's so funny?" I ask as I set the food down.

"Izzy. She just sent a picture of her seatmate sleeping on her. Look."

Odette shoves her phone in my face, and the photo is just as she described.

"She's on her way back, then?"

"Yep." Odette wiggles in her chair, clearly excited about reuniting with her best friend. "She's flying into New York, spending a day doing touristy stuff, then we'll pick her *and* her boy toy up from the airport on Thursday."

"Boy toy? She's bringing someone back?"

"Yes, because she loves me and wants to have a date for the wedding." Odette gives me a pointed look.

"I have a date."

Odette's mouth drops open, and even Noah is looking at me in disbelief.

"What?" I shrug. "I'm capable of getting a date, you know."

"Who? Who is it?"

"Me," Summer says.

"Yes!" Odette cheers. "It's about time!"

I want to ask her what she means by that, but I'm too distracted by Noah. His eyes are trained on me, and he's giving me a look that reminds me a lot of the one Summer's father gave me at the iceplex.

Knowing.

I look away.

"Chill out. We're just friends, and Ezra's doing me a favor so I don't show up alone, and he's got to do all those best-man duties anyway," Summer says as she grabs the stack of small plates she got out earlier and starts to line them up.

"Um, he's doing *you* a favor? Pfft. Please." Odette laughs. "You're hot. The favor is all yours."

"Hey, I'm hot too," I argue.

She ignores me. "Anyway, I'm glad you two took my advice. It's going to be so fun. We're going to dance all night."

"I don't dance."

"You will, or I'll bust your kneecaps," Odette threatens me.

"I can't have busted kneecaps *and* dance."

She grabs a piece of food off the nearest tray and launches it at me.

"Hey, hey!" Summer interjects. "Stop throwing my food. We're supposed to be eating it."

"Yeah, *Odie*, grow up."

She launches herself at me, but Noah's quick to hold her back. I just laugh.

Summer rolls her eyes, but there's still a smile playing on her lips.

And I realize then that this is fun—hanging out with Noah and Odette and Summer and being here with them. It's actually, truly fun.

Is this what I've been missing out on all this time, being angry? Is this what I could have had? Is this what I want?

"I'm good, I'm good." Odette smooths a hand over her hair as she settles back down on her chair, Noah watching her like a hawk, making sure he doesn't need to interfere again. "Sorry, Summer. Present us with the menu."

"Thank you." She clears her throat, then points to a pile on the tray. "First up, as Ezra guessed, we have pork belly bites. They're smoked, then glazed with your own Empty Net cider and homemade barbecue sauce to really punch up that pear and peach flavor."

She puts a few pieces on everyone's plates, and though I haven't had it yet, I already know I'm going to need more.

"Next," she says, scooping up some of the fried food I was hoping would make the final cut. "Mac and cheese balls. We already had a version of this, but this is better. It actually has flavor. And bacon."

"You added bacon?"

She grins at me. "I added bacon."

She continues going over everything she's cooked up, and by the time she's done, it's clear she's thought of everything. There's something for everyone here, from the pork belly to the brussels sprouts that are out-of-this-world good to the three different kinds of sandwiches and even the salmon bites. There's even simpler stuff, like sourdough pretzel sticks that are served with beer cheese, a charcuterie board featuring local meats, and our beloved Seattle-style hot dogs that nobody can ever seem to get enough of.

It's exactly what we were looking for—a little bit of new, some old, and something very local.

"Enjoy," she says when she's done presenting everything, and I don't think she even finishes talking before we're all digging in.

The sounds coming out of all of us are borderline pornographic as we bite into our meal.

"This is incredible," Odette says through a mouthful of the pulled pork that's been slow-cooked in our green-apple Face Off cider. She chews, then swallows. "I can't remember the last time I had something this good. Remind me again why you're not catering our wedding?"

"Because you never asked me."

She mumbles something about how she should have, then shoves another bite into her mouth.

I eat, and I enjoy every bit of it, but what I like more is watching Summer watch us. Her eyes are shining with happiness, and I can tell that this is fulfilling her in a way she's missed far too much since she left Chicago.

I could do this forever.

I freeze for a moment, then pretend that thought didn't cross my mind and keep eating. If I act like it never happened, then I don't have to question why the idea didn't scare the hell out of me.

I know I like Summer. That much is obvious. But it's nothing more than that. It can't be.

You're enough, Ezra. For me, you're enough.

I don't think I've ever been enough for anyone before, least of all myself. But Summer said those words with such sincerity that it's hard not to believe her.

Her words never leave my mind. Not as I finish up the best meal I've had, maybe ever, and not even when I gather the dishes and take them to the kitchen, letting her relax with our friends because she deserves it.

Once I have everything on the counter, I let the water run for a bit to get it hot so I can give the dishes a rinse before putting them in our new dishwasher.

The door opens behind me, and I don't even bother looking to see who it is.

I know.

"When did you start sleeping with your employee?"

"Hello to you too," I say to Noah as I take off my watch and set it aside, deciding to hand-wash the dishes instead. I need something to do if we're going to have this conversation. "Want to help?"

"No."

But he does anyway, coming to stand next to me and grabbing a towel.

We're quiet for a while. I wash, he dries, and so many unspoken words float between us.

"Well?" he prompts after we've let too many silent minutes pass. "When?"

I sigh. "I don't know. About two months ago now?"

I catch him pause from the corner of my eye.

"Jesus," he mumbles as he resumes his duties. "And you didn't think to tell me?"

I level him with a stare. "Like you have any room to talk, Noah."

It wasn't all that long ago when Noah brought Odette on to help renovate our barn to turn it into a wedding venue. If I recall, they snuck around for just about as long as Summer and I have been before being found out and admitting they were in love.

Noah has no business scolding me for keeping this a secret.

"You're right. I did do something similar. But Odette wasn't actually our employee. Summer is."

"Maybe on paper, but we both know that I never would have hired her if it weren't for Sheriff Turner blackmailing me."

"That's a bullshit flimsy excuse if I've ever heard one," he scoffs.

He's not wrong. It is. But it's all I have to cling to that will explain why I'm doing something that's so clearly wrong.

"So," Noah says, leaning against the counter beside me. "I'm guessing it's serious, then?"

"What?" I look at him like he's grown another head. "No. Why would you say that?"

"Because you're hiding it."

"I'm hiding it because, as you pointed out, she's my employee. I'm her boss. Not like I want to advertise that."

"Or you're hiding it because you have feelings for her and you're afraid to admit it." He shrugs. "That's why I hid my relationship with Odette."

"You hid your relationship with her because you were afraid of Izzy finding out."

"Yeah, because how the fuck was I supposed to explain to my younger sister that I'd fallen in love with her best friend?" He leans in conspiratorially. "It's okay if that's what happened, Ez. I'm not going to judge you."

I glower at him. "Fuck off."

But there's no actual bite behind the words. Not when he's hitting so close to the truth.

I *am* keeping my . . . whatever this is with Summer secret because she's my employee and people are nosy, and it truly is nobody's fucking business.

But maybe . . . just maybe . . . there is a small part of me that's hiding it because I'm no longer feeling like this is something that's happening just to pass the time. I'm not falling into bed with her damn near every night just because she's there and I'm lonely. I'm doing it because I want to.

Because I want *her*.

When the hell did that even happen? *How* could that happen? How did I go from swearing I'll never burden anyone with this damn weakness of mine to letting myself get tangled up with Summer like this? I'm not even sure if she's planning to stay in Port Harbor. Yeah, she just created this menu for Stick Taps, and she's about to start training new staff, but we both know that running a kitchen for someone else isn't her dream. She deserves bigger than this, and I'll be damned if I hold her back from that just because I went and developed feelings when I swore I wouldn't.

Noah laughs, and this time when I glare at him, I mean it.

"What?" I snarl.

"You're so in love, dude."

"I am not."

"Oh, you are too. And I fucking love it. I never thought I'd see the day that Ezra 'I Don't Do Love' Rawlings finally fell victim to the love bug, but here you are."

I turn away from him, mostly because I can't stand the way he's grinning at me like I'm some sort of fool. I certainly fucking feel like one.

"Shut the fuck up."

He just laughs again, harder this time, and it pisses me off.

"Get the hell out of here," I snap. "Leave me alone."

"All right," he says. "I'll go. But only because you clearly need time to process all your *feelings*."

He pushes off the counter, still fucking smiling, and I have the strongest urge to spray him with water.

I resist—but only barely—and focus back on the task at hand.

The door creaks back open, and I exhale for what feels like the first time in minutes.

"Hey, Ez?"

I don't look at him. I don't even stop washing. But he knows I'm listening.

"It's okay that you love her. And it's okay to let yourself be loved. There's nothing about you that isn't deserving of that."

Then he's gone, and I'm left with nothing but cold, dirty dishwater, and the realization that I am irrevocably fucked.

CHAPTER TWENTY-TWO

Summer

The menu is a hit. We haven't even officially launched it yet, but we've been secretly testing it on select nights, and everyone is over the moon with the changes.

And my staff? I would have killed to have people like this backing me up at Lore. It's like a night-and-day difference. Only a few of them are professionally trained, but it doesn't matter. They're all so eager to learn that I'm looking forward to running the kitchen with them.

"I'm home!"

I smile as the front door closes behind him.

Ezra gave me the code to his place a few weeks ago, saying it was so I could lock up after him when he had to take off for doctor's appointments in Seattle, but I don't fully believe that was the reason.

I think he likes having me around more than he wants to admit, and honestly, I like being around.

"Sunny." He grins at me as he comes into the kitchen.

I've been working on a new recipe for a few hours now. It's like whatever was lying dormant inside me after I left Chicago has been woken up, and the old flame that I had for cooking is burning brighter than ever.

It's making me want to rethink trying to buy Sunnie's. I've walked by it no fewer than ten times since the for sale sign went up, and I've asked just about everyone who has come into the cidery how they feel about the sale. They want the business to stay local, and I couldn't agree more. It has my wheels turning and fingers itching to make a move more than I'd like to admit.

I'm inspired and elated and so many other pretty words, and I have a feeling it has everything to do with the man who just pressed his lips to my cheek.

"How was your day?" he asks, then picks up a piece of balsamic broiled halibut I've been working on and pops it into his mouth. "Holy shit. That's incredible." He buries his face in my neck, and I giggle. "Have I mentioned how much I love having you in my kitchen?"

"You love me making you food. There's a difference."

He pulls away. "Uh, no. I meant what I said. I love having you in my kitchen, even if you're not actively cooking."

There's something in his eyes that has my breath catching in my throat. It's something that wasn't there before a few days ago, since the tasting with Noah and Odette. I don't know what it means, but it makes my heart flutter in a way it never has.

I can't deny that it makes me nervous. What if I'm reading too much into things? What if I'm just seeing what I want to see? What if . . . What if what I feel for him isn't casual anymore?

So I paste on a smile and tease, "It's still the apron, isn't it?"

He grabs my waist, pulling me closer, his lips ghosting over mine. "Damn right it is."

Then he's no longer flirting with kissing me. He's *really* kissing me. It's like he's starved and hasn't eaten all day.

I'm more than happy to feed him.

I wrap my arms around his neck, tugging him closer, and he clings to me like he's afraid to let me go.

I'm lifted off the ground and placed on the countertop, and I've come to realize it's one of his favorite places to have me.

"Missed you at the cidery today," he says between kisses as his fingers undo the strings on the apron. "You should have seen how mad Tootsie was when she realized she couldn't escape."

After fixing the coop last week, we had to go back and do it *again*. I think we got it this time, though.

"She's a handful."

"Speaking of a handful . . ." He slips the apron off over my head, then cups my boob and lifts his brows suggestively.

I laugh. "You're incorrigible, you know that?"

He shrugs unapologetically. "I know what I like, Sunny." He kisses the tip of my nose. "And I *really* like you."

It's the closest he's come to revealing how he's feeling about this thing we're doing, and I can tell in the way he pauses momentarily that he realizes it at the same time I do.

So when he takes my mouth again, I know it's a distraction tactic, and I let him have it because it just feels too good not to.

I kiss him back with just as much fervor, and before I know it, I'm sitting on the counter with my dress pushed down over my breasts and Ezra's lips wrapped around my nipple as I ride his fingers.

"Fuck," he says with his mouth still on me. "I love the way your pussy squeezes my fingers, you know that?"

"I think you've mentioned it before."

"Have I mentioned how much I love having my face buried between your thighs?"

"Maybe, but feel free to remind me."

He chuckles darkly as he kisses his way down my body, dropping to his knees in front of me.

Worry over his hip tingles in the back of my mind, but I tell myself that I have to learn to trust him in knowing his limits.

And honestly, all my worries fade when he swipes his tongue against me.

"Oh god," I moan, practically coming off the counter, eager for more. "That's . . ."

"Good?" he asks, pulling away.

"Yes." I grab his hair, dragging him right back to where I want him.

His laugh rumbles through me, and it feels so good I could cry.

We've done this so many times before, but somehow each one is just as good as the last. I'm not sure I'll ever get used to it, and if I do, how could I ever move on after that, whenever what we're doing is over? I don't think I can.

I don't think I'd want to.

He pushes his tongue into me, then draws it up to my clit, sucking the pulsing bundle of nerves between his lips. He flicks his tongue against me quickly, and my orgasm rushes into me unexpectedly. My body shakes again and again, and he doesn't let up for a moment. It doesn't matter that I'm pushing at him, trying to close my legs to get a reprieve. He keeps going, and I'm damn thankful for it when the second wave hits, and I'm shaking once more.

When he finally pulls away, his face is wet with my arousal, and it might be the prettiest thing I've ever seen.

I grab him by his shirt, jerking him to me and kissing him because I need to. He tastes like me, and if I hadn't just come again, I might a third time.

It makes me want to drop to my knees and take my turn worshipping him, but he doesn't let me. Without warning, he yanks me off the counter and spins me around until my ass is in the air, slamming into me before I can even register what's happening.

"Fuck," I cry out, my face resting against the cold countertop. "Ezra . . ."

"That's right, Sunny," he says, his voice gravelly and dark as he bends over me, his lips kissing the shell of my ear. "Tell me who's in you right now. Tell me who's fucking you."

"You, Ezra. Always you."

"Always me," he says through gritted teeth.

He's pounding into me with a force I've never felt before, so rough that my face is pressed against the counter so hard that I'm certain it'll bruise. And I take it. I take it because if I don't, I might do something really reckless, like tell him how there's a chance I might be falling for him.

"God, you feel so good," he says.

Thrust.

I like you.

"You feel like heaven."

Thrust.

I want more from you.

"I'll never tire of this."

Thrust.

I think I could be in love with you.

"Fuuuuuuck." He draws the word out, and it's the only warning I have before he comes with a loud grunt and a string of indiscernible words.

He wrings the last of his orgasm out, and I lie there, trying to catch my breath and trying to hold everything I'm feeling in.

I think I already am, I say to no one, and I only wish I were brave enough to say it out loud.

"Try the Cap'n Crunch with the Smacks. It's weirdly good."

He passes me a box, and I pour a small amount into my bowl, skeptical of this combination, though he's never steered me wrong before. Not even with the Apple Jacks–and–Fruity Pebbles combination that was way better than it sounded.

It's two in the morning, and we're both starving after our workout in the kitchen despite the halibut we had earlier.

I take a bite, pleasantly surprised by what I'm tasting.

"Okay, wow. That is actually really good."

"Right?" he says excitedly, and it's so cute how much he looks like a little kid right now. "The flavors work well together."

I grab the box, loading my bowl with more crunchy honey-coated pieces, and snuggle down further into the bed.

Before Ezra, I was always a bit of a night owl. Working in a kitchen kind of requires it. But since he's way worse than I am, I'm now used to staying up so late. I even look forward to it. There's something about the wee hours of the morning that feels so magical and far away. Everyone is asleep, and we're in our own little world.

Tonight is no different as we watch Pam and Jim from *The Office* try to fight their love for each other.

The irony doesn't escape me, but I try not to think about that too much.

"We might have to extend the opening-night party for the new kitchen," Ezra says.

"Oh?"

"Yeah. We're getting interest left and right for entertainment. Talked to Noah today about adding another band, maybe tacking on another hour of food and drinks."

"I'm game if you are."

He nods. "We are. Have I mentioned how excited I am about this?"

"A few times. Though you mostly just talk about the potential profits."

"Hey, I like making money. More money means adding to my car collection and being able to pay my lawyer to get me out of speeding tickets." He shrugs. "But it's not just that. I'm excited that everyone in Port Harbor will finally get to try your cooking. I've been feeling a little spoiled by it lately."

"Oh, I'm sorry. Should I stop cooking you elaborate meals?"

He cuts me a glare. "Don't you dare."

I grin, then finish off my cereal before setting the bowl aside.

"Speaking of people eating your food . . ."

His words are so casual that they aren't, and I'm instantly on edge.

He slurps up the last of his milk, then sets his bowl on his side table before turning to me and continuing.

"Sunnie's still doesn't have a buyer."

I swallow the lump that's sitting in the middle of my throat. I had a feeling that's where this was headed.

I sit up a little more. "Ken, uh, mentioned something earlier this week when I stopped by for fritters."

Ezra cocks his head to the side. "You talked to him about it?"

"I didn't say that. I just said he mentioned it."

It's not entirely a lie. Sure, he brought it up *after* I asked him about it, but still.

As bad as it sounds, I was excited when he said he didn't have a buyer yet.

I've been letting myself do that lately—get excited by dreaming, and it's because of how good it feels to be cooking again. I want to keep doing it. Not just for myself, Ezra, my dad, or the cidery even. I want to keep doing it for the younger me and for the dream she had. And I think I want to keep doing it here in Port Harbor.

Ezra blows out a breath, running his hand through his hair, and I love how messily it lies on his head. "Fuck, Summer. I don't know what to say next. I'm scared you're going to shut down on me."

I frown, but it's a fair thing to say. That's what I've done in the past.

But I'm done shutting down. I'm done running from what I want. Working on the menu, seeing how people are receiving this thing that I built, and falling in love with cooking again . . . it's scary, and I'm absolutely petrified that I'm going to fall flat on my face again, but I *have* to try. I don't think I'll forgive myself if I don't.

"I'm not going to shut down."

He doesn't look up. He just continues picking at the blanket wrapped around him.

"I'm going to the bank tomorrow."

He pauses, holding his breath. Waiting.

"I'm going to ask them about a loan," I continue.

His eyes snap to mine, and I see the hope filling them.

"And I'm going to try to buy Sunnie's for myself."

He doesn't move, not right away, and I think he's waiting for me to say *psych*. But I don't. I mean it. I've been thinking about it a lot, and I can't help but feel like I have to at least try.

When I say nothing, Ezra launches himself at me.

I giggle as he peppers kisses over my face. My nose, my chin, my cheeks, my forehead. Every inch is covered as he slides on top of me, all his good parts lining up with mine.

"Fuck, Sunny. You don't know how happy that makes me."

"Really? Because I'm pretty sure I can feel it," I say, driving my hips up into his very obvious erection.

"To be fair, I'm *always* that kind of happy when it comes to you." He kisses the corner of my mouth, then pulls away, his eyes turning serious. "Are you sure, though? I don't want to pressure you into anything you don't want to do."

"You're not. I've been thinking about it for weeks now. I can't stop, actually. Having my own place has been my dream since I was a kid, and I can't keep denying myself that dream just because I'm scared. I have to try, or I know I'll regret it if I don't. But don't get your hopes up too high. I haven't even been approved for anything, and I don't know if I will be. I have decent savings, but waterfront property is expensive. Who knows if I can even afford it?"

I tell myself it wouldn't be a big deal, but that's a lie. This location is perfect for everything I'm already dreaming up.

Ezra swallows. "I'll help you."

"What?" I laugh. "Don't be ridiculous."

"I'm not. I'm being serious. I'll help you."

"Ezra . . ." I shake my head. "You can't. You . . ."

"Believe in you, Sunny. I believe in you, and I know you can do this. In fact, I have so much fucking faith in you that I want to be your first investor."

Another disbelieving laugh tumbles free. "Come on, Ezra. You can't be serious."

"I am."

"Isn't our *situation* complicated enough?"

It's the first time we've brought it up in a long time, probably too long, but it doesn't mean it's not something I haven't thought about. Especially not with how my heart is starting to war with my head.

"I—" Ezra starts, and he snaps his mouth closed because he doesn't have a good answer for that, and he knows it. He exhales slowly. "Can't you just let me help you?"

"No."

His green eyes narrow. "Stubborn brat."

"You like it."

"I do," he says, nuzzling his nose against mine. "I really fucking do."

Our lips meet in a searing kiss, but that's all we do, despite his noticeable excitement, and there's something so simple in that.

Could we always be like this? Could we make out like we're eighteen again and never get tired of it? Could we have something like this for real?

I . . . I think I want it. Maybe more than I realized, but I do. I want Ezra to come home to me at night, make love to me in the kitchen, then snuggle me in bed at two in the morning. I want laughing until we cry over nothing at all, inside jokes, late-night car rides, and kissing just because we can. I want it all, and I want it with him.

At some point our kiss slows to the point that we're just resting there with our lips against each other, not really moving.

Eventually Ezra rolls off me, and I snuggle against him like I've done so many nights before. His arm goes around me, his fingers grazing over my back in long strokes.

"Summer?"

"Yes, Ezra?"

"I meant it. If the bank says no and you need help, I want to be the person who gives it to you, okay?" His voice is soft, pleading even, and dammit if I don't want to give in.

But I can't. Not when I still don't know just what this is we're doing.

So I settle for "We'll see. Now go to sleep. We have an early day tomorrow."

He hums, accepting my answer for now, and pulls me closer, his fingers still stroking over me.

That familiar warmth that always fills me when we lie like this spreads as I listen to his breathing even out, and sleep begs to take hold.

I'm just about to the point of giving in when I hear the faintest sound.

"Ezra?"

"Hmm?" he says sleepily.

"Do you hear that?"

"What?" He shuffles around, jostling me. "Hear what?"

"I don't know. It sounds like a buzzing."

"It's your phone," he says, squinting over at the device sitting on the dresser.

What? Who could be calling at this hour?

I push the blanket back, and a chill racks through me at the sudden cold. I pad over to the dresser just as my phone goes black again.

Right away, it brightens once more as it shakes against the wood.

PORT HARBOR HOSPITAL

My heart sounds like the drum line at a college football game.

Bumbumbumbumbumbumbumbum.

"Who is it?" I faintly hear Ezra ask, but I don't answer him. I can't.

Shaky fingers wrap around the phone, and I slide my thumb across the bar at the bottom, pressing the device to my ear.

"H-hell . . . o?" The word is so unsteady, I'm surprised I even got it out.

"Is this Summer Turner?"

"Y-yes?"

"Hi, Summer. This is Crystal Andrews with Port Harbor Hospital. Your father is being admitted to the ICU for a heart attack. I—"

I don't hear the rest of it.

Everything goes black.

CHAPTER TWENTY-THREE

Ezra

I have never broken more speeding laws in my life, and considering my track record, that's saying something.

My tires squeal as I take off from the red light I hated to stop at.

Summer sits beside me in the Porsche, her hands folded tightly in her lap as she stares out at the dark road.

Other than muttering "dad" and "hospital," she hasn't said anything since the call, and that scares the shit out of me on a level I hadn't realized I was ever able to reach.

Seeing her break the way she did . . . going catatonic, essentially . . . fuck, it wrecked me.

I never want to see her like that again. I can't. I'm not sure I could survive it.

I still don't know exactly what's going on, but whatever it is, it's bad. It's why I had to help her back into the dress I had impatiently taken off her just hours earlier, put her shoes on her, and lead her to the car. I even had to buckle her in, tears rolling down her cheeks as she refused to look at me.

When I finally pull up to the hospital, I park right in front of the entrance.

"Sir," the security guard says as I help Summer from the car. "You can't park here, sir. This is a loading and unloading zone only."

"Then tow it!" I tell them, tossing them the keys over my shoulder as I trail behind Summer as she practically sprints through the sliding glass doors.

Her sneakers squeak against the floor as she skids to a stop at the front counter. I barely keep myself from running into her. My hip aches, but it's the last thing I'm focusing on right now. This is all about her.

"Daniel Turner."

The woman sitting behind the counter raises one perfectly shaped brow. "Is that your name or the person you're looking for?"

"Yes. Wait, no. Yes. I—I—I—" She huffs. "I don't have time for this!"

Oh fuck. She's losing it.

I step up behind her, placing my hand on the small of her back. She leans into the touch for only a moment before jerking away, almost like she's catching herself doing something she shouldn't be doing.

I pretend I don't notice as I turn to the receptionist. My eyes flash to her name tag.

"Good morning, Drea." She smiles at me, and I know right away she's more likely to listen to me than to Summer. "We're looking for Daniel Turner. *Sheriff* Turner."

"And you are?"

"I'm Ezra. Rawlings. This is Summer, his daughter."

"You're his daughter?" the receptionist asks Summer.

She nods, her lips trembling as she holds back tears.

I fight the urge to reach out to her, to make sure she's okay. "We received a call that Daniel was admitted here. Can you help us sort out where he is, Drea?"

"All right. Let me see." Her nails clack against her keyboard, her eyes flying over the screen. "Right. He's still in surgery."

"Surgery?!" Summer shrieks.

"Yes, and that's all I can tell you for now. You'll need to wait for his doctor for more information." She points down the hall. "There's a waiting room around the corner. We have coffee and vending machines in case you get hungry."

She looks back at her computer, dismissing us, and I know if I don't get Summer out of here soon, she might explode.

"Come on," I say to her, tugging on her arm. "Let's go sit. Hopefully his doctor will be out soon."

Summer glares at Drea, and I almost feel bad for her. But I'm too busy being worried about Summer to truly care.

We make our way to the waiting room, and the first thing I notice is the quietness. It's almost eerie. There are several people spread around and plenty of empty seats. We take two near the back.

For a while we just sit there. Summer stares at nothing in particular, and I stare at her.

The urge to reach over and hold her is so fucking strong, but I don't. I'm not sure what she needs right now, but I'm waiting for her to tell me.

"Do you want anything to drink?" I ask her after thirty minutes have gone by.

She shakes her head.

I rise from the chair and make my way to the vending machine and pay far too much for a bottle of water. When I peek back over at her, she's still staring blankly, and I can only imagine the thoughts racing through her mind. I'm sure they're the same going through mine.

Is her father going to be okay? Will he survive this? Will he ever be the same if he does? How fucking long is this surgery going to take?

I grab the water from the dispenser, crack it open, and gulp it down. I refill it from the water fountain, then resume my spot next to Summer.

She moves for the first time since sitting down, and it's to slump back in her seat.

She's tired and defeated, and I don't blame her one bit.

Her head falls into her hands, and I know instantly she's crying. Her shoulders shake, her little whimpers ringing in my ears, and it fucking hurts. Seeing her like this, going through this. It's literally making my chest ache.

I press on it, trying to suppress the feelings, but it's useless.

So, instead, I turn to her and rub her back.

"He'll be okay," I say softly. "He's Sheriff Turner, for crying out loud. There's no way he won't be all right. Besides, if he's not okay, then who the hell is going to yell at me for speeding, huh?"

"Deputy Jenkins."

"Fucking Jenkins."

She laughs lightly, but it turns into more sobs just as quickly as it comes, and I have to close my eyes. Seeing her like this is too hard.

She eventually falls over into me, her head practically in my lap. I let her stay like that, running my fingers through her hair, wanting so desperately to wipe away her tears, but I don't.

One hour goes by, then two.

From the window, I can see that the sun is beginning to peek through the Cascades. The colors streaking through the sky are objectively gorgeous, but nothing feels pretty in this moment. Not with Summer lying in my lap, her heart breaking into tinier pieces by the second.

We're nearing three hours when a new face finally steps through the doors.

I look up immediately, but Summer stays where she is. I feel her slipping, losing hope, and I wish I could give her all of mine.

"Summer Rawlings?"

My heart stutters, doing a goddamn somersault right in my chest cavity.

Fuck, that sounds good. Too good.

"That's me."

She rises to her feet, pushing her bangs out of her puffy eyes. I follow behind her, pain shooting from my hip into my groin. It's fucking electric, and I grit my teeth against it.

"Well, sort of. It's Turner. Summer Turner. Is my dad okay?"

The doctor gives us a warm smile. "Hi, Summer. I'm Dr. Swift. Your father is doing just fine. The surgery to remove the blockage in his heart was successful, and he's currently in a room resting."

Summer exhales, her shoulders relaxing marginally.

"What happened? I thought he was okay. He was on meds, and he was eating better and—"

"Hey, hey," Dr. Swift says. "Let's tackle one question at a time, okay?"

Summer nods, wringing her hands together in front of her. "Okay. All right. I just . . ."

"I know. This is hard. I get that. It's all very overwhelming." The doctor sighs. "First of all, we don't know why it happened. Sometimes it just does, even with proper medication. It could have been a number of things, or it could have been nothing at all. All we know is that the blockage is gone. He's breathing on his own, and his vitals are stable. He's sleeping, and right now that's what we want. His body is tired. Mine would be, too, after going through all that. We're going to let him get some sleep, and we'll run more tests and develop an action plan when he wakes up. Sound good?"

Summer nods, her bottom lip trembling as she fights the tears that are teetering on the edge of her brown eyes. "Sounds good." She sniffles. "Can I . . . Can I see him?"

"Of course you can. Just remember—rest."

We both nod, then trail behind her as she leads us through some double doors around the corner.

Summer stares ahead the entire time, and while I'm dying to reach out and touch her, I shove my hands into the pockets of my joggers instead. She needs space, and I need to respect that, no matter how badly it's killing me not to be there for her.

"This is it," Dr. Swift says as we stop in front of what looks to be a private room. "Before we go in, I do want to warn you that he looks a bit pale. But he's just undergone surgery, so that's not surprising. Just try to remember that it won't last, okay? I'm sure he'll get his color back within a day or two."

Summer takes an encouraging breath, then nods.

The doctor pushes open the door, then steps aside to let us pass, and my heart leaps into my throat at the sight before me.

I don't know Daniel Turner well, but he's always been this larger-than-life presence, even though I have a few inches on him. It's never mattered. He's a figure in this town. Hell, he's *the* figure.

But right now he looks small. Tiny, even. He's lying in the middle of the hospital bed, machines surrounding him, and he looks frail. Weak.

How could I ever think I was weak when I never looked anything like this? I might have lost my career, but I still have my life. I still have time. I still have so much fucking future ahead of me.

I can't believe I spent all those years being angry when I could have been living.

I could have been loving.

I look over to Summer just in time to see her face crumple.

"I didn't see it," she whispers, staring at her father, tears brimming in her eyes. "I didn't see it. He said he was okay, and I let it go when I should have known better. I let him suffer. I let him . . . I let this happen." The tears spill over, her shoulders hunching inward. "I did this."

I trail my fingers over her back. "Summer, you didn't. You—"

She lurches away, and it's cutting right down to my fucking core. Especially when she looks at me like she's done.

"No, stop." Her face is hard, unlike anything I've ever seen. "You don't understand, Ezra. I did this because I haven't been paying attention. Because I've been . . . I've been distracted. I haven't been home enough. I've been focused on everything else. Because . . . because I went and fell in love with the one guy who isn't capable of loving me back."

Her words nearly knock me over.

Summer . . . loves me? How? When?

"I wasted all my time here on things that weren't important. I should have been there for him. I should have seen it, and I didn't. I failed as a chef, and I failed as a daughter. That's all I'll ever be—a failure. A fraud. An absolute fucking disappointment."

I want to scream at her. I want to tell her how wrong she is. She's none of those things. She never fucking was.

She sucks in a deep breath.

"You should go, Ezra." Her words are like a slap to the face, even though I know she doesn't mean them. "I'm sure there's plenty to be done around the cidery for the wedding."

How could I possibly leave knowing she's here hurting? That she's sitting here chewing on those gorgeous lips I love so much, waiting for the worst news? How could I ever leave her?

I can't.

So I don't.

I interlock my hand with hers, squeeze it tightly, and wait.

She's trying to push me away, and I'll be damned if I'm going to let her.

◆ ◆ ◆

Daniel wakes up mid-Saturday, and Summer bursts into tears instantly.

I step out of the room to give them privacy, and when I come back, they're both asleep again.

I stay the rest of the day and night, my hip shrieking over me sleeping in the world's most uncomfortable chair. It's happy for the break when I go home for a few hours to shower and change on Sunday.

As I'm headed back to the hospital, I hook a left instead of a right and go to Summer's, using the code she gave me when she was sick. I grab her a change of clothes, the book sitting on her bedside table, a phone charger, and her tablet, just in case.

A little bit later I walk through the double doors of the main hospital entrance, a duffel bag of clothes slung over one shoulder and a paper sack full of food in the other hand.

The receptionist waves at me as I pass, and not a single nurse stops me as I waltz through the ICU back to the room where Daniel is.

Summer does a double take when I enter.

"You're back?" she asks, her eyes falling to the bag from Dickie's Gourmet Burgers I have in my hand.

"I'm back."

I hand it over, then set her duffel beside her on the floor before folding myself back into the uncomfortable chair.

I stay there that night too.

On Monday, I convince Summer to go home and shower.

She's resistant at first, but when her dad chimes in about how bad she smells, she heeds my instructions and goes.

I hand her my Porsche keys—which they didn't tow, thank fuck—and I take her spot next to her father.

We sit in silence for a long time. Daniel still drifts in and out of sleep because, apparently, a heart attack at his age really takes it out of you, and I scroll through the emails on my phone. The cidery is buzzing with the upcoming wedding this weekend, and my staff— and Noah—are keeping me informed every step of the way.

"Did I ever tell you I used to be a fan of yours back in your playing days?"

I look over at Daniel, who is staring at me from his bed, still looking far too pale. "No, but I knew it anyway."

"How?"

I shrug. "You never gave me a ticket before."

He laughs. "Yeah, that's fair." He closes his eyes once more, exhaling heavily, like even just this short conversation has worn him out. "I'm still a fan, you know."

"Even with my lead foot?"

"Even with that. My daughter is a fan too. She's having a hard time with this, but she's glad you're here. *I'm* glad you're here."

I'm glad I'm here too, I want to say back, but I don't.

These last few days, being next to Summer like I've been and not being able to touch her, hold her, or tell her that I love her, too, has just about killed me.

Because, yeah, despite trying at every turn not to, I've done the dumbest thing I've ever done before—I've fallen in love with her, and I'm not about to let her give up on us before we've even really started.

My thoughts spin into overdrive, and Daniel's snores fill the room.

I stay the night again.

CHAPTER TWENTY-FOUR

Summer

Ezra has been with me every day for a week, and I'm not sure whether I'm touched or irritated by it.

He is the one who said he didn't do relationships. *He* is the one who said he didn't do love.

This certainly feels like both.

Dad is home, and the only reason Ezra isn't here right now is that I finally forced him out last night.

I couldn't take another moment of his longing looks or his sad eyes, mainly because they were working.

I love him—*of course* I love him—and deep down I'm glad he's been right by my side through all of this. I'm not sure I could have survived it otherwise.

But he's also a reminder of just how badly I fucked this whole thing up.

I should have called my father's doctor the second he mentioned heartburn. Maybe it wouldn't have gotten so bad that he had a heart attack at his desk.

He was alone.

That part gutted me when I found out. I cried for two hours straight until I couldn't cry anymore.

It was Deputy Jenkins—*thank you, Jenkins*—who found him just a minute or two later. They performed CPR on him until the ambulance arrived, where they stabilized him and rushed him to the hospital.

I was eating cereal. I was giggling. I was fucking making out with my situationship.

What kind of person does that make me? What kind of daughter? I moved back here for him, and I've been so wrapped up in someone else that I let his health get to the point of major surgery and a multiday hospital stay.

I've let everyone down, including my biggest cheerleader and the man who has been the only family I have had since I was eight.

I'm not going to let anything distract me again. Not Ezra, not Stick Taps, and certainly not some romanticized idea of opening my own restaurant.

Odette was beyond understanding when I told her I wouldn't be able to make it to her wedding. She didn't even mention how it would ruin the symmetry of the table if Ezra didn't have a date.

And we're swimming in flowers to the point that I had to tell the ladies down at the flower shop to start donating every order that comes through. Our fridge is exploding with casseroles, and our counters are overflowing with baked goods. I eventually had to put a sign on the door and had the powers that be blast it out to the citywide newsletter that we cannot accept any more visitors.

It's safe to say that if my father chooses to continue his campaign for reelection as sheriff, he won't have any trouble getting Port Harbor to rally behind him.

Selfishly, I hope he doesn't. I hope he retires and settles down. We still don't know what caused the blockage, but I doubt the stresses of his job helped.

"How are you doing? Do you need anything?"

My father sighs from his favorite recliner, then points the remote at the TV, muting it. "I love you, kiddo, but if you ask me those questions—or any variation, for that matter—again, I might have to kick you out on the curb."

I grimace. Shit. I guess I have been asking him those same questions over and over.

"I'm sorry, Dad. I'm just worried about you. You did just have a heart attack, after all."

"I am well aware of what happened and how serious it was, Summer. But I'm okay. I am going to continue to be okay. I have a great team taking care of me at the hospital, so you can stop fretting over me every second of the day."

I sigh, then nod.

"Besides, don't you have a wedding to be at?"

"I'm not going."

"Why the hell not?"

I point to his heart. "Uh, hello?"

"Well, I'm not having a heart attack *right now*. And I don't plan to have one tonight either, so go. Have fun for both of us. Maybe bring me home a slice of cake."

I roll my eyes. "Just hush and turn the TV back on. I'm happy where I'm at."

Truthfully, I am bummed to be missing the wedding. I was looking forward to it. I wanted to see Odette in her gown. I wanted to see Noah cry as he watched her walk down the aisle. Ezra and I even had a bet placed on it. I want to see Izzy, too, since it's been so many years, and meet her French boyfriend.

But most of all . . . most of all, I wanted to dance with Ezra.

I know he said he didn't dance, but I have no doubt I could have convinced him to do it.

My heart tugs at the thought of him being there alone. Is he sitting there with that perpetual frown lining his face? Is he slinging back too many ciders? Or is he having a great time, a break from all my moping?

I don't know, and I guess I won't.

I wiggle down on the couch, pulling my blanket higher and getting comfy for a night in.

My eyes grow heavy, my breaths begin to slow, and I'm just about asleep when a loud noise wakes me up.

I look over at my father, who is wide awake.

He shrugs. "Don't look at me. I wasn't the one who rang the doorbell."

With a groan, I throw the cover off and push my feet into my slippers before heading for the front door.

"This had better not be another well-wisher," I mutter. "Can't they read the sign?"

I yank open the door, ready to tell whoever it is to get lost, but all the words get stuck in my throat.

Because standing on my front porch is Ezra—and he's wearing a tux.

He looks like a vision. An absolute dream come true, and maybe he is.

I love you.

The three words echo in my head, and I want to say them so badly, but I can't. Not when my ailing father is right in the other room, proving to me that I don't deserve this. Not when I failed him like I did.

"What are you . . ." I clear my throat. "What are you doing here?"

"Not doing a promposal, whatever the fuck those are," he says. His lips twitch just ever so slightly, and then he tucks his hands into his pockets. "I'm, uh, here to pick you up for the wedding."

I narrow my eyes. "I'm not going to the wedding. I already talked to Odette about it."

"Right." He nods. "But see, I *also* talked to Odette about it, and she wants you there."

"Ezra, I—"

"And Noah and Izzy and the entire town. We all want you there."

"You talked to the entire town?"

He scrapes his shoe against the top step. "Well, it wasn't the entire town, but the point is the same—the people want to see you."

I sigh. "As sweet as that is, I can't leave. I—"

"Can. You can leave."

I turn to find my father walking slowly toward us, leaning on his cane for support.

"Dad." I rush to this side. "What are you doing up?"

He waves me away. "I'm fine. Been walking on my own for longer than you've been alive."

"But that was *before* the heart attack, remember?"

"Did you say fart attack?"

I scowl at him. "Dad."

"Summer."

We stare at each other in a heated standoff.

He's the one to cave first.

"Just like Ezra talked to Odette, I also talked to Ezra. That's why he's here. He's taking you to the wedding because I want you to go. I *need* you to go. I love you to death, but I need a few minutes alone. You've been up my ass—which I appreciate, by the way—since the surgery, and sometimes a man just needs a minute to breathe, you know? So go. Go to the wedding. Have fun. Take the night off. Get wasted." He gives Ezra a look. "But no drinking and driving."

Ezra holds his hands up innocently. "Wouldn't dream of it, sir."

"Good." Dad looks at me again. "Please, Summer. Do this for me, will you? We need someone there to represent the family. Might as well be you. I don't know if you remember this, but I did just have a heart attack. I'm not much in the mood for dancing."

He winks at me, and I want to scream and cry and throw my arms around his neck and tell him how much I love him.

Instead, I settle for a peck on the cheek. "All right. I'll go. I just . . . shit," I mutter. "I was going to curl my hair and wear a dress and . . . and . . . I don't have time. The wedding starts soon."

"You have time," Ezra says. "And I'll help."

"What? How are you going to help?"

"I don't know?" He shrugs. "I'll . . . I'll . . . I'll curl your hair while you do your makeup."

I lift my brows. "You know how to curl hair?"

"No, but it can't be that hard to figure out, right?"

My dad whistles lowly. "Oh boy. Don't know what you got yourself into with that one." He points to the recliner with his cane. "I'll just be over here."

Ezra curling my hair sounds so ridiculous that I have to see it.

"Fine," I relent. "Follow me."

He closes the front door behind him, and I notice he leaves a wide berth behind me as we make our way farther into the house.

I tell myself it's for the best, even though it doesn't *feel* like it is.

I grab my makeup kit and curling iron from under the sink and take them both to the vanity in my bedroom.

I usually just wear lipstick and maybe a few swipes of mascara if I'm feeling it, but a wedding definitely calls for a full face.

I plug the curling iron in and let it heat up. Then I settle onto the stool in front of the mirror.

Ezra sits on my bed, looking comically big, and I begin my routine, pretending he isn't there as I spritz my hair with heat protector.

It's pointless, though. I can feel his eyes on me with every move I make. It's distracting, and I put way too much primer on, but I push through.

After a few minutes he stands and settles behind me.

I try to keep my head as still as possible as he grabs a chunk of my hair.

It's ridiculous. He's just touching my hair. But I swear he's touching every part of me. It's been too long since I've been in his bed, since I've felt his arms around me, since I've had his lips on mine.

I miss it. I miss *him*.

His brows furrow as he tries to figure out how it works. It's cute. *He's* cute, especially in that tux that fits him like a dream.

When he sorts it out, he wraps the hair around the barrel and squeezes tightly.

I laugh. "You don't have to hold it so hard. You'll give me creases."

"Shit. Sorry." He drops the level, quickly pulling away. "Ow! Fuck!"

"Are you okay?" I ask as he sucks his finger into his mouth. "Let me see."

"I'm fine," he says, pulling his hand away when I try to reach for it.

The gesture stings, but it's only fair. I've done the same to him all week.

I turn back around, resuming my routine, and he gets the hang of it fairly quickly.

"How have you been?" he asks when we're about halfway done.

My first instinct is to say, *You've been with me all week, you know how I've been.* But that wouldn't be fair. While Ezra has been there, I haven't. Not really.

"I'm okay."

His green eyes, which always make me feel like I'm the only person in the room, narrow for only a moment before he nods.

"Your dad seems like he's better, even just since last night."

I smile. "He is, I think. Or at least I hope."

"He's going to be okay, you know. He's strong. And so are you."

He says the last part quietly, but it feels loud, and that's probably because I needed to hear it more than I knew.

"There," he says after a few more wraps around the curling iron. "I think I'm done."

I look at his work. It's not perfect by any stretch of the imagination, but it'll do with the time crunch we're on.

"Thank you," I tell him.

He nods, then resumes his spot on my bed as I finish my makeup.

When I'm done, I go to the dress I have hanging on my closet door.

I don't bother asking him to turn away or go into the bathroom as I strip off my pajamas. He's already seen every part of me. Has touched every inch. What do I have to hide now?

I feel Ezra's eyes on me as I grab the silky dress—a burnt-orange midi—and step into it. There's a zipper, and there's no way I'm going to be able to get it up myself.

"Can you?" I ask, peeking over my shoulder.

Ezra crosses the room to me, his steps determined and even. His knuckle grazes across my back, and it sends a shiver down my spine.

"Sorry," he mutters, but I'm not.

It's the most alive I've felt in days.

He steps away the second he runs out of track, putting a healthy distance between us again, and I release the breath I was holding since he stepped up behind me.

After sliding on my shoes, I turn, running my hands down the front. The material is cool and soft against my skin, but it's not what causes the goose bumps to break out over my arms. It's his stare, the way he's taking me in like he's looking at me for the first time.

"Well?" I ask when he doesn't say anything.

He swallows once, then twice.

Finally, he says, "You're a fucking vision, Sunny."

My cheeks flush, and my body ignites for the first time since I got the phone call about my father.

He holds his hand out to me. "Shall we?"

And I place my palm in his.

◆ ◆ ◆

Noah and Odette are officially husband and wife, and I don't think I've seen two people look more in love than they do.

The ceremony was beautiful, and I'm so glad I opted for waterproof mascara, because it was a necessity after those vows.

Now we're all seated in the recently renovated barn on the Stick Taps property, and the cider is flowing. The food is great, but it could use a few tweaks to become incredible, and the people are just what I needed.

I think I've spoken to every person here, and they've all inquired about my father. It's been emotional, and I've had to excuse myself more than once.

The whole time, Ezra's stood by my side. Quietly, most of the time, but just knowing he's there has made leaving my father behind a little easier.

Well, that and the texts he's been sending every half hour.

Dad: Still alive.

Dad: No heart attacks yet.

Dad: Yep. You guessed it. I'm alive.

Dad: This is not a ghost texting you.

He's lucky he's not here, because I'd yell at him for that last one.

"Summer!" Izzy calls out, and I grin over at her. "Have I told you how incredible you look?"

Only five times. I'm pretty sure she's had a few too many ciders, but it's cute. She's clearly happy for her brother and best friend.

"Ezra, doesn't she look hot?"

"She always looks hot," he says, and I don't have to look at him to know his eyes are on me. I feel it. I have all night.

"Well, if you think she's so hot, ask her to dance."

"He doesn't dance," I say automatically.

"He can. If you want to, he can."

I turn to Ezra. "Really?"

"Yes." He stands, towering over me, and holds his hand out.

For the second time tonight, I take it.

I shouldn't. I know that. I should be putting distance between us, because this can't continue. I mean, I told him I loved him last week, and he never said anything about it. That has to mean he doesn't feel the same, right? That I've been imagining that this thing between us could be more?

I can't keep putting myself out there. I don't have anything left to give, not after this week.

Ezra leads us to the dance floor, and "The Way You Look Tonight" begins to play.

"I love this song," he says as he draws me into his arms, and I fall against him like it's where I belong.

"I didn't take you for a Sinatra kind of guy. He's a bit sappy for you, no?"

"Maybe. But remember when I said I have flashes of what my life was like with my parents?"

I falter in my steps, but if Ezra notices, he doesn't say. He just holds me close, getting me back on track.

"Them dancing to this song is one of them," he continues. "They'd put a record on long after I'd already gone to bed and sway in the kitchen. They thought they were being quiet, but they weren't. I'd hear them from time to time and tiptoe out to the hallway to watch them. It's stuck with me all these years."

Tears spring to my eyes.

How can someone who witnessed that not believe in love? How can he not want that too?

His hand tightens on my back, pulling me closer.

"I'm glad you came tonight," he says into my ear. "And I'm glad you came with me."

I can't. I can't do this.

I can't listen to him say sweet words into my ear, not when I feel the way I do about him and not when he can't give me more.

So I run.

"Summer!" he calls after me, but I don't stop.

I keep going. I need air. I need to not be inside. I need to not be in his arms. Not when he's looking at me like he is.

"Summer!"

I push through the crowd, undoubtedly drawing attention, but I don't stop. I can't.

The cool new autumn air slides over me, and I gulp in breath after breath as I rush as far away from the people and noise as I can.

I just need a minute. I need to think. I need to be alone. I need—

"Summer, please!"

I carry on.

"Fuck, I love you!"

I stop.

But I don't turn around. I can't. Because if I do, I'm going to give in to him, and I can't do that.

"I know I said I didn't believe in it—and maybe I still don't—but I believe in you. I believe in this . . . in us. It's real, and what I feel for you is really fucking real. Being close to you this week but not being able to touch you . . . it killed me. I feel like I'm dying, and I'm not ready to. I'm not ready because I want so many more years with you. I *need* so many more. Just like I need you. You . . ." I hear him suck in deep breaths. "You make me feel whole again. You make me feel like I did when I was still playing. You give me purpose. You give me strength. Fuck, you make me feel like I matter, and I haven't felt like that in a long damn time. I love you, Sunny. And I don't want you to push me away. I don't want you to shut me out. I just . . . I love you."

My vision blurs on the edges, and I worry I might pass out for a moment. I realize it's because I haven't taken a breath—not a real one—since he started talking.

I don't use my words lightly. I don't say things I don't mean.

That's what Ezra said to me once, and I believed him then.

I believe him now too.

I turn to him, and the second I do, I can see it in his eyes, the ones that are begging me to say something. The ones that are pleading with me to trust in him.

And I do.

Ezra loves me.

I take a step toward him, then another.

He meets me in the middle, and though I can tell he wants to reach out to me, he doesn't.

He stands two feet away, his stare boring into me.

"Sunny?" he says after a few quiet moments.

I let out a shaky breath. "I told myself when I came here that I was just coming here for my father. That was it. Then you happened. You walked into that police station, and you irritated the hell out of me. You also called me on my shit. You pushed me when I needed it the most. And you were so unapologetic about it, and I respected that. I respected you. I . . . loved you. I *still* love you."

His entire face lights up, just like it does when he's on the ice or when he's speeding down Harborview Boulevard. "Yeah?"

I smile. "Yeah. And I'm sorry I've pushed you away this past week. I—"

"No, don't apologize. You don't have to."

"I do," I tell him. "You need to hear this."

I inhale slowly, then exhale.

Then I do it again.

"I was scared," I say simply. "I saw my dad lying there in the hospital bed, and I thought, *This is my fault.* I came back to Port Harbor for him, to take care of him. But I also came back because of what happened in Chicago. They blacklisted me there. Did you know that? I was running the kitchen at Lore, and I couldn't handle the pressure. I . . . I couldn't take it."

The words leave me in a rush, and once they're out, I realize just how badly I needed to say them. To come to terms with what I did and try to move on.

I'm ready to do just that.

"It's okay, Summer. It happens."

"It wasn't, though. Okay, I mean. I blew up. I freaked out on everyone. It was *bad*. There were videos of it circulating in the industry, and I was ousted before I even made it home that night. I will never be able to work in Chicago again, maybe anywhere other than Port Harbor, for that matter. I know you know what it's like to lose your dream, but that wasn't your fault. You had no control over it. But *me?*" I point at my chest—aching for what I lost, and what I hope to recover. "*I'm* the one who burned mine right before my own eyes. *I'm* the one who threw it all away because I was having a bad week. So, when I came out here, I promised myself that I was done. I wouldn't try again. I had my shot, and I wasted it. I was moving on, and I was going to focus on my father." I sigh. "But then Stick Taps happened. *You* happened. And all those promises fell by the wayside. I don't regret it, but I did at first. When I saw my father, I did. But how can I regret something that feels so good? So right?" I shake my head. "I can't. So I'm sorry. I'm sorry I tried to push you away. I'm sorry that I tried to run again. But I am not and cannot be sorry that I love you."

I take a step toward him.

"I'm still scared, but I'm willing to try if you are."

He doesn't say anything for a long time. He just stares at me, and try as I might to read his gaze, I can't.

My fingers begin to itch, and everything in me starts to buzz in a way it hasn't since I was standing in the kitchen at Lore, knowing I ruined everything.

Did I ruin everything here too?

Then finally, he speaks.

"Can I kiss you now?"

A laugh bubbles out of me, relief flooding every inch of me. "Yeah, Ezra, you can kiss me now."

He hauls me into his arms with lightning-quick speed, and his mouth crashes to mine in a kiss that I can feel in my toes.

And it feels like coming home.

It feels like every piece of me that broke off over the last week is coming crawling back and sliding into place.

I'm not sure how long we kiss, but it's so long that I'm not sure who is holding up who anymore.

"I'm scared too," he says when we finally pull apart. "I have been since I saw you sitting at that metal table, looking smug. I knew even then that you were going to rock my world. I just didn't know how. But now that we're here . . . fuck, I don't know. I can't picture it any other way. This is it for me. *You're* it for me, Summer. I'm yours."

I grin. "It was my brattiness that did it, wasn't it?"

"And the apron helped too."

I laugh, then pull him back in for another kiss.

"I love you," he says against my lips.

"I love you, too, Ezra. Thank you for not giving up on me."

"Never."

I know deep in my bones that he means it completely, and I'm never going to take that for granted again.

"Want to dance?" he asks.

"With you? Always."

"Always sounds good to me, Sunny."

He takes my hand and leads me back inside, where I spend the rest of the night in his arms, then his bed.

Something tells me that no matter what, we're going to be okay.

And maybe even forever.

EPILOGUE

Ezra

"Can we please be done with weddings now?"

"What? You're not having yours on the property too?" Noah jams his elbow into my ribs with a grin. *"Mr. Engaged."*

I roll my eyes. He's been calling me that for weeks now, ever since I proposed to Summer.

We were walking along Harborview Boulevard, and it just hit me out of nowhere—I wanted to marry her.

Maybe it was the way the mountains looked against the sunset-colored sky, or perhaps it was just that I'm so in love with her that I can barely keep my hands to myself. Whatever it was, I knew. I had already planned on spending the rest of my life with her, but I wanted it to be official. I wanted her to be *mine* in every sense of the word.

I spent the next two weeks looking at rings until I found the perfect one—a brown pear-cut diamond encrusted by several smaller white diamonds—and then I set the plan in motion. I would cook her dinner, then afterward we'd take a late-night drive to do some stargazing, and I'd ask her there.

None of that happened.

I came home to find her in my kitchen in the tiniest pair of shorts, a cropped tee, and an apron. One look at her and all my plans went to shit.

We didn't make it out of the kitchen for another hour, and I had my dinner on the countertop. Later, we snuggled in bed with our cereal instead of going for a drive, and at nearly 2:00 a.m., I reached over to the side table drawer, pulled out the ring, and asked her—milk dribbling down her chin and all.

Sometimes I wish I could have waited and made it more romantic, but it just felt so *us*. And based on the way Summer is showing off her ring to literally everyone tonight and gushing over the story, I think it's safe to say she feels the same.

"I don't know where we're getting married. We haven't discussed details yet."

"But you're hiring Odette as your planner, right?" Noah's eyes narrow threateningly.

I chuckle, clapping him on the shoulder. "Yes, your wife will be our wedding planner, even if she is the most obnoxious little sister I never had."

"She's not obnoxious. She's perfect."

His eyes track her from across the room. She stands in a circle along with Izzy and Summer. They're all giggling and sipping on champagne.

"I can't believe my sister is married," Noah says, a grin plastered across his face as he watches them too. "I can't believe *I'm* married and have been for two years now." He laughs. "If younger versions of us could see where we're at now, they'd flip."

"Maybe. Or they'd just be really damn happy for us."

"Shit, Ez. That was kind of romantic."

I glower at him. "Don't you ever say that again. I'll punch you."

"You boys wouldn't be causing trouble over here, would you?"

We both turn to find Daniel Turner sipping on a glass of what looks to be punch.

"No, sir. I mean *Sheriff Turner*. I mean *sir*." Noah stumbles over his words, and it's comical to watch him squirm. "We never cause trouble."

"Mm-hmm, sure you don't," the older man says, his eyes falling to slits as he looks at me.

I certainly cause trouble. While I don't speed nearly as much as I used to, I've still been pulled over five times in the last few years. I'm pretty sure if I didn't make his daughter so damn happy, I wouldn't have a driver's license at this point.

"And it's just Daniel now," he reminds Noah.

"Sorry. I know you're retired now, but it's a tough habit to break."

For a split second, he looks pained when Noah says *retired*, but it disappears as quickly as it came on.

After the heart attack, I think everyone expected Daniel to withdraw from the race for sheriff, even with all the well-wishes. He didn't. He won and served for another six months before announcing that he was stepping down to focus on his health.

I know a lot of that had to do with Summer deciding to stick around Port Harbor.

"Dad!"

Speaking of Summer . . .

"Dance with me," she says, more than a little tipsy on all the champagne that's flowing.

He rolls his eyes but heeds his daughter's request.

She tosses me a wink as he leads her out onto the dance floor, and I watch as he twirls her around.

It's sweet, and since Summer and I have been together, I've been privileged to witness many moments like this between them. Their bond is special, and his unwavering support is a big reason Summer kept going when the sale of Sunnie's fell through the first time.

Summer was devastated, though she didn't want to show it. She was so close to getting her dream—it was right there within her reach—and it was ripped away, all because the bank wouldn't back her without a cosigner.

I jumped in, ready to help her, but she refused me at every turn.

Ultimately, it was Daniel who stepped up and made it happen.

While they're technically co-owners of Sunnie's, he's only around to make repairs and run errands whenever a supplier inevitably screws up. Otherwise, the place is all Summer's, and I couldn't be prouder of her.

"Ezra!" Daniel calls, waving me over. "Come take over, son!"

Son.

That's something he's taken to calling me lately, and I can't deny that warmth fills my chest every time I hear it. Sure, I have my uncle who raised me since my parents passed, but this feels different, like Daniel's *choosing* me.

I like being chosen.

"Duty calls," I say to Noah, patting him on the back before pushing my way onto the dance floor.

Before, you couldn't have paid me to do this. I would have made up a reason to say no or use my hip as an excuse not to, but that's no longer the case. Now I can't imagine anything better than leading Summer around to some sappy love song, showing her off to everyone. Even when my hip pinches as I step onto the floor, I don't mind it. I'll take all the pain if it means having her in my arms.

I grin when Summer spots me, and not just because she's already smiling back at me.

No, it's because her eyes light up like they do every time I see her.

She loves me. She's *in* love with me. And I've never been fucking happier in my life.

"Thanks," Daniel says, then kisses his daughter on the cheek before hurrying away.

"Hey!" she shouts over the music.

"Hey, Sunny," I say back.

Then I swoop her into my arms, and she comes to me easily, like we've done this before. We have. So many times, and I'll never tire of it.

"I feel like I haven't seen you all night," she says with a pout.

"I've been around. Watching you."

"I know. I can feel it."

"Just like you're feeling the champagne?"

She giggles, then shrugs. "I'm letting loose. That's what you said to do, wasn't it?"

It was. Ever since Sunnie's opened back up with Summer as the owner, she's been working nonstop. I get it. I was the same way after we got Stick Taps up and running, and the iceplex too. Hell, for the following years as well. Which is how I know she'll burn herself out if she keeps going at the rate she is. If she's not running around the kitchen in our home, she's dashing around the one at the restaurant.

She needs a break. Part of me says that because I miss her, but the other part says it because I need her to realize this is a marathon, not a sprint, and that her dream isn't going anywhere. It's right here, right now. It's happening, and it's okay if she lives in the moment a bit.

"It is. Guess I'm just shocked you're actually listening to me. You're usually far too obstinate to do so."

"You like it when I'm stubborn."

"I just like you, Sunny."

She grins, twining her arms around my neck. "Yeah?"

"Yeah."

She nuzzles her nose against mine. "Well, I more than like you, *fiancé*."

"Is that so?"

"Yep. Which is why I can't wait to marry you. Did I tell you that? That I want to get married sooner rather than later?"

"No, you haven't mentioned it."

"I do. I think we should elope. Let's leave the country and go somewhere beautiful and say our vows. Just us."

I laugh, hugging her closer. "I'm pretty sure Sheriff Turner might murder me if we did that."

Her nose wrinkles. "Yeah, maybe. But you could totally take him."

"Are you encouraging me to fight your father, Sunny?"

"Maybe." Another giggle escapes, this time with a little hiccup following behind it. "I think I'm drunk."

"You most definitely are," I agree.

"You must be drunk, too, if you're dancing with me."

"We stopped dancing minutes ago. That's just the room spinning."

"Is not," she argues, because *of course* she does.

"Is too." I press a quick kiss to her lips because I can't help myself. "Now, tell me more about how you want to run away and marry me."

She sighs happily. "I don't care where we get married, honestly. It could be in the gas station parking lot. I just want to marry you. I want to be Summer Rawlings."

A low hum of approval moves through me at the sound of that. "I want you to be Summer Rawlings too. But with a proper wedding, so your dad doesn't bury me six feet under before we can say *I do*, yeah?"

"Ugh. Fine. You win."

"I always win."

"You do not. I just let you think you do because I like how cocky you get."

I bark out a laugh. "Is that so?"

"Yep. I'm just nice like that."

"You're something, you know that?"

"I know." She smiles. "But you like my something."

"I *love* your something." I press a kiss to the corner of her lips. "I love *you*."

She sighs. "I love you, too, Ezra. Pretty sure I have since you first saw me in those handcuffs."

I dip my head closer, my lips ghosting over her ear. "Did I ever tell you how much I liked that look on you? Been thinking we should re-create that."

"Ezra!" She pulls away, blushing. "Not now."

"But later?" I quirk my brow.

She giggles. "Later. We have time."

"Not just time, Summer. We have forever."

She grabs my dress shirt, pulling me to her and planting her lips against me in a quick, hard kiss.

"Mine," she says.

"Yours, Sunny. Always yours."

And nothing about that scares me anymore.

Not when I have us.

Not when I have her.

And not when I plan to never let her go.

ACKNOWLEDGMENTS

As Chuck Shurley (from *Supernatural*) once said, "Writing is hard."

This is especially true when you're dealing with a mess of health stuff. That's how I spent my entire 2025—in and out of doctors' offices and going to appointments, which is why it was so refreshing to escape to Port Harbor with Ezra and Summer.

I hope that's what this book was for you, too—an escape. Maybe even a funny, sexy, and sweet escape.

This book wouldn't be any of those things without a few people . . .

My husband, who has supported me through every step of my author career. You make me delicious meals, take me to all those endless appointments, and make me laugh. I am forever grateful you talked to me on the school bus all those years ago. I love you, and I'm sorry that you can relate to Ezra's story of chronic pain in the way that you can. Thank you for being my sounding board when writing his experience.

The team at Montlake. I appreciate you taking this chance on me more than you know. And thank you for giving me such a great editing team, who helped whip this book into shape.

Park, Fine & Brower, thank you for always being in my corner.

My VPR team . . . I couldn't function without you, and you ladies all know this. *Thank you* isn't even close to enough for all you do.

And, of course, my lovely readers who took this journey with me. Your support means everything to me. You've given me a life I could have never dreamed up, which is funny since I dream up stuff all day for a living. That just means it's that incredible. Just . . . thank you.

Finally, a huge thank-you to Kali, my adorable, sweet, and oh-so-attention-starved half-assed Siberian husky. You sat at my feet through this whole book, and I felt your warmth (literally) and love through it all. You can't read, so you don't know this, but you're getting extra snackies tonight.

ABOUT THE AUTHOR

Photo © 2019 Perrywinkle Photography

Teagan Hunter writes steamy romantic comedies with lots of sarcasm and a side of heart. She loves pizza, hockey, and romance novels, though not in that order. When not writing, you can find her watching entirely too many hours of *Supernatural, One Tree Hill,* or *New Girl.* She's mildly obsessed with Halloween and prefers cooler weather. She married her high school sweetheart, and they currently live in the Pacific Northwest. For more information, visit www.teaganhunterwrites.com.